SHATTERED ILLUSIONS

J. C. JACKSON

SHADOW PHOENIX PUBLISHING

Shattered Illusions

J.C. Jackson

Copyright © 2017 J.C. Jackson

Published by Shadow Phoenix Publishing LLC

ISBN-13: 978-0-692-90218-9, 978-1-7322835-2-7

Cover designed by J. Caleb Design

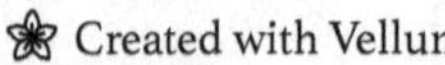 Created with Vellum

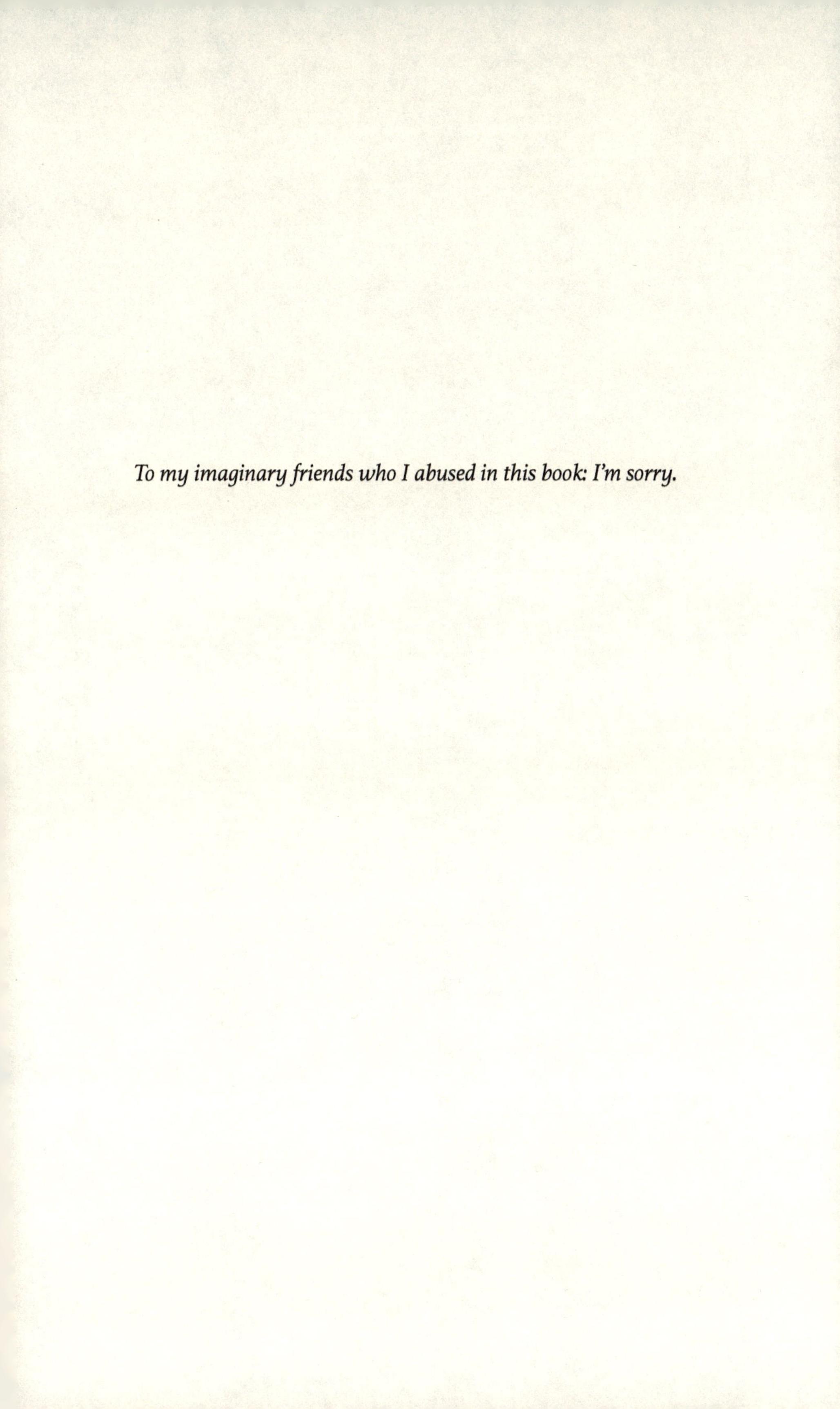

To my imaginary friends who I abused in this book: I'm sorry.

1

THE ELEVATOR DINGED FAR LOUDER than my head wanted to process and I winced at the sound. Rubbing the bridge of my nose, I needed to pull myself together before I got to my destination. I did not feel like fielding questions about why I looked so tired again.

I had gotten enough grief from Silver last night over our video call. "Ketayl, you need to take better care of yourself," he said far too many times. Right now my soon-to-be partner trained in Ocean's Edge, but the badge ceremony was scheduled to take place tomorrow afternoon and soon after he would be here in person giving me a hard time about my long hours.

I might have to start locking the doors to the lab.

Scratching the back of my ear near the pointed tip, I yawned and tried to muster energy as I made my way down the hall. I wanted to blame my current state on needing to get up early to submit my final work for the semester with the Elven Arcana Consortium, but truthfully I had been plagued with memories which eventually turned into nightmares of late.

"When were you planning on telling her?" I heard Lockonis' voice from around the corner. "You don't have much time left before she finds out in a way you don't want her to."

I paused, not sure if I should interrupt her conversation. Tucking a stray lock of dark auburn hair behind my ear, I then attempted to push it back into my bun. I looked back behind me at the elevator and debated turning around and leaving, but I came here to get my paperwork for tomorrow. Fletch kindly offered to plan my trip to Ocean's Edge and I just needed to get my travel packet from him.

"Soon. Seriously, why are you on my case about this?" It surprised me to hear Kitteren's voice. Why were my sister and Lockonis outside of Vince's office?

"Because I agree with the big guy that you've been handling things poorly." I knew "big guy" was how Lockonis often referred to Vince, the director of the TIO. "I understand your team for the assignment is also divided on how to handle a certain aspect. I know you're desperate, but think this through - you could lose a lot more than you gain." With my curiosity piqued I contemplated casting my invisibility spell so I could get closer and watch, but Lockonis would easily sense the arcane usage.

It surprised me she had not noticed my presence. I reminded myself not everyone could sense people with an arcane presence, but I thought Lockonis could. I thought just the sound of the elevator would have gotten her attention.

I shook my head. I should not be hearing this at all. My feet would not move though.

"I know, dammit, I know. What else would you have me do? We've all been chasing these guys for years. We need to do something - the lack of information has stalled us out." My mind pictured Kitteren running a hand through her bangs, exasperated. I previously caused her to do it a number of times on my own. "Look, I really don't like this plan either, but I've got it covered."

Lockonis sighed and then said, "Just know if this aspect goes all to Hells, you'll have only yourself to blame. I'm going to assign the extra security we discussed."

"That'll blow the whole thing for certain!" Kitteren cried. "I told you I'm already working on a detail."

Lockonis firmly told her, "This is not negotiable - I'm assigning the extra security. You aren't the only one who will lose if this goes bad. I don't like the odds and you're gambling with a highly valuable asset."

This did not sound like any of the assignments Kitteren told me she was working on. I needed to move before I got caught eavesdropping.

I straightened my loose cream-colored shirt and pressed the wrinkles out of my tan calf-length pants and stood up taller before I forced myself to walk around the corner. I needed to get my paperwork and get to work. Maybe eat somewhere in there.

Lockonis faced me and tilted her head to see around Kitteren better with a broad grin on her face - the Elven woman only stood a few inches taller than my sister. The fiery red tail of her hair swayed behind her. Her bright blue eyes betrayed nothing of the conversation I interrupted. If nothing else, she seemed amused by my presence.

Once Lockonis saw me, Kitteren turned around to follow her gaze. "Oh, hey, Ket. What are you doing here?" She played nervously with her dark auburn hair which matched mine.

"I'm just picking up my paperwork for tomorrow. I wanted to read through it over breakfast," I tried to keep my voice neutral.

"Oh, Ket, before I forget, you'll be awarding a second person. Finally found someone to fill that new assistant position in the lab we talked about." Lockonis smiled. "Surprisingly a recruit was a far better candidate than any of the current branch lab techs. I'm just glad to be done with that headache."

I wrung my hands nervously. I knew she used the word assistant, but I felt like I might be replaced. "I'm okay, I really don't need help."

Lockonis rolled her eyes and sighed. "Ket, you need one. Especially where you're transitioning to a new team." She walked past me and patted my shoulder as she went. "Enjoy your time off, Ket. Later Kitty."

I heard my sister growl. "Don't call me that. It's Kitteren."

I looked back at her retreating form confused. "Time off?" I asked Fletch to plan my trip so I took an overnight flight out and another overnight flight back the following evening after the ceremony. I had too big of a backlog in the lab to spend more time in Ocean's Edge. Otherwise I would have waited and accompanied Silver back. Though the thought made me unsure about spending so much time in a confined space with him.

"Heh, about that..." Kitteren trailed off.

I slowly turned back to my sister. "What did you do?" Her surprises so far had been tame, but if she interfered with work...

"Ket, come on. You've been working practically non-stop - you need a break. It wasn't hard to get her and Vince to authorize vacation time," Kitteren said, nervousness still laced in her voice.

Was that what they were initially talking about? No, their conversation had been about an assignment. Taking a deep breath to calm myself, I firmly told her, "I can't take time off. I'm backlogged as it is. This run to Ocean's Edge is already going to put me farther behind." Even I could hear the anger seeping into my voice as I spoke - my words started to sound sharper.

"I did just mention the two who signed off on it, right?" Kitteren pointed in the direction Lockonis went and then to Vince's office. "And you're getting an assistant. That'll help for when you get back."

She knew with those two signing off I could not fight the decision. I simply glared at her unsure where else to take this conversation.

"And I'm going with you to Ocean's Edge," Kitteren smiled broadly. It did not help.

I found a question to try and gauge how irritated I needed to be with her. "How long?" A day or two I guessed I could manage. If I could get rest that is. Then I could come back with more energy.

"Not counting our stop in Ocean's Edge, 10 days."

"What?!" came out of my mouth before I could stop it. "No. No no no. No, that's way too long." I started pacing. I bit the tip of my thumb, trying to mentally work out the logistics while my power pushed against my weakened control. Ever since I encountered the necromancer's spell six months ago I fought to regain my full control. I needed to calm down, but Kitteren only made it worse bouncing around in front of me.

My sister forcibly stopped me. "Easy, Ket. Lockonis is going to take over in the lab while you're gone."

"She has better things to do," I shot back. The Director's second did not need to be wasting her time in the lab. I felt awful the times she would come in to give me a hand.

"Uh, no," Kitteren said. "She's going to use the time to find out why you keep getting inundated. You need downtime in the worst way. It'll be you, me, and our parents. And your birthday is coming up. You shouldn't be working on your birthday."

I sighed and pinched the bridge of my nose. I did not like being this passive, but if our adopted parents were involved, I figured it could not be bad. I knew it would take me a while to find the positive side of this sudden change in my schedule. I also knew I had a soft spot when it came to Kitteren and let her get away with more than I should allow, but I could not bring myself to change things and potentially push her away.

Shaking my head, I let myself into the reception area of Vince's office where his assistant, Fletch, sat with Kitteren hot on my heels.

"Hi, Ketayl. Here for your travel packet?" Fletch asked, smiling. The Human man's brown hair stuck out above his forehead, defying gravity. He rolled his wheelchair back to reach the packet on the desk behind him.

"Yes, and thank you for doing this," I said as calmly as I could. I forced a smile.

"Not a problem," Fletch said handing me a bound packet. "I've also included information about the people you'll be presenting badges to."

I opened it to check the flight information since I traveled commercial this time and read it twice. "This isn't right. I can't... I'm not supposed to be going to Mystic Port." I heard the panic in my voice.

Fletch looked surprised and then over at Kitteren. My sister said, "That would be because I asked him to change it."

"Mystic Port?!" I said through clenched teeth. I could not return there and she knew I always turned down both her and our adopted parents offers to take me. Why would she force this on me? I did not want to be reminded of the destruction I caused.

Kitteren smiled and waved at Fletch before tugging me out the door. We were a few yards down the hall when I dug my heels in and ripped my arm out of her grasp.

My power spun like a raging storm that I barely kept contained. "No!"

"Ketayl, listen to me first, okay?" Kitteren pleaded. Her emerald green eyes were wide with fear. "First, you're doing that weird color-changing thing with your eyes again."

I took a deep breath and tried to calm my power. What Kitteren referred to had been the most my power manifested itself when my emotional state became too strong, but I did not know what it looked like exactly. I also still did not know how to control it. I had a long battle ahead of me to get it to be mostly settled, which was its normal state nowadays.

"Second, you need to go this time. Papa has been practically begging to see you. His time is limited." Kitteren spoke slowly as if she thought it would help calm me down.

I paused, considering her words. Who she referred to as Papa, which I never figured out why she called him that, was a Human man named Donald Blair. When we were both little, we hid in a beat up shack in the forest on his property.

Memories continued to flood in about how Don managed to keep us hidden. His attempts to care for a constantly sick Kitteren. My daily need to go down into the city and steal food and money to try and keep the both of us alive. That I knew made no sense now as I could have gotten some from his stores, but I already felt indebted to him.

And now she implied Don was dying. My brain did not want to wrap around the concept. It kept rejecting it, knowing emotions far too strong were behind that door.

I felt my anger drain away and I felt empty. I opened and closed my mouth a few times, never finding the words to say. Even my power stilled.

"I'm sorry I didn't tell you sooner. I just..." Kitteren trailed off. "Please, don't fight with me on this. I promise everything will be fine. And maybe you can tell me about the fairie while we're there, show me..."

"No!" I cut her off, my anger back immediately. I told her time and time again I would not talk about that part of our lives and I meant it. I tucked the packet under my arm and strode down the hall. I needed to get away from my sister.

"Ket. Ketayl. Wait!"

I had already punched the button to call the elevator by the time she caught up with me.

Kitteren got herself between me and the open elevator doors. I thought about pushing her so I could get back to work - while she stood only a couple of inches taller, physically she was far stronger than me. "Shit, Ket, just stop already. No one remembers. I know you're upset, but you'd be curious too if our places were reversed."

I admitted to myself I would be if I was in her position. It did not mean I would relent on my decision to keep the information private. "You're already forcing me to go to Mystic Port with you. At least respect when I told you no about the fairie, I meant it. That person was a monster."

Or as my control strained, I was still a monster. The truth hid beneath a thin illusion of relative normalcy. I still might be capable of the destruction I accidentally wrought and that fact alone scared me.

KITTEREN FOLLOWED me until she realized I planned on skipping another meal and then worked on redirecting me toward the dining hall. I should have fought her as my appetite had left given the morning's revelations, but I did not have the energy left to do so. I obviously needed to refuel if I wanted to continue my protests.

I poked at my food, not hungry still. Kitteren talked about something or other in Mystic Port we should go see while we were there. I still struggled with what she said about Don. There had been nothing from her or our adopted mother, Lindale, previously. Was it sudden? Were they trying to keep the news quiet from me? My mind ran in circles.

"Geez, what did you say to her?" Retanei asked as she sat down next to me, waving a hand in front of my face.

I blinked and sat up to get away from the ebony hand of my Dark Elf friend. When had she gotten back from her assignment?

I needed to focus - I had work to do still and then I needed to pack. I had to rethink my plans for that as well - this would no longer be a quick, simple trip anymore.

"I kind of surprised her with a vacation. She's still mad at me," Kitteren answered. Then I noticed she typed away quickly on her phone. I rarely ever saw her with her phone and she would ignore it when we were together. She shrugged as if none of what just happened was a big deal to her. It only made me more upset with her, but I reigned it in. Fighting with her might push her away and I could not lose her from my life as much as I was unhappy with her at the moment.

Retanei leaned into my field of vision and smiled. "Most people look forward to vacations, Ket."

I looked down at my plate. Today apparently would be a day of things that were going to irritate me. Why did people always assume I needed to be reminded of how the world worked? I knew Retanei meant well, but I did not want to put up with it today.

Kitteren tossed her phone down on the table. "We are talking about Ket."

I glared at my sister again and gave up the pretense of eating. I accomplished nothing sitting here. I quickly excused myself, needing space from people for a while.

Once I got back to the lab, I found the three Arcane College pins had come back from the EAC earlier this morning. I started processing some of the backlog, but made my way over to the pins as I knew they would keep me distracted from the morning's events.

While all of my machines ran samples of other things I tried to figure out this puzzle. I had been staring at the pins through jeweler's lenses for a while, flipping them over, when I noticed they all bore a seam on the side which made no sense. It was not part of the design itself - the two with gems had an obvious separate cage to contain them and my student pin was only metal.

I started with my student pin since it was not direct evidence in the case and pried it apart gently with a tool. Being older and not as good of quality as my Researcher's pin, it did not take much effort. What I found inside surprised me. Then again, I did not know what to expect.

A mix of arcane and divine text had been etched in letters so small that if not for the lenses, I would not have been able to make out. The only part I could understand listed arcane ranks. The rest of it I would have to ask Silver when I got back. I knew each rank listed wore a different style of pin. They became bigger and more elaborate as someone went up the ranks in the Arcane College. Having been a Researcher, my pin appeared almost the same as my student pin. Only the gems in the background of the Researcher's pin set them apart.

Repeating the process, I managed to get the other two pins apart with a little more effort. My Researcher's pin contained identical arcane text, but the Archmage's was different. His list had only one on it: the Circle of Magi.

I found it odd that nowhere did I see Magus listed. At least I thought the Arcane College had a Magus. I could not remember who it was.

I looked at the other side of the pins and saw a circular line of something embedded in the metal. The two which belonged to me looked like they each held a strand of my hair coiled in the metal.

Brown's appeared to be what I remembered his hair looked like. Testing my thought would likely be a chore itself. One I might not be able to spare the time to pursue for a while.

Pushing the lenses up on my head, I sat back on my stool and contemplated. I really wanted an answer now, but Silver would be in the middle of training. I would get a video call from him every couple of days, but I tried not to bring my work into it. He had enough to deal with in Ocean's Edge without me dropping work from the main office on him as well.

My computer started making noise at me, signaling someone requesting a video call. I only hoped it was not from one of the branch lab techs who made sport out of insulting me. I did not think I could bite my tongue today.

Once I wheeled my stool over, I raised an eyebrow at the name and punched it up to the larger screen behind the computer. "Hi, Rathal." I heard from him regularly, but like Silver, he usually did not call until after normal hours - unless he was trying to get an update. He had become a friend over the last few months.

"Heya, cutie. How goes?" Rathal smiled broadly. "I'm bored and hoped you had something new."

Then there was that - calling when he had nothing to do, though these were rare. I rolled my eyes at what he called me. He still called for an update, but more to just have someone to talk to.

"Who are you harassing now?" I heard Savanas' voice. A moment later she walked into view of the camera. "Oh, hi, Ket. Is he bothering you?"

I shook my head, the heavy glasses sliding awkwardly so I took them off and smoothed down my hair. "No, I've got something new, but I've hit a block."

Rathal grinned broadly at my statement. "See, totally getting an update," he said to Savanas.

Savanas rolled her eyes before she reached forward to hit a few buttons on Rathal's keyboard and suddenly my view changed to where their large screen sat. Outside of the rest of Savanas' team, I could also see the recruits moving about. I felt self-conscious as a few stopped to look. A sandy-haired Halfling seemed most interested, but kept moving after hesitating a moment.

Savanas stepped in front, followed quickly by the others. "What do you have?"

Focusing on the task at hand, I rolled my stool back to where I left the pins. "I've been examining the Arcane College pins when I noticed a seam which didn't make sense. I pried my student pin apart and found a mix of arcane and divine text inside." I grabbed the tray with the pins and wheeled myself back.

"Why would there be divine text on an Arcane College pin?" Brad looked confused. Arcane and divine text rarely ever appeared together. They were two very different types of magic. I found it surprising anyone ever figured out how to use both energy types at the same time.

The necromancer spells were the only ones I had seen merging the two, but even then Brown's arcane and divine notes mostly remained separate.

"I don't know," I said, turning on the microscope and getting my Researcher's pin lined up underneath before reaching over to add the image to the video feed. "This is the pin I wore. It bears the same inscription as my student pin as far as I can tell. The other side looks like it contains a strand of hair embedded in it, but I haven't been able to test that theory yet." A machine behind me beeped, reminding me I had other tasks to deal with.

"The only part in arcane text is a listing of ranks," Rathal observed. He turned to look at someone off screen. "Hey, Silver, you got a minute?"

"Dawnseeker, I've told you time and time again you can't just borrow my recruits," an annoyed female voice came from the side.

Savanas rolled her eyes and turned in the direction of the voice. "I'm authorizing this one, Faring. If you've got a problem with it, talk to Vince." Then she muttered something too low for me to hear.

"Sorry I don't have more information. I haven't had a chance to learn how to read divine text yet." I had it on my list of things I needed to do, but I felt like I barely had time to breathe lately. I understood the dangers of learning divine, but if I could at least be able to read the text, it would help speed processing this case along faster.

A few seconds later, Silver strode into view. I still found it odd to see him outside of the garments of his order no matter how many video calls we had. He wore a light blue, short-sleeve, button-up shirt tucked into khaki-colored pants. He still wore the gauntlets, belt, and a few months ago reforged his circlet into ear cuffs.

Silver bowed slightly, before saying, "A pleasure to see you, Ketayl." The formality caught me off-guard. His attention quickly shifted to the side of the screen the video from the microscope displayed.

He also seemed distracted. All the other times we spoke were after he completed his training sessions for the day. I must have caught Silver in the middle of something.

I shifted uncomfortably, adjusting my lab coat. I had not wanted to bother him with this. He needed to be able to focus on his work. Though, I began to wonder why my own training had been so vastly different.

"What is this from?" Silver looked at me, confused.

"My Arcane College pin - the Researcher one I wore," I said quietly. Why did I shy away from facts? It made no sense. Maybe I was ashamed I did not know about this.

Crossing his arms, Silver studied the image. "It looks like it's meant to enhance a spell. To control the wearer? The wording is a bit flowery and old. What's the arcane text?"

Rathal stepped in, "It's a listing of ranks. You said this one and your student pin were identical, but what about Brown's?"

"The list is shorter." Having something to do, I regained my confidence. I swapped the pins out to show them the Archmage's. "His only has the Circle of Magi."

Savanas pursed her lips before she said, "Makes sense. You don't want someone lower being able to control someone higher up. Does it say anything about causing the wearer pain if they fight it?"

Silver nodded, reading the text again. For such a small pin, there was a lot of text. "It's not gentle, that's for certain. It explains Ketayl's reactions though fairly well. Did you feel like you were having a hard time breathing?" He looked at me, concern plain on his face.

I nodded, looking down to fiddle with the other half of my Researcher's pin. I found annoyance at Kitteren's avoidance of the topic every time I tried to talk to her about it and here I was doing the same thing.

Darius said, "I have to ask, but are those things safe for you to handle? I mean, we're talking about spells to control people."

Looking back up, I nodded. "These pins are inactive. My student pin was dead when Lockonis and Magus Engelil looked at it and I broke the spell on my Researcher's pin. With the Archmage dead, I don't think they were able to get a good understanding of how it worked."

"So we need someone alive and with an active pin to get a full picture," Savanas summed up. "It won't be an easy task."

"Could be fun though," Darius commented. "I specialize in pissing off Arcane College mages."

"You failed with that one," Rathal pointed at me.

"She doesn't count. Ket is one of us."

Silver had been reading through the text again. He said, "This looks a lot like the way those necromatic spells were written. Can you get me copies of the text on each pin? I'd like to try to cross-reference them when I get a chance. There's some older language used in there I can't quite make out."

"I'll have the images uploaded to the case file by this evening," I promised. It would not take that long, but I would rather give myself a little breathing room.

"Who else has been apprised of this new information?" Savanas asked.

I bit my lower lip. I had not thought through revealing this to them without consulting anyone else first. "No one. I found it shortly before Rathal called."

"Okay..." Savanas started to say.

Another voice in my lab cut her off, "Ket, you should be packing. What are you doing in here?" Kitteren let herself in.

I turned to glare at her and tilted my head at the large screen on the wall.

"Oh, hi, sorry. I'm not here," Kitteren said and took a seat on a stool at the back of the room. However, I did not miss her narrowing her eyes when she noticed a particular person in the group on the screen.

Kitteren still blamed Silver for me getting hurt and no amount of telling her it had been my choice would change her mind. She very loudly voiced her dislike of him when she found out he was being assigned as my partner.

Savanas followed where Kitteren moved behind me and did not speak again until my sister seated herself. "I'll let you finish with Rathal. Thank you for the update, Ket."

Standing up, I bowed to the group as Rathal ran back to his desk to return the feed to his computer. As soon as he settled back in front of his camera, he smirked, "So, working yourself to death again?"

Rolling my eyes, I tossed back, "I'm backlogged. Lockonis has been coming in to help. The pins came in this morning and I wanted to take a look at them before I left."

I glanced back when another machine beeped. They would all be demanding attention now.

Rathal smirked. "Just so you know, I'll be picking you up at the airport. I promise not to make an ass out of myself this time. Is anyone else from the main office coming with you?"

I pointed back at Kitteren. She took it as a sign to come forward. I had not paid attention to the fact she wore her physical training attire. The green sports top and black calf-length pants showed how toned she kept herself. I still preferred baggy shirts to hide how scrawny I was.

"Rathal was it? Not in any official capacity of course. We're headed for vacation after the ceremony." Kitteren's tone was odd and I could not place it.

"You must be the sister I've heard about," Rathal said and smiled.

"Half-sister, technically," I muttered just loud enough to be heard.

Kitteren patted my head and I elbowed her in return. Not hard, but enough to re-enforce my aggravation with her. She said, "She's just mad because I got Vince and Lockonis to sign off on it."

Rathal looked up from his computer and then hushed as he spoke again, "I better get going. The boss lady is glaring at me. I look forward to seeing you lovely ladies in person soon."

The connection cut.

"You have some good looking contacts," Kitteren mused, smirking down at me. Then it finally clicked as to her behavior.

Shaking my head, I set about getting the images Silver requested. "Rumor has it Rathal likes to chase women." I still did not know why Darius insisted on telling me during one of our calls.

"Hm, could work to my advantage." I did not need to look up to see the sly grin I knew would be on my sister's face. I knew more about her love life than I wanted to. She had taken a couple of lovers in the time I had been with the TIO and insisted on telling me about them. And then some past ones. Though she had not been with anyone for almost a year now.

I tried not to think too hard about her desire to join with Rathal. I had gotten to know him in the following months after I returned - when he was not under the influence of a necromatic spell. He seemed like a decent person. Talkative. Rathal had been concerned about what I thought of him during the investigation, but given my own problems...

Well, we found common ground and I tutored him so he could be more effective as an Arcane Investigator. Especially now that the arcane camera filters had gone into production for the branches. Ocean's Edge received the first one.

I glanced at the box of blank filters sitting on my desk in the office which would have to wait until I got back. I tried to get at least 10 done in between everything else during the day, but I fell behind there also. Taking a vacation now would only make the backlog worse. My biggest problem had become certain branches kept breaking theirs. I wished we could have used plastic, but it did not take the spell as well as the glass filters did.

"Ket, what's wrong?"

I sighed, returning to the microscope, trying to line up the last pin to take an image of. "I really don't think taking a vacation now is a good idea. I've got so much work to do."

Kitteren put her hand on my shoulder and squeezed lightly. "It's precisely the time for it. Ket, you've been working yourself harder than ever before. The lab, physical training, studying who knows what - you need a break. You need more than a few hours to get away so you can come back fresh. Now come on, let's go get you packed and then we can spend some time in Great Tree before our flight."

Sitting back, I sighed. "Give me an hour to get everything in and shutdown." The logical part of my brain kept agreeing with Kitteren. Why did she have to be right?

2

DROPPING my bag on one of the beds in the hotel room, I took a moment to stretch. We flew out late last night and had a long layover in Chained Lakes. I still did not care to fly and it would be a longer flight to Mystic Port.

I pushed back thoughts of what I would encounter there. I needed to get through today first.

At least this time, with the help of headphones and some music, I got some rest on the second leg of our trip. Perhaps requesting overnight flights had not been the wisest option.

Rathal picked us up as promised. He and Kitteren seemed to hit it off fairly quickly and I sat silently in the backseat of his car. He dropped us off at the hotel and excused himself - citing work he needed to complete this morning.

Kitteren quickly retreated to the bathroom with her carry bag when we arrived. This was the same hotel I stayed in the last time I had been in Ocean's Edge, but this room had not been designed for an extended stay. It contained only a bedroom with two beds, a desk, and the attached bathroom.

I wished my sister would hurry up - I wanted to go to the Hidden Flower again to get breakfast. I would make the trip to Lou's bakery, but I did not remember how to get to there from here. Not to mention everything looked so different being green and alive instead of snow-covered and frozen. We were on a floor just high enough to see over the canopy of trees. Odd I paid them little notice during the winter.

Digging through my suitcase, I searched for the clothes I planned to change into. I could just use my power to clean the clothes I currently wore, but I figured I might as well put on something more appropriate for the ceremony this afternoon. I debated trying to get more rest, but it seemed every time I stopped trying to distract myself, my mind inevitably turned back to what Kitteren said about Don. I could not afford to deal with those thoughts right now.

Only a few items in the suitcase looked like the clothes I packed. Did I have the wrong bag? I checked the tag and it said this one belonged to me.

Something inside the suitcase caught my attention. Picking up the dark blue material, I let it unfold, turning it around to get a better look at it.

The dress was soft and silky. It would come up over one shoulder with the waist coming up just under the bust. Two offset layers formed the skirt part which came down into points. A wide sleeve half-attached to the one side left the shoulder exposed.

It reminded me of the dress I wore when Mother found us. Of course it had more or less been barely held together rags at that point. My old dress originally had both sleeves, but I lost one along the way when I needed something to fix the sled I pulled Kitteren in. The third and longest layer of skirts I had torn off a year prior in order to give my sister some extra warmth.

"Mom made it for you."

I jumped. I had not heard Kitteren come out of the bathroom. Quickly folding it back up, I put the dress away. "She shouldn't have. I really don't need more clothes."

"She wanted to." Kitteren came and sat down on the bed next to my suitcase wearing only a towel around her torso. "It's for the Summer Solstice. You need to let yourself remember things about that time, Ket. Talk about them. Mom wants to try and help us find out where we came from, but I was too little and too sick to remember much of anything. Not to mention with your birthday being near the Summer Solstice, she wanted to get you something."

"It's not really my birthday." The year Mother declared it, the Summer Solstice fell on the 21st of the sixth month, this year it was on the 20th. I still did not understand the reason it had been chosen.

I returned to trying to find something to wear for the day before the conversation went where I did not want it to. The past would be better left alone.

Where did the outfit go I packed for the ceremony? "Kitteren, did you repack my bag?"

"Yes. Come on, Ket. You have the worst sense of fashion. You always wear that over-sized stuff. You've got a nice figure - you shouldn't hide it." Reaching into my suitcase, she pulled out a purple sleeveless top and a pair of black dress pants. "Wear this."

I made a face of annoyance at her and grabbed the rest of what I needed to change and freshen up. This trip was not starting well. I wanted to speak further about her repacking my bag, but I needed to eat and there was no point in arguing now. The deed was done and I trusted she would not have put anything in there I would completely refuse to wear.

"Hey, Ket, can I get some help before you go change?" Kitteren said as I reached the bathroom door. Turning, she held up a lock of wet hair in my direction.

Rolling my eyes, I shifted everything to one arm and opened my now free hand in her direction. I focused my power on drying her hair. While not as long as mine - it only came down between her shoulder blades - it was just as thick and would take long to dry on its own. Especially in this humid environment.

"Good?" I asked after a few seconds.

"You're the best," Kitteren said, smiling at me broadly. She picked up her brush and started working on getting the tangles out.

Shaking my head, I went into the bathroom. Clean up, get food, and then maybe I could find some time to read before I needed to check in with Savanas.

<hr>

AFTER BREAKFAST, Kitteren navigated us through the underground public transit. I wondered if Retanei used this to get back to the office after dropping the truck off with me six months ago. I had not even realized this existed, but I supposed that would be the point. Great Tree went to even greater lengths to keep their local public transit from being a disruption of the surroundings.

Now lush green trees lined the streets and the dense green foliage surprised me, though it thinned out the closer one got to the water-front. Government, corporate, and tall apartment buildings stuck out over the tops of the trees - anything roughly three stories or under remained hidden beneath the canopy.

Adjusting the form-fitting top again, I trotted to keep up with Kitteren. My thin slipper-like shoes were not really built for this. At least the doors to the Ocean's Edge TIO office were in sight. I left the packet Fletch gave me back at the hotel on my sister's insistence.

"Quit fidgeting, Ket. You look fine," Kitteren tossed back and then slowed down when she saw I had a hard time keeping up with her quick pace.

"I don't like it. Makes me look smaller," I whined. I really wished she had not repacked my bag. I did not need to appear smaller and more fragile than I already did.

Kitteren stopped and put her hands on my shoulder, holding me at arm's length. "No, it doesn't. Actually, it makes you look stronger, more confident. Besides, you've developed a nice tone on your arms and legs, you should show it off."

Rolling my eyes, I batted her away, suddenly grateful for the long pants. "Let's just get this over with." I started to wish I had not put my hair in a bun - then I could use it to hide. But down would not have looked professional given the length. Kitteren wore a similar outfit - her shirt a deep red, but she opted for a narrow black skirt instead. I guessed she planned on going to the ceremony with me.

We entered the lobby and Melody greeted me before the second set of doors closed, "Ketayl! I forgot you were coming!" She hustled over, giving me a hug. "It's so good to see you. Who's your guest?"

I smiled and tried not to show how much I did not like people touching me. Kitteren I had gotten used to, but most everyone else outside of family still bothered me. "This is my sister, Kitteren. She's also from the main office."

Kitteren pulled her shirt up enough to show the badge clipped to her waistband. "I'm just here to make sure she doesn't get lost."

I raised an eyebrow at her and shook my head. I was more than capable of following directions. Better than her at least. I forced back my annoyance at Kitteren's surprise vacation again.

"Come on and I'll get you two checked in. Hey, Roh, you be nice now." Melody turned her attention to a puppy who came over to sniff at us.

He looked like someone dropped a bucket of black paint on his tan fur. Brown eyes stared out of the small ball of fluff at me - one ear flopped over while the other tried to stand straight up.

Melody returned to her desk and sat down, typing away quickly. "This is Savanas' new companion, Roh. After losing Big Black, she wasn't sure she would take another, but I think she got lonely. He won't grow to be the size of Big Black, but Roh will still get pretty big. The local law enforcement has been using this breed for years and she got Roh from a litter they had a few months ago."

Roh sniffed at my feet and I knelt down to pet him. He turned to lick my hand. It tickled and I moved my hand out of the reach of his tongue. I briefly entertained the idea of asking Savanas if she would let me play with him for a while.

"Savanas is letting him stay down here when she's not actively training him. I think she just wants him to get used to the place. Plus she dotes on him too much," Melody chimed cheerfully. I had a feeling she might be spoiling Roh more.

It did not take long from there and we headed upstairs. This time I guided Kitteren. The elevator dinged and I got off first. The office was far less busy than during my video call yesterday. Only the agents assigned to this office were present.

"Ket! I was wondering when you were going to show up," Darius saw me first and then saw who stepped off the elevator after me. "Looks like double-trouble."

The Ocean's Edge team had their attention on us and I let Kitteren get ahead of me. I smiled and wrapped my arms around my waist, holding my tongue and quietly following. The attention made me uncomfortable.

Kitteren's confidence showed in how she walked and interacted with people as she strode up to where Savanas came over to greet us. It looked like she belonged here.

Savanas caught us as we reached the area sectioned off for her people. She held her hand out to Kitteren. "Savanas Farstrider. What can I do for you?" She reached over and patted me on the shoulder, giving me a smile, but quickly returned to business with my sister.

"Kitteren. I would like to discuss something with you pertaining to an ongoing assignment. Is there somewhere we can talk?"

I blinked in confusion. Why did Kitteren not tell me she also had business here? I forced myself to keep my face neutral and my tongue silenced. Maybe she told me, but I had been too aggravated with her on other things to listen.

Savanas thumbed up toward the floor above. The skylights were visible from this floor because the next floor only bordered this room. There were more rooms up there, but I paid them little heed before. "This is the time of year my actual office gets used." She turned back to me. "Go ahead and make yourself at home, Ket. You're a bit early."

The two headed upstairs, leaving me with the three remaining agents. "Um... hi."

"You're not part of that?" Brad asked as soon as we heard a door close.

Looking up at the floor above, I bit my lower lip for a moment. "I didn't know Kitteren had business here. I thought she just tagged along." Why had she claimed she was not here in any official capacity? Perhaps I did not understand what Kitteren meant.

"Aren't you two heading for the Northern Isles after this?" Rathal asked.

I nodded, unsure what to do being the center of attention. Then I found something to distract myself with. "Did you get the update to the case file?"

"Yes," Brad said, "Silver said he wasn't able to get a chance to look at them last night because he needed to study for this morning's test."

I frowned. I really had not wanted to add to his workload. "I'm sorry, I should have held off working on..."

"Easy, Ket. He's been worried about you taking on all of the work yourself," Brad said. "Silver was relieved when you came to us with the new information. He's taken the being your partner thing seriously. Though it has been driving him mad he can't tell the others in his class he's already been assigned."

Darius smirked and commented, "The guy has taken everything seriously. The testing this morning is just a formality and to give their teams an idea of what they need to work on. All of them have been assigned - they're going to have the ceremony to hand out the assignments at the Waking Dawn this afternoon."

"Yeah, I plan on not attending the ceremony this time as much as I want to check out the new place." Rathal explained, "Faring needs to keep a better leash on her recruits. At least on *that* one."

Darius started laughing, "I never thought I'd see the day a skirt chased you off."

Rathal glared at him. "I have standards. Now this cutie here is another story." He got up and stood next to me, putting his hands on my upper arms. Then he squeezed a few times before saying, "Ooh, you've been working out."

I stepped away from him and rubbed my arms. Why did it seem like people wanted to touch me?

"This cutie could also knock you into next week with a thought," Darius advised. The comment concerned me - I wondered if he truly understood how dangerous I was. I reminded myself his knowledge could only be as far as what he saw six months ago. I did not think I shattered the illusion of relative normalcy I created.

"Geez, I was just joking," Rathal pouted. "Sorry if I made you uncomfortable, Ket."

I nodded, accepting his apology.

Brad shook his head and turned his attention back to me. "Rathal's right, you do look like you've been working out."

Feeling the heat rising to my face, I wrapped my arms around my waist. "I learned my lesson about skipping physical training the last time I was here."

The men laughed and I ducked my head, somewhat ashamed I needed to learn that particular lesson the hard way.

"Just make sure you don't try to measure yourself against anyone else, okay?" Brad advised.

"What do we have here?" another voice joined the conversation. I had not heard the elevator.

I turned and saw Doc standing behind me. He came closer, handing a folder to Darius.

Doc bent down to look more closely at me. Standing back up, he smiled and said, "I'm glad to see you're doing well, Ketayl. You haven't been overworking yourself again, have you?"

Savanas answered, "Of course she has. I'd be concerned if she wasn't."

I looked up to see both Savanas and Kitteren leaning over the railing. That was a short meeting. I wondered what they could have talked about.

"Come on up you guys. We'll use the media room. Doc, you don't mind entertaining the visiting agents, do you?" Savanas said and waved at us to come upstairs.

I looked at Doc. I guess I needed to stay down here since I fell under visiting agent, well, as close to an agent as a liaison could get. He answered, "It would be my pleasure."

Rathal got behind me and started pushing me toward the stairs. "You can't miss this one, cutie."

I moved away from him and followed the group up the stairs.

"Savanas, are you sure…" Kitteren asked, trailing off as she saw us reach the top.

"My answer remains the same. I'll give you the support I can, but it's going to take time," Savanas crossed her arms. "And I echo what Vince and Lockonis warned you about. This is a gamble I don't think you want to take. Given the events already in motion, I suggest transparency with everyone involved." Her eyes slid over to me for a moment on the last part.

It did not sound like the meeting went the way my sister hoped, but I noted the similar statements I overheard between Kitteren and Lockonis. My curiosity started to get the better of me and I wondered if I could find out why she came here.

The skills I learned as a child trying to survive the streets had not completely left me, but I would not be able to employ them now in an attempt to find out what she was up to. I had needed to keep up those skills to survive at the Arcane College. It allowed me to avoid the attention of the ranked mages and to keep an ear on the rumor mill.

Though I had never been successful in listening in on the Circle of Magi.

No, I should not do that. I let Kitteren believe I lost or forgot most things from back then. I only wanted to keep her safe. I did not want her to know the monster I could be. Mother knew a little more of my capabilities, but still not all of it.

"Well, since our favorite Arcane Investigator is here, I think this calls for a late dinner at my place," Savanas announced. She looked directly at me, before she said, "And I won't take no for an answer. Say 1900? The ceremony should be well over with by then."

I bowed graciously. Our next flight did not leave until very late again and I would admit to myself I could not turn down Savanas' cooking.

Darius held the door open to the media room and started ushering the others in. Savanas held me back for a moment.

"Just remember you're among friends - you have no reason to be nervous," Savanas said once the door closed.

Her words only made me more nervous. "What's going on?"

Savanas grinned broadly. "Just something which should have happened quite a while ago." She moved and held the door open for me. I waited for her to let me in the second security door as well.

I looked at my surroundings while the system beeped and the door unlocked. I guessed the small gray room between the hallway and the media room acted as a buffer for sound. I vaguely remembered Darius saying he had been reviewing footage up here six months ago.

The others were all seated in the theater-style arrangement except for Darius who sat along the far wall from where I entered. He spoke too quietly into his headset for me to hear and turned to look back at us. He tossed a thumbs up.

With the room decently lit I took a moment to glance about. The wall in front of the seats held a large screen spanning the full size of the wall. It currently showed the TIO logo. The bank of stations Darius sat at likely controlled the system.

Brad said, "I called down and Faring said some of them are still testing and as soon as they're done, she's going over the ceremony. She won't release anyone."

Savanas looked at him with a raised eyebrow. "I'm assuming that's the nice version."

Brad nodded silently.

I moved toward the seating, assuming I needed to follow the others. The three rows of eight seats each separated down the center by an aisle with the back row being an exception and having another seat there. I spotted an empty spot next to Kitteren and went to go sit down next to her.

"Over there," Kitteren pointed to where Savanas stood.

Now I was completely confused. I looked over at Savanas who pointed at a spot on the floor to her left. What did I do?

Savanas stood halfway between the seats and the screen, she leaned over when I took my place and whispered, "Nothing to worry about. I'll walk you through it."

I took a moment to look at where the others were. Brad, Rathal, and Kitteren occupied the front row. Darius remained at the control station, but faced us. I shifted nervously being the center of attention again.

Savanas dug into her pocket and pulled something out with a long, silver-colored chain. She put the chain over my head and I looked down to see a gold-colored badge hanging on a black leather board. The simple shield design bore the organization's name fully spelled out in dark blue with a stylized dragon in the center.

I did not understand. I looked up at Savanas, hoping she would explain. Maybe I needed to borrow one for the ceremony this afternoon? I previously thought it odd to have a liaison giving a badge, but said nothing at the time. But then why go through all of this?

Savanas said, "I promise there is nothing hiding in it. Place your left hand over the badge and raise your right hand."

I focused solely on Savanas and blocked everyone else out as she walked me through the swearing in. It was not a long oath to be taken, but one which made me unsure of where I now stood within the TIO. Perhaps a walk-through of the ceremony for later? But then why would everyone else be here?

I blinked when Savanas held out her hand to me. Tentatively taking it, my focus widened and I heard the others clapping.

"About damn time," Lockonis' voice came from seemingly everywhere in the room and I jumped.

Savanas turned and nodded to Darius who reached over and punched a button. The screen changed to show Lockonis and Vince on one side of the screen and Retanei on the other.

Brad came over and handed me a wallet. "Your new ID is in there already."

I raised an eyebrow at him and opened it. My picture appeared on a TIO card. My normal ID listed me as a liaison - the word "agent" took its place on this one. I flipped the center piece of the wallet and saw a spot to put the badge in on the other side when I was not wearing it.

"I think Ket is still confused," Kitteren noted. She got out of her seat and came to stand over my shoulder.

"Ketayl," Vince said and waited for me to look up at him. "You've more than earned that badge. Savanas asked for the privilege of swearing you in."

I glanced at Savanas who I would have sworn blushed for a moment before she looked down at her watch. "I'm afraid I might have to cut this short. I've got agents gathering downstairs for the briefing."

"We'll speak more when you return," Vince said and his connection cut quickly. Retanei gave me a quick friendly salute and ended her side as well.

Kitteren took the opportunity to give me a hug before moving away. I went through the motions of shaking hands with the others as well, not actually understanding what just happened. They all began filtering out of the room. I felt pulled in so many directions lately.

It kept me mostly distracted from what still lay ahead, but this added a layer of complexity I did not think myself ready for.

As Darius walked away, I started to follow, my eyes still down on my new ID, but Savanas' hand on my shoulder stopped me. "You stay, but this time you can take a seat. Brad will gather the visiting agents and bring them up in a few minutes. Often they like to get a feel from my guys first about the group of recruits as a whole."

I folded the wallet closed and put it in my pants pocket before I took a seat. Could I actually be what they said I am now? What was the difference between what I was and what I am? I stared down at the badge I cupped in my hands. What did this mean? I only confused myself more the longer my train of thought went. Being the only liaison I knew of, I had never quite been certain of where I stood within the organization.

"Ket," Savanas said softly and came to kneel down in front of me. "Don't think too hard about this, okay? I realize the last insignia you wore tried to kill you, but this is just a piece of metal. I've had the same badge since the day I took my oath and the worst that happened was it stabbed me in the hand when I changed wallets one time. That was before the leather backboards."

I grinned at the image as Savanas laughed at the memory. "Okay."

Savanas stood up and glanced at the door. "Well, at least in taking your own oath this morning, you'll roughly know what you're walking into this afternoon. I spoke with Lockonis before you arrived and she said she already alerted you to Sparky."

"Sparky?"

"Yeah, I can never seem to pronounce his actual name. He..." Savanas trailed off when she heard the door beep and unlock.

The door opened and Brad stuck his head in. "Ready?"

"That was quick. Yeah, send them in," Savanas said and patted my shoulder before walking over to the control station.

"Oh, what's this? Playing favorites now?" an older male Dwarf asked as he came in and spotted me. He took a seat next to me, grinning. His hair was striped dark gray and white.

"No, Stoney. This is Ketayl's first time and I asked her here early to go over a few things," Savanas said. She sounded as if she had gone through this conversation a number of times before. She reached over to the control station and punched a few buttons.

The lights dimmed as the others filtered in.

A Human woman commented, "Don't you mind Old Stoney, honey."

"Wait," Old Stoney said. "Are you Ketayl from the main office?"

I nodded shyly and prepared for someone else to have a problem with me.

"Oh Gods be good. Girl, you have my undying gratitude for handling my lab work until I can get a replacement." Old Stoney patted me on the back. "Anything you need, I've got you covered."

I grit my teeth against the unexpected movement. I forced a smile, still confused. For so long I dealt with other lab techs who only saw the label of the Arcane College. Even after I stopped wearing my pin many would still lace their requests with insults.

"Ket also handles my tougher cases. Not to mention how many other branches send work to you?" Savanas asked as she watched everyone else settle.

I shrugged - I did not keep track of the number. "It fluctuates," I offered as a response. Some needed to because they did not have the equipment or personnel on hand to process the evidence, but others did it simply because they thought me undeserving of the position.

"Looks like everyone is here," Savanas said, taking in those of us seated.

"Only 10 of us? Small group this time, eh?" Old Stoney commented as Savanas wheeled a cart in from the closet.

Savanas leveled a look at him. "More like you're all getting multiple recruits." She picked up a handful of the packets. "Ketayl is new with us for this ceremony so I'm going to cover more than I normally would. Also, as thanks, Trevyn Lavabasher has offered us the use of his establishment. Directions to the Waking Dawn will be in your packets."

"Can we drink this time?" a male voice from the back asked.

"Within reason, Dustin," Savanas warned. "He's promised us samples for after the ceremony, but after that you have to pay for your own drinks. Just because we're not considered on-duty doesn't mean we shouldn't still set a good example."

A female voice from behind me commented, "Well, it will make this one more entertaining."

"I've already got the orders and badges packed up in my car to bring over." Savanas handed packets out as she spoke. She only paused to see where someone was seated.

I stared at mine, not sure how I was going to read anything in here. Or how she was able to tell which one belonged to who. I was glad I got to go over the two profiles ahead of time on the flight here.

"The ceremony is simple. I'll be reading off the recruit's name and they'll come up from the left side of the stage, then you guys will have to remember who you have so you can come up from the right," Savanas continued. The other agents sat quietly.

I wished I only had to deal with one. I sat nervously while I heard pages flipping from the others.

Savanas continued, "Put the badge on them, *then* hand them the packet. Got the order, Stoney?"

"A guy tries to mix things up once..." Old Stoney said, making the rest of the room laugh.

Savanas shook her head, picking up a remote. "Shake their hand and head off the right side of the stage. They'll know to filter back to center front and with any luck, Faring will direct them from there. We're going to swear all of them in at once."

"Thank the Gods," another male voice from the back said.

Savanas smirked and pushed a button on the remote, checking the screen behind her as it lit up with the TIO logo. She commented, "Yeah, I'm not going through it 25 times."

"What's the order?" the woman from before asked.

"Whichever one I grab first," Savanas tossed out tentatively. "No? Okay, just because I want to piss Faring off, we're going by scores. Lowest first. Also, it won't put poor Ketayl up right off the bat."

I sank further into my seat at having been singled out.

Old Stoney inquired, "I take it your training coordinator didn't work out well this round."

"I still can't find a use for her," Savanas said offhand. "As soon as they finish their testing this morning, Faring is supposed to be doing a run through of the ceremony with them."

Murmurs started amongst the agents. "Can we get to the recruits?" A female voice asked this time. I regretted my decision to sit in the front - I could not see who spoke.

Savanas clicked a button and the screen changed to a profile. A Human woman with curly dirty-blond hair and blue eyes stared out of the corner of the profile. "I've put this in the order they'll be called. First up is Holly Campbell."

Old Stoney groaned, "Did you have to give me the bottom of the barrel?"

The others laughed. I stayed still and silent, wondering where my two fell. Silver boasted at being in the top of his class, but I did not know if his words were true or not. If I understood correctly, this was a general training - the specialization training would happen with the teams they went to. It dawned on me the task now fell to me. I bit my lower lip nervously.

Over the next couple of hours, Savanas went through each profile and answered any questions the agents had. So far she had not called either profile I held.

Then the Halfling man who hesitated as he walked past the video call yesterday appeared on the screen. Looking at the jumble of letters, I mentally tripped over the name again. I hoped he liked being called Sparky.

"This is..." Savanas paused. "I still can't pronounce his name even after hearing it a few times. He's earned the nickname Sparky though, which should make things a little easier."

"How'd the kid get that?" Old Stoney asked. Admittedly I was curious, but I did not want to ask and I had not thought anyone would ask a question on my profiles.

Savanas held up a finger while she took a drink from a bottle of water she pulled out of the cart earlier. "Now this is going to make Ketayl worry as he's being assigned to the lab in the main office. The first day in the lab here, he managed to short out one of the machines. Don't ask me which one because I don't remember. Apparently it was a spectacular display. He hasn't lived it down since."

The other agents laughed and Old Stoney elbowed me lightly. I forced a smile, but Savanas was right about me being concerned.

She continued her story, "Despite a rough start, Sparky has

shown great aptitude and interest in the area. He was approved by Lockonis." Savanas directed the last part at me.

I understood the reminder, but I still feared the security of my job despite the badge hanging around my neck. It would not take much to send me back to the Arcane College.

"Which leads us to the top of the class: Silver Blaise."

I found some comfort in the familiar photo staring back at me.

"Okay, which of you lucky bastards got him?" Old Stoney asked. I clutched my closed packet tightly.

There were murmurs around and worry about their reaction held my tongue.

"Silver is assigned to Ketayl," Savanas said.

"How come she gets the top two?" Old Stoney whined.

"It's an odd set of circumstances. Ketayl was assigned Silver before he started training due to his specialization in the divine. He had been a consultant on a case with her roughly six months ago," Savanas said and stopped any further commentary. She pushed a button on the remote again and it returned to the TIO logo. "This briefing is over. I'll see all of you at 1400 in the Waking Dawn."

Her cutting off any further questions surprised me.

I waited for the others to leave before getting up. Savanas caught me before I got far, "Sorry to put you on the spot there, Ket. Anyone getting the top two would have that lot whining. They'll be over it by the time the ceremony takes place."

I nodded and bowed. I had not taken more than a step before she spoke again.

"What's wrong? Is it getting Sparky?"

I stopped, but did not turn to look at her. There were a lot of things wrong lately. "I didn't know Lockonis found a replacement until yesterday."

"I warned her about this," Savanas said softly before speaking normally again, "Ket, you're being transitioned to form a brand new team. You've been needing the help in the lab as it is. How do you expect to juggle even more work?"

Savanas had a point and I realized she echoed Lockonis' words. I said, "Lockonis didn't tell me she approved a time-off request from my sister either." I felt betrayed for some reason. It did not make sense and I tried to push it away.

"That, I don't know anything about," Savanas admitted. "I'll put in a call to her to get some answers. If I know her as well as I think I do, she meant nothing harmful."

I looked at Savanas. "You don't have to do that." No need to get the second of the TIO involved.

"Yes, I do. Lockonis can completely forget to mention things," Savanas said, "I may not contact you like the others do, but I consider you a friend and you can call me if you ever need anything. Now why don't we go see if your sister has survived those three downstairs."

"I'd be more concerned about if they survived her," I said flatly.

Savanas laughed as she directed me out the door.

"Hey, Savanas, mind if I take our guests to lunch?" Rathal called up as soon as I could see them. "I was thinking of heading out soon to avoid the chaos."

It looked like the other agents from the briefing had already left. I looked at the folder in my hands. I could not hold any sort of grudge toward Sparky - he had been picked by Lockonis and she demanded the best.

Kitteren looked down at her phone, as if her messages were more pressing. What was so important she had become attached to the device?

Savanas made a face before relenting, "Yes, go. Better to let you have the rest of the day off than to have Faring screaming about you borrowing her recruit without authorization again." Under her breath as she passed, I heard her say, "I'm still going to have to deal with her."

"Great, let's go you two," Rathal said gesturing at both of us to follow as he strode by with his gear bag over his shoulder.

Savanas pulled me aside out of view of the floor below. She formed her mouth into a thin line and looked at the stairs leading down quickly before she said, "Just watch yourself, okay?" Then she waved me off. She called out to Rathal as I was halfway down the stairs, "You better make sure Ketayl is at the Waking Dawn on-time for the ceremony."

Rathal threw back some half-hearted acknowledgment.

I waved at the others as I followed Rathal and Kitteren. Why would Savanas give me that kind of warning?

3

RATHAL DROVE us to a restaurant near where we attended the memorial service for those who fell to the necromancer six months ago. Kitteren took my badge from me and put in my pocket, but left it on its chain as I would need to be wearing it again soon.

Once we were inside and seated, I tore my eyes away from what I considered an impressive view of the harbor to ask, "What was that yesterday about borrowing a recruit?" I tried to deflect the conversation from their ribbing about my being classified as an agent now since ignoring them was not working.

I did not think it possible for Rathal to look embarrassed. He took a sip of water before answering. "Well, it's not what you think. Yesterday when I called Silver over was a different situation. See, there's this one woman in the class and she keeps coming over and hanging around me whenever she gets a chance. And if it's not me, then it's Silver. I think she has a thing for male Elves and this class was mostly devoid of us."

A flash of an unexpected emotion shot through me upon hearing about Silver, but I did not know what it was. I pondered it for a moment. It had been too fast to really catch it. I knew for certain it could not be jealousy.

Jealousy was when I lived on the streets and saw a child throwing a temper-tantrum at their parents over not getting some sweet while I starved - my own biological parents dead. Seeing how well the ranked mages at the Arcane College were treated for enlisting a Researcher to do their work for them. Never getting recognition myself.

The last one, I had long become numb to, but for some reason it bothered me today. Perhaps I had grown too used to hearing praise for my work within the TIO.

Kitteren smirked, "And here Ket said you knew how to charm a lady."

"Wait, I never said..." I tried to correct and looked down at my hands to cover my embarrassment.

Rathal laughed, "I know how to be a professional. Besides, like I told Ket, I have my standards. Though, I do enjoy the company of small, power-packed ladies such as yourselves."

I put my face in my hands and groaned. This had been a bad idea. I should have just gone back to the hotel and tried to get some rest.

"Just so you know, I don't have my sister's arcane talents," Kitteren said.

I looked up in time to see Rathal give Kitteren a sly grin. "Power comes in different flavors."

I gave up. Really I did. Trapped in the booth between my sister and the window I did not have many options. I turned my attention back to the menu. I let them flirt and forget I was there.

Finally settling on something by the time our server returned, I then turned my gaze back out the window and watched the nearby sailboats gently bobbing in the water where they were moored.

"It may almost be summer, but the water is still far too cold for most people to be out swimming or participating in other activities," Rathal said. "It was a pretty bad winter and most people didn't start putting their boats back in until a few weeks ago. Brad wanted to go fishing so badly he went early and nearly froze himself."

I did not understand why someone would take a boat out of the water except for repair, but I said, "It makes for a pretty view." Well that sounded boring. I glanced over to the other two at the table.

"It really does." Rathal did not look at either of us, but out over the water. Turning back to us, he asked, "I know what Ket is doing here, but what was your business with the boss lady?"

"Classified," Kitteren said. What on Terra could she be hiding?

"It's for an ongoing assignment. We're in a bit of a lull - I'm just setting things up for the next run. Perfect time to grab her and get away."

Lunch continued with the two of them flirting. I felt like the odd person out. I started thinking about how much work I still had at the main office to keep from getting overwhelmed about the ceremony coming up and then the trip to Mystic Port.

I would be working very long days to try to catch up when I got back. And I needed to make sure Sparky settled in and understood how the main office's lab ran. Or was it learning to deal with me?

The Arcane College pins still bothered me. What *would* something divine be doing in a pin for a group dedicated to the arcane? Silver said something about it being for control. I could not recall any other time I felt as if something held my tongue and made it hard to breathe as when my pin activated. I had also not seen the thread until within Silver's aura, suggesting something divine about it.

I started tapping the tip of my fork lightly on my plate while I thought about it.

It would make sense if they wanted to have control without anyone knowing about the secrets hidden in the pins - divine would not be noticed. But then how many within the Arcane College dabbled in necromancy? Or could it be something which had always been done and they continued the practice out of habit with only a few recognizing the truth?

Kitteren lightly smacked the back of my bun. "You're supposed to be on vacation - stop thinking about work. Don't make me steal your hair pins." Kitteren pulled one out. "You wear your hair in a bun all the time - you really need to change things up and relax."

"I'm here on official business so I'm not on vacation yet," I shot back quickly, glaring at her and reached out to snatch my hair pin back. The server coming to check on our table held my tongue and further attempts to reclaim it.

"I don't know - the last time I saw her let her hair down she ended up in the hospital. Does she really work that much?" Rathal asked, looking at Kitteren who cringed at the reminder. "I know when I call she's usually still in the lab, but I figured it was my luck."

Cutting my sister off, I commented, "I just don't quite have enough hands or hours in the day to get everything done. I haven't had much time to actually work on trying to track down the group." I felt like I failed in my job which would be one more reason to replace me. Hopefully things would work out with this Sparky and I could get more accomplished.

"You could have asked Silver for help you know. Just because he's in training doesn't mean he's unavailable," Rathal advised. "He's probably the only recruit ever to be assigned *before* starting."

Kitteren made a face of disgust at the mention of Silver.

Rathal raised an eyebrow at my sister's reaction before continuing, "Don't feel like you can't ask for help from the rest of us either. We know this case as well as you do."

But they were not the ones tasked with finding that group. If I could not find them, how do I find out what they might be planning?

The server delivered the check while I thought. Rathal took it before I could reach for it.

"I said I was treating you ladies, remember?" Rathal chided.

Sighing, I pulled the folder off of my lap and glanced at Sparky's profile again. I had no idea what this person was like. Though, I did not even have a short profile to look at before I got stuck working with Silver. Surely it could not be bad. At least I could try to get a feel for his personality after the ceremony.

"That's not who I expected," Kitteren said, looking over my shoulder.

"He's being assigned to the lab," I said and regretted not checking my tone of voice. I sounded depressed.

Rathal gave me a confused look before he put his finger on the edge of the folder so he could see what we were looking at. "Oh, Sparky. Good kid. Damn smart. Very friendly though a little odd. He'll be a good addition to you. He's not trained in the arcane or divine, but he should be able to keep up with you otherwise."

Addition. I could handle that word. Far better than thinking Lockonis wanted to replace me. I wondered why Rathal's word got through better than what Lockonis and Savanas tried to tell me.

Rathal got up as soon as the server came back with his card. "Come on. If you're late the boss lady will have my hide."

Once he moved a few steps away, Kitteren leaned back, smiling broadly. She whispered, "I want his hide."

"I know," I said flatly, pushing her gently to get her to move faster.

As we stood outside of the Waking Dawn, Rathal said, "I'm not going to the ceremony. I'm sure Darius or Brad will be there though. When it was held at the office, we usually attended because, hey, free food, but I'd like to avoid a certain recruit this time."

Kitteren picked at her collar, giving Rathal sidelong glances.

I knew what Kitteren hoped for, but I did not want her to think she needed to stay with me. I said, "I think I can survive this on my own. Thank you again for lunch, Rathal."

"Are you sure, Ket?" Kitteren looked concerned. "How are you going to get to Savanas' house later?"

"I'll be fine. I can probably catch a ride with someone. If not, I'll call." I bowed to both of them and started making my way toward the entrance.

Kitteren quickly followed me, telling Rathal she needed a moment. She pulled me aside and asked quietly, "What's going on?"

"Kitteren, I don't want to mess up your chance with him. Go, have fun. I'll be fine. I have Savanas to go to if I need it," I explained. I was not stupid - Rathal may have made fun of me saying I was blind when it came to myself, but I had gotten decent at reading others. Granted, even blind it would have been hard not to notice the attraction between these two.

Kitteren smiled and hugged me. "You're the best, sis. I'll catch up with you later then." She practically skipped back to Rathal, hooking her arm in his and whispering something quick. They both got in his car and I watched quietly as they left. I may be annoyed with my sister, but I was not about to stop her from enjoying herself out of spite. After what she went through early on in life fighting Neschal's Disease, I only wanted to see her alive and happy.

My mind returned to her words of Don's time being limited. I shook my head - I did not have time right now. I needed to get through this ceremony.

Taking a deep breath, I looked up at the building which had previously been destroyed. My mind overlaid how it looked six months ago with the arcane remnants and the souls tied screaming on the floor. Coming here had been a bad idea also.

It took a moment for the image to clear to the present. No arcane remnants and Silver would be here soon to prove there were no souls trapped here. I watched him release them, but I still worried perhaps we missed someone.

Tucking the folder under my arm, I went up to the door and tried it, finding it locked. I glanced at my watch and found I was quite early. The sound caught the attention of a male Dwarf I had not met and Savanas who were inside talking near the front.

Savanas reached the door first. "Sorry, hadn't expected anyone so early. Want to help set up?" I almost did not recognize her. She wore her black, wavy hair down - it brushed her shoulders. The green collared shirt hung loosely over black dress pants. Her badge hung from a simple silver chain around her neck.

I nodded. It would help keep my mind off the past.

"Ketayl, this is Trevyn Lavabasher, owner of the Waking Dawn. Don't let him talk you into any of his 'special' brews. Those things pack a punch," Savanas warned.

He leveled a look at her before sizing me up as he held out his hand. "The name sounds familiar," Trevyn said, offering his hand. He kept his burnt orange hair neatly braided back and his long beard bound tightly about every hand's width. His entire outfit was black.

I reached down to take his hand, not sure why he would know my name.

"Ketayl is one of the agents who helped in the investigation," Savanas clarified.

"Aye, you've more than earned my deepest thanks an' appreciation. Whatever you want is on me," Trevyn shook my hand firmly and smiled broadly. "Don't feel right havin' yer people help set up, but if yer gonna help, we should get you an apron. Don't want those nice clothes gettin' wet or dirty." He waved for me to follow him.

The layout looked roughly the same from the last time I had been here. A stand-alone wall sat behind the hosting station which stood tall enough to give some privacy to the diners. Booths lined the outside walls, though the tables were pushed together behind the stand-alone wall to form a much larger table. A small stage had been set up in the back with a podium. The bar sat along the side next to the kitchen. Screens were mounted to the walls. Wine glasses hung by their bases above the bar.

We made our way to the kitchen where platters sat ready to go out and other trays of food waited to be baked. A couple of his employees were busy getting things ready.

Trevyn reached up to unhook a black apron and handed it to me. "To start, let's get these glasses brought out to the bar. Two trays should be enough." He walked over and pointed to the trays of shot glasses. "After that, I'll show you where the regular glasses go."

Testing the weight of one tray, I decided it best to take them out one at a time. I could use my power to levitate them both out at once, but I did not want to possibly unnerve Trevyn. Magic had previously been used to destroy his establishment after all.

I put the tray down on the bar. Not sure where else to take it without further instruction.

"Perfect," Trevyn said, coming up from the other side of the bar. "I'll start pourin' the samples during the ceremony."

I nodded and went back for the other tray. Then I brought a tray of regular glasses out and Trevyn showed me where to store them behind the bar.

I busied myself putting the glassware away when I heard a familiar voice. "Ketayl?" Silver asked.

I wiped my hands on the apron since this set of glasses was still a bit damp from being washed. I turned to look up at my partner. He wore a black suit with a blue dress shirt, the top button undone, with the tail of his braid sitting over his right shoulder. I had grown relatively comfortable with our video calls, but seeing him again in person made me nervous. Not to mention I forgot how much taller than me he was.

"I thought I recognized that bun," Silver teased. "What are you doing?"

Gripping the apron, I felt the need to look away for some reason. "Just helping."

"It's good to see you again. You look very nice," Silver said. An awkward silence fell between us before he found something else to say, "This whole thing seems silly to me."

"Who are you talking to?" I recognized the Human woman who slid up next to Silver as the first profile in the briefing this morning. I struggled to come up with a name. Her hand snaked around his arm. "Oh, you know the bartender? How cute. You should come over with the rest of us - the ceremony will be starting soon." She began pulling him away toward the group of recruits. I noted where Sparky stood among them. He wrung his hands and looked around.

Silver pulled his arm from her grasp. "I've told you not to do that, Campbell," Silver said sharply. He tossed me a frustrated look. "We'll talk later."

As soon as he started heading over to the others, the woman glared in my direction before turning her back to me.

I cocked my head to the side, not understanding. What had I done?

"Don't you worry about losin' yer boy. He ain't interested in that slime," Trevyn said softly next to me. He never stopped getting the glasses organized on the bar.

"What do you mean?" And why did he call Silver my boy? Perhaps I was not familiar enough with the slang in the area.

Trevyn pointed at the group with his chin. "Been tendin' bar for enough years to be able to read people pretty good. Yer boy barely tolerates her behavior and I'd eat my beard if her interest wasn't only skin deep."

Savanas came over, her face unreadable. "Ketayl, come on. Let's get ready." I followed her back into the kitchen where I left my things, but not before I saw Campbell grinning as she watched me follow the head of the Ocean's Edge branch.

Taking the apron off, I hung it up and straightened my shirt. I was still uncomfortable in the clothes Kitteren chose, but there was nothing I could do about it at the moment. Savanas quickly tucked her shirt in before grabbing a black suit coat.

I started for the door when Savanas stopped me. "Ket, your badge."

I stopped. I almost told her I did not have one, but the weight in my pocket reminded me. I dug it out and put it back around my neck hesitantly - I was not sure if this was right or not.

"Take a deep breath. Most people will be focused on me. And actually, I'm not sure who is more nervous - you or Sparky. Just remember you have a lot more friends around you than you think," Savanas advised. There was that phrase again. She fiddled with getting her badge to lay right. "While the oath taking is serious, we try not to get too wrapped up in ceremony."

I closed my eyes and did as she suggested. It helped to center myself. I should have tried to get more rest this morning, but I was too aggravated after finding out Kitteren repacked my bag on top of everything else.

"I will admit I am looking forward to the moment Holly realizes she mouthed off at an agent. In any case, we have a minute to talk. I called Lockonis," Savanas said, standing to the side of the door just enough she could still look out at the gathering crowd.

I was not sure I was ready to hear what she had to say. I certainly was not ready to deal with what sat beyond those doors.

"She didn't tell you about the time off for a couple of reasons. First, Kitteren asked her not to. Second, she was going to use your sudden disappearance as a chance to deal with the problem branches. See, nothing to worry about," Savanas assured. "Though sometimes I think she has far too much fun in baiting dead-weight. One of these days I'm going to figure out how she manages to handle so much."

I took a shaking breath. She was right, nothing to worry about. Except what was out there. I did not know how to deal with a partner. Her comment to me when I left the office came back to mind again. "Why did you warn me earlier?"

Savanas shook her head. "We need to get going right now."

Nothing more was said as we made our way out of the kitchen and toward the small stage set up in the back of the large room. I hid behind the other agents. If I could not see the recruits, they could not see me, right?

Brad found me anyway, but he was a tall man and stood next to a table where packets and badges were spread out on this side of the stage. "Hey, Savanas probably forgot to tell you I'll be handing you the badge and packet, okay?"

I nodded nervously.

"Don't you worry, young man, we've got her covered," Old Stoney came over and reached up to pat me on the back.

I stiffened - I really did not like being touched.

"You got two men so you just need to clip the badge to their pockets," the Human woman with gray streaks of hair turned to tell me over her shoulder. "Though if I hear right, we likely won't see you at one of these again. Not for a while at least."

"Oh, specialized team - makes sense to get the top two now," A male Gnome with bright blue hair squished himself back to our conversation.

"Not to mention we're all used to getting the ones who need a bit more polishing," Old Stoney said. "Finish training them in a team and transfer them to where they'll be the most effective."

"Thank you all for being here," Savanas said, "This is a very important day to many of you and an important day to the rest of us as we welcome new recruits into our family." She stood at a podium placed at the back of the stage and spoke further about the TIO and its history, obviously having given this speech a number of times before.

I peeked through the other agents. Holly stood at Silver's side, smiling broadly. Silver scanned the agents and stopped when he saw me. He visibly relaxed. Sparky wrung his hands nervously looking from one agent to the next.

I started to feel sorry for the Halfling.

Soon enough Savanas started calling names and agents moved to place the badges on the new TIO member and hand them their orders. I carefully watched the others go, trying not to be obvious with my unease. As the list got toward the end, the other agents who awarded all of their new members pushed me to the front of the group.

Brad nudged me and cocked his head in Holly's direction. She was down in the center next to the others Old Stoney awarded, staring at me in disbelief and worry.

"Harvenshr... Oh Hells, Sparky, get up here." Savanas gave up on trying to pronounce his name.

Brad handed me my things before I went over and had to kneel down to clip the badge to the Halfling's pocket. Or rather a ribbon someone had sewn on for the occasion as it would not have fit. Standing back up, I handed him his packet and forced a smile, offering my hand. My movements felt stiff as I could sense eyes on me.

Sparky took it nervously and he followed me off the stage. Maybe he was just unsure of where he was being assigned. Savanas was not calling out our names or anything to identify where we were from.

Brad handed me the last badge and packet as soon as I got in reach.

"Silver Blaise."

I turned around. I thought I had been nervous before, but it only spiked now. This time I was eye-level where I needed to clip the badge to Silver's coat pocket. I could not meet his gaze. Quickly I offered him the packet and my hand.

It felt like he held my hand too long. When he finally let go, I moved quickly to get off of the stage. I might disappear to the bathroom later just to try and wash the weird feeling off my hands.

"If you would all stand before the stage with the agent who gave you your badge," Savanas said. She waited patiently as everyone moved to the front. I followed the other agents examples and turned my back to the stage so Silver and Sparky could stand in front of me. Sparky looked up at Silver and visibly relaxed. Perhaps they had become friends and knowing they were headed for the same place helped calm him. I probably read too much into it.

Savanas started the swearing in process similar to mine. No sooner had she ended the ceremony then Silver took my hand and tried to kiss the back of it. I pulled away, remembering my earlier thought of wanting to retreat to the bathroom. I forgot how much of a tactile person he was and glared at him. My actions only seemed to amuse him.

Sparky opened his packet and read the information there. He looked up at me with uncertainty. "Is this real?"

"May I?" I opened my hand in request so I could read the papers myself. Quickly glancing at the information I handed it back to him and nodded. Everything looked to be correct - orders to start in the lab about a week after I was scheduled to return.

"This is awesome!" Sparky actually jumped.

I had not expected his reaction.

Silver laughed while he opened his packet. "Sparky has been dreaming about getting a spot in the lab in the main office."

"I figured I was going to have years ahead of me before I managed to work my way there if at all," Sparky started then paused and looked up at me. "Do you know Ketayl?"

Silver started laughing again and I glared at him. Why did he find this funny?

"I'm Ketayl," I said quietly.

The Halfling stared at me for a moment and tilted his head before shaking it. "Wait. No, I'm still in bed. Dammit," Sparky said and began to pace.

I looked up at Silver confused. Savanas made her way over to us, coming up behind Sparky. She asked, "What's wrong with him?"

"He thinks he's dreaming," Silver answered before I could open my mouth.

Savanas rolled her eyes. "No, Sparky, you've really been assigned to the main office."

"Assistant, yeah, I got that. Also telling me *the* Ketayl is right here also. It's too much." Sparky waved a hand in my direction.

Now I was really confused. How would he know about me?

Savanas laughed. "Ket's real." She looked at me to explain, "In the lab, they review closed cases. The Parsing's case is one of them."

"Oh," I said, not sure what to think. It had been one of the first cases I worked on alone in the lab which brought me to my current chaotic method of processing evidence. I did not know why the case would be relevant to recruits.

"It was a stroke of genius. Agent Farstrider even let me read some of your other case files. I can't wait to get started!" Sparky bounced. I had no idea how to handle this.

Tucking a stray lock of hair behind my ear, I admitted, "You may regret saying that. I'm really backed up in the lab."

"I hate to break up this conversation, but, Ketayl, can I talk to you privately for a minute?" Silver asked. His serious tone concerned me.

I nodded and excused myself. Finding a relatively quiet spot, Silver simply handed me his paperwork. He had it flipped open to the last page.

I read the information three times to make sure I was not seeing things. "Why would they need to send you to Mystic Port with me? It's not an assignment."

"Why didn't you tell me you were heading for Mystic Port?" Silver sounded hurt or angry - I could not tell which.

Looking up at him, I realized this had to be the worst way to start this partnership. "I'm sorry, I didn't think to message you. I only found out I was going yesterday. Kitteren managed to force the time-off and she planned the trip."

Silver looked at me in surprise. "You're taking a vacation?"

"Unfortunately," I admitted.

"No, you need it. You looked really worn out yesterday during the call." Silver took the paperwork back. "What's in Mystic Port?"

"Nothing," I said quickly as I spotted Holly walking over. "Um, if you'll excuse me I need to get something to drink."

I made my way over to the bar where Trevyn stood happily. "What can I get you? I can recommend a particular sample brew based on yer tastes. See if you like it first."

"Thank you, but I can't drink. Can I get a glass of water?" My already weakened control and alcohol sounded like a bad combination.

Trevyn grinned and went to fill my request. I took a moment to breathe and realized I forgot to ask him how much it was.

"You win," a female voice came from behind and startled me.

Turning around, I saw Holly standing there, her face hard to read. "I'm sorry, I don't understand."

"Well, I probably should have started with I'm sorry about my behavior earlier and you win."

I looked at her confused. "It's okay, but win what?"

"Hm, well, that explains it," Holly smiled and then offered her hand. "It was a pleasure meeting you."

I took it, still lost as to what just happened. She left after, returning to her new team. I really needed to talk to Savanas. She had to know why Silver received those orders.

A glass of water appeared on the bar. I pulled my wallet out and Trevyn waved me off. "I told you it was on me. Not that I would charge for water anyway. Go get yerself somethin' to eat. Bloody scrawny Elves."

I gave him a quick bow of thanks. Turning around, I did not know what to do. Savanas spoke with a mousy-looking Human woman who appeared to be getting more angry by the second. I refused to step into the middle of that.

I should talk to Sparky more I guess. At least let him know what he would encounter, but I did not know what would be left.

Where had he gone?

"That was impressive," Sparky said. I had not seen him approach. He had a sample glass in his hand. "Do you mind if I ask about what you're working on now?"

I took a sip of water, thinking about my answer. "I'm not sure what I'll be going back to. Lockonis said she's dealing with the backlog. I know I'll still have the Brown case."

"Brown. Brown. Can't say I'm familiar with that one, but obviously it must still be open," Sparky said, tapping the side of his glass with his fingernail.

"It is. Most of what is left is arcane and divine specific."

Sparky pouted. "No fair. I'm not familiar with either of those areas."

I shrugged. "That's where me and Silver come in I'm afraid."

"Okay," Sparky said sounding dejected, "Anything I should know about the main office?"

I pursed my lips while I thought. "I'm not sure what would be useful. Lockonis will probably do an orientation with you when you get there. I'm unfortunately going to be away."

Silver wandered back over to us, also carrying one of the sample glasses and raised an eyebrow at my water. He should understand by now my personal restriction on alcohol and I leveled a look at him.

"Wait, do you two already know each other?" Sparky asked.

"Yes," Silver said before I could open my mouth. "I'll tell you later, but she was the one I was calling to help me study."

Silver stood rather close and I hated the fact I only came up to his shoulder.

"Ma'am, if you will ignore what I'm about to say..." Sparky said to me, pausing for a moment before directing his attention to Silver. "You freakishly tall ass - that's not fair having an agent tutor you."

Should I mention I needed to learn a lot of what they had been training for to help him? It cut into some of the time I tried to allocate to helping the cyber team. I wondered what they turned up. Lockonis would always tell me they did not have anything of note. The main group could have decided to go into hiding after what happened with Brown and his group.

My mind quickly circled back to the pins. The text, the hair - why? And I did not know for certain that the strand was hair. There had not been enough time to run tests. Did the Circle of Magi know about it? Could someone else be attempting to influence the school? But then why the shortening list of ranks for a higher level mage? The Circle of Magi must know or maybe the Magus of the Arcane College? Trying to recall a face or a name for the Magus, I found I could not.

"Are you okay, ma'am?" Sparky asked.

Blinking, I returned to what was currently going on. "Yes, sorry, I guess I'm a little distracted by something I was working on in the lab."

"The pins?" Silver asked.

I nodded. "But it can wait. You two should go enjoy the party - I fear I'm not good with social events."

"Neither am I," Sparky admitted. Then he took a sip of his drink and winced. "You guys should try this stuff. It packs a punch."

I held up my hand to signal I would pass on the idea.

"When was the last time you ate?" Silver asked. Mentally I groaned and outwardly I sighed in resignation. Was he going to always be like this?

"Yeah, you definitely owe me a story metal-boy," Sparky mused over his drink.

Silver rolled his eyes. "You're never going to give up calling me random names, are you?"

"Nope and now you're stuck with me at the main office."

I hid my amusement at their antics behind my hand. I could live with this.

"What you need to know about Ketayl is she will work herself to exhaustion and skip meals if no one reminds her to take them." Silver said, looking at me expectantly.

I sighed and said, "I had lunch a little while ago. Rathal and Kitteren are my witnesses."

"Kitteren is here?" Silver asked, looking around nervously.

I shook my head, knowing his concern. During the short time Silver stayed at the main office earlier in the year, my sister would always pull me away from talking with him. "She elected to spend the time with Rathal." And now I had a reason to be more grateful I waved her off to go enjoy herself.

Sparky raised an eyebrow and remained silent.

As the conversation continued between Silver and Sparky, I found myself now debating Silver's orders. His schedule was off by an unknown number of days, but his orders were to go to Mystic Port with me. Bad enough Kitteren and our parents wanted to dredge up the past, but I did not need Silver finding out. I wanted to keep up this illusion of normality. I liked feeling I belonged somewhere even though I kept everyone at arm's length for their own safety.

How could I maintain the illusion if they were determined to dig up the monster?

DINNER AT SAVANAS' house was a quiet affair. Lou sent his apology about not being able to be away from the bakery this evening. I sat quietly outside - decorative lights lined the backyard giving it a gentle, comforting air. My adopted parents decorated their outdoor space in a similar fashion and I always found it calming, but not tonight. Not with what lay just beyond the horizon.

I rode with Silver, who seemed all too happy to be free of the group. When he handed me his packet to hold while he drove I asked if I could read it again. It kept me distracted from him driving.

Everything else in the packet I expected, but I was uneasy about the fact I ended up listed as the team lead. It was a team of two after all.

Before this, it felt like nothing would change and I just talked to him from a distance. Now I had this Elven man in my life. A partner - something I had not dealt with previously. For some reason it still did not feel real.

Nothing more had been included regarding his orders to go with me - it just said further details pending. This included his flight information.

I watched as Silver spoke with Brad and Darius on the other side of the yard. He was the only one of the recruits invited to Savanas' house. Well, I guess they were all agents now. Kitteren and Rathal had not yet arrived, but we followed Savanas and gotten here much earlier than she suggested this morning at the office.

Standing up, I decided I needed to find Savanas. Roh saw me move and came over to bounce around my feet for a moment before returning to play with Melody. His ears flopped around in the most comical fashion as if they were too big for his body.

Through the sliding glass door, I saw Savanas still in the same outfit she wore to the ceremony minus the jacket, but with a simple black apron over it. She took something out of the oven and looked at me curiously.

I let myself in quietly. "I'm sorry. I don't mean to bother you, I..." I trailed off, uncertain how to broach the subject.

"Ket, relax, I'm not going to bite. Just say what's on your mind," Savanas said gently.

I fidgeted for a moment and blurted out, "Why is Silver being sent with me to Mystic Port?" I paused and then added, "Sorry, I don't know if you know and..." I trailed off again because I started to ramble.

Savanas stood up straighter, looking at me confused and then it seemed something clicked for her. "Ket, what I say stays between us and even then I can't give you an exact reason." Something on the stove caught her attention and she turned to deal with it.

I walked further into the kitchen, trying to stay out of her way. Her words set me on edge.

Savanas gave me a sidelong glance, "Look, we just want you to be safe and it'll give you and Silver a chance to get reacquainted."

"Is something going on?" Could Mystic Port possibly be more dangerous now than back then?

"I can't say," Savanas said and I could not tell if she actually knew or not. It was a vague enough statement to go either way and her face betrayed nothing.

I folded my arms and looked out to her backyard where Silver told a story to Brad and Darius. He made grand gestures with his arms and the men laughed. While I enjoyed the same antics during our video calls, this trip to Mystic Port was too personal and my concerns overrode any amusement I might find from it at the moment.

Savanas sighed loudly, which drew my attention back to her. "Lockonis advised me about how much you've been working lately. You've taken a lot on in a short period of time. I'm not sure you've even had time to truly process what happened six months ago let alone be prepared for what is ahead. Just take this time and enjoy it. Silver will watch your back so you can relax. Provided you let him that is," Savanas said and smirked at me. "The orders came from Lockonis and she'll follow up with him shortly. He'll still have the right to refuse as it's really more of a request, but she needed to do it this way to be able to get Personnel to play nice if he agrees."

I frowned and looked back out the window at my partner. Why did she not say anything to me before I left? It was useless to wonder about it now - Lockonis likely had much on her mind and Kitteren could distract anyone.

How was I going to explain this to my family? Should I convince Silver to turn down the request? It seemed the most logical idea.

"Go outside, enjoy the evening. Food will be ready soon enough," Savanas advised. "Talk to Silver, but don't try to change his mind - you'll only make him decide to go. He has to be one of the most contrary people I know and I deal with Rathal on a daily basis." She made a shooing motion at me with her hand.

I started to think she could read my mind somehow, but shook off the idea. As I let myself back out and returned to my previous spot, I could not shake the feeling Savanas tried to tell me more. Either that or I spent far too much time digging for more through each case I processed.

Stretching in my chair, I then needed to adjust my shirt again. Maybe I should have spent some time this afternoon picking up a couple of outfits instead of going to lunch. But I hated spending money on myself if I did not need to. I could make do with what my sister packed.

"You seem uncomfortable," Silver said as he came over and sat down next to me. At some point he shed his jacket and rolled up his sleeves. The lights played off of the metal bracers he wore. I briefly wondered if he would be changing the style of those eventually as well.

Now I remembered Silver previously told me he reforged his circlet into ear cuffs because Rathal would knock it off before he could draw his weapons when they sparred together.

"It's not what I usually wear. Kitteren repacked my bag," I said, wrapping my arms around my waist.

Silver leaned forward, toying with the end of his braid, smirking. "I think it looks good on you, but I'd rather see you comfortable."

I fidgeted with my hands, letting silence fall between us before finding another topic. "Sorry I haven't been able to get more done and now I'm going to fall further behind."

Silver put his hand over mine to get me to stop. "Ketayl, you've been taking it all on your own. I'm sorry I haven't been around to help more."

I moved my hands away and sighed, pulling my knees to my chest. I caught Silver look up out of the corner of my eye. Patting my shoulder, he stood and said, "I'm going to go see if Savanas needs help. It looks like your sister wants to talk to you."

Not exactly the person I wanted to deal with at this moment. As soon as the thought crossed my mind, I kicked myself for even thinking it. Kitteren was simply being Kitteren.

A few moments later, my sister plopped into the seat Silver vacated. "Ugh, who invited him?" I had grown tired of her attitude toward him, but I could not change her mind and arguing made it worse. She patted my bun and asked, "What's wrong, Ket?"

"Just tired I guess. It's been a long day. Did you enjoy yourself?" I asked, unfolding.

"Mmm..." Kitteren smirked, her eyes finding Rathal. "He's quite good. I almost feel bad stealing him from you."

"Kitteren..." I warned.

My sister rolled her eyes. "I know, I know. You really should consider taking a lover. Just not that paladin partner of yours, okay?"

Where did her statement come from? I did not even remotely have a relationship like that with Silver. Sighing, I looked around to see where everyone else sat, but erred on the side of caution and changed to the dialect of common my sister and I used since most people could not understand it, *"I've told you before I can't."*

Kitteren raised an eyebrow at me. *"Why not? You've never actually explained it."*

"Because I'm dangerous. I can't afford to get too close to someone. You know I have to control my emotions because my arcane abilities are tied to it." I already walked the line caring about those I did. I did not know what would happen if I lost any one of them. I could not process what Kitteren said about Don and I had not seen him for half a century.

I pushed the thought back as it tried to come forward again. Tomorrow, I could deal with it tomorrow.

Kitteren sighed. *"You won't know your true limits until you try."*

"I can't take the risk," I snapped at her.

Savanas and Silver came out with dishes and started placing them at the large table on the patio. "Hope everyone is hungry," Savanas chimed happily.

Kitteren moved first and I hung back, watching where everyone sat around the large table on the patio. I caught the attention of a few people who turned to look at me. Especially Kitteren and Silver. I was going to end up being the buffer between them. It was not where I wanted to be.

I reminded myself that after this, I would head back to the hotel to rest for an hour or so and then off to the airport. But then I would start worrying about returning to Mystic Port.

4

THICK FOG COVERED the city and the harbor. I felt like as soon as it lifted, the truth would be revealed and the magic gone. Likely how this place came to be named Mystic Port.

The sun had not quite made its appearance yet to burn off the fog, though the sky continued to lighten announcing the oncoming dawn.

I remembered these type of mornings - I used them to my advantage in getting an early start to scrounge up food. It rained often and I never quite knew which way it would go when the day started like this.

Rubbing my arms in the cool early morning air, I let my feet take me where they willed. The bag on my hip bounced lightly - I only brought the essentials with me and a small snack. I had not been here for half a century and so much had changed. By the look of the buildings, I seemed to have wandered into the historic district as they started becoming more familiar with what I remembered from 50 years ago. I kept seeing what I remembered overlay what was before me. The fog must be playing tricks with my mind.

The few other people out and about at this hour paid me no heed. Perhaps Kitteren told the truth and no one remembered. Unfortunately, I still did.

I left my younger sister at the hotel - she pestered me again during the flight here to talk about the past. She also made my hair pins and elastics disappear during the short time I took to clean up before we left Ocean's Edge.

More and more I began to see the places I once traveled. Where I knew I could score easy food and who to avoid. If I cut through the alley there and jumped onto the trash cans, I could get up onto the short roof to hide while whoever chased me thought I jumped the fence.

I had been able to avoid this visit for a couple of years when the idea had first been brought up soon after I transferred to the TIO. My words to Kitteren and Mother for my remaining away was because I wanted to keep from bringing further trouble to Don's doorstep. Reality quickly revealed it to be a fear of facing my past.

I struggled again with the concept of Don dying - my mind continuing to reject it. I never truly felt I had been able to repay him for his kindness during a time when we were getting turned away by everyone else because of our race.

Sighing, I shook the thoughts from my head and found myself heading toward where I remembered the open market being. Local vendors would rent out the stalls to sell their goods. My mind wandered as much as I did and for once, I did not feel the need to stop it. I had been careful when stealing back then and tried to not be seen. Granted, I had not been able to get away from everyone.

I could not entirely be certain why I decided to pick Mother's pocket back then. I knew I needed to test my abilities for what I planned, but why her specifically, I could not remember. I got away initially, but eventually she tracked me down. All things considered, I do not think anyone could have predicted her choosing to take Kitteren and I as her own.

Pushing my hair back, I found myself annoyed yet again at Kitteren. The dark auburn mass was too long to wear unbound, but I had not the patience to wait and pester her. I still did not understand why she insisted on forcing these changes on me. I tugged at the hem of my dark blue shirt - it clung too tightly to me and came too short for my comfort.

Moving farther into the market area, I started to see sections I recognized. The shops may have changed and the buildings updated, but they managed to maintain the rustic look from back then. The shops became smaller, the streets narrowed, and then the massive single level structure holding a number of stalls took its place. I wondered if the open courtyard still stood in the center or if they covered it to add space for more sellers. I noticed a sign designating it as a farmer's market.

I felt torn between finding comfort in the familiarity or shame as it only served to remind me of a past I would sooner forget. The fog thinned out as I entered the building.

It was still too early for the shops to be open. Vendors were getting things ready for the day, especially the ones serving food. I caught sight of a small form snagging an apple from a fruit stand and taking off as fast as their short legs could carry them while the shop-keeper attended to other tasks.

She stopped as soon as she broke sight of the stall and took a bite - a Human girl with dirt covering her well-worn and somewhat tattered pale yellow shirt and what I thought were once tan pants. Filthy curly strawberry-blond hair topped her head as she ate quickly. Too much did I know what that life was like and felt torn between bringing her before the shopkeeper or just letting her be.

Coming up with a third option, I dug into my pouch and pulled out the wrapped fruit bar while I strode over to her.

Pale blue eyes turned my way and she realized I had seen her. She turned to run and then stopped when I held out the item. She took hesitant steps over to look at it, snatched it up, and disappeared down the next turn.

The fruit bar would quiet her stomach for a little while.

I closed my eyes to the memories of when I stood in her place and pushed back the rising turmoil of my emotions. It would only unsettle my power again. While there had not been any unwanted manifestations of my power, I feared it none-the-less. To me, it would only be a matter of time if I could not figure out how to regain my full control.

I took a deep breath and opened my eyes, trying to focus on something else. Earlier I passed people beginning to set up for various events around the city.

The Summer Solstice was about family and sharing tradition. I was interested to see what the different cultural displays and festivities would be. Reading was a poor substitute for the real thing.

Perhaps, when I got back to the hotel, I could look up a schedule online. I might as well make the most of the unexpected trip.

The headline on one the the newspapers at a newsstand caught my attention: "Child Disappeared". Immediately my mind returned to the past when slave traders gathered orphaned children in the area to sell. My hand gripped the scar hiding under my shirt on the left side of my torso from that fight. Were the slave traders taking children again?

"Ket!" Kitteren called and I heard her running toward me. "There you are. Why did you leave without me?" She sounded out of breath and somewhat panicked.

I dropped my hand and shrugged, not bothering to face her. Telling her I needed time to see the city for myself and think seemed too heavy of a topic for this hour, but I also could not tear my eyes away from the picture of the smiling Human boy in the article.

"Must be a slow news day if they're reporting runaways." She nervously rocked back on her heels a couple of times, the movement of her arms telling me she wrung her hands behind her back. "We should get going. Mom and Dad are arriving today."

I made a face at her for her uncaring attitude and moved away from the newsstand heading in the direction of the courtyard. The fog began getting thicker again as I walked. If I said anything about the article, then I would have to tell her things I did not want to.

I also knew our adopted parent's itinerary, "They aren't arriving until this afternoon. I don't want to spend..." A bronze statue made me lose my train of thought.

There were two children cast in bronze, one curled up, crying, and the other comforting. The one who sat beside the distressed child caught my attention - fairie-like wings sprouted from her back and long hair fell unkempt around her. Her dress was torn and tattered.

Getting closer to see better through the thick fog hanging in the courtyard, I peered up into the fairie's face. It was a child's face, but not one I recognized. Elven-like ears poked out from under the mass of hair.

I turned on Kitteren then, angry, and slipped into the common dialect we grew up with, *"You told me no one would remember."* I kept my voice low and fought to keep my emotions in check, but I felt betrayed.

Kitteren put her hands up defensively. *"I didn't lie. This has fallen into legend. It's a story, that's all. Those children that you and Mom freed back then eventually grew up, but then the details were like a myth. This was put up almost 25 years ago, Ket. I have the same hair color you do and no one has ever accused me of being the fairie."*

Hair color? What else did she not tell me? What was still being told? Narrowing my eyes at my sister briefly, I then turned to lean forward to read the plaque. It spoke of the fairie being a mischief maker and a thief, but would only take enough for herself. That part was wrong: I made sure I always got enough for Kitteren.

It went on about how the fairie looked after the lost and forgotten children of the world. Where had that come from? Admittedly, I had no reason to try and free the others, but it was not right for them to have their chance at a better life taken away. They had already been shunned once by the church which originally took them in. To then be taken for profit from the people who stepped up to care for them - I could not let that stand.

But Kitteren spoke true - just a story. One which had a base in reality, but had been overly embellished in the following years. Something told me Mother was involved in the story telling. She often enjoyed trading tales and this sounded like something she would construct.

I decided to drop the topic for now and move on - this was a reminder of the past and for me, walking away from the statue was as close to moving forward as I could manage right now.

I heard a sigh of relief from behind me. It did not mean I would forget this or let the matter drop completely, but I did not want to continue our conversation in the presence of the statue.

After getting out of sight of it, I sat down on a bench. Kitteren sat next to me - her movements slow and cautious.

Eying her for a moment, I leaned back and crossed my arms over my chest. There was a chill in the air, but I had always gotten cold easily. I admitted to her, "I shouldn't be here."

"Ket..." Kitteren groaned, exasperated.

I just wished she understood how much work I had to do. It felt like the lab work at least tripled and then there was trying to balance everything else. I could not afford time-off, yet here I was.

Silver might also follow me here sometime in the next few days. I still held a sliver of hope he would turn down Lockonis' request. We had work to do now that he completed the basic part of his training. Both of us being away made no sense.

It made even less sense for him to be sent here with me. The orders he received said little more than further information coming. I had not yet brought the question up to Kitteren, unsure if she even knew anything about it, but I had too many things to deal with and kept getting easily distracted.

Just the recent discovery I made with the Arcane College pins alone would normally have kept my attention back at the main office. Certainly I would be pulling even longer hours trying to work on those and the backlog at the same time. Then I needed to deal with Sparky...

"I'd rather have you whining about not wanting to be here than working," Kitteren said, breaking my train of thought.

Sighing, I rubbed my arms and decided not to start another fight right now. "I just... I don't want to remember this part of our lives. Living on the streets, barely alive."

"Yeah, and look at us now." She puffed up her chest proudly. Deflating a little, Kitteren looked around. "Sometimes it helps to remember where you came from to better appreciate where you are."

I remained silent, trying to think on Kitteren's words, but my mind kept drifting back to the article I had seen. She might be right and the child had simply run away. I had not actually read it.

My sister took a deep breath and leaned forward - her eyes dead ahead. "Ketayl, I really don't remember anything about where we are from. I barely remember this place. I keep pestering you for information to try and fill-in some of the gaps."

Losing the last of my anger, I looked down at my feet. "It isn't surprising - you were sick and slept a lot. I'm just glad you grew out of it."

"Yeah, having Neshal's Disease sucked. Lost a good 10 years," Kitteren said. "You could have left me for dead to try and make a better life for yourself, but you didn't."

"You're my sister." I had a duty to look after her to the best of my ability. Even if it meant leaving her in another's care.

Kitteren turned toward me and smirked. "And you remind me I'm technically your half-sister when you're mad at me."

I shrugged. We sat in silence a while, and I gave thought to her words. I still could not shake the feeling being here was wrong. As if history would repeat itself because of my presence.

I DRAGGED along behind Kitteren down a familiar dirt road later that morning. The road had been widened and better maintained, but it was still dirt. Why had she seemed nervous about being in the open market area earlier? If anyone should have been avoiding it, it would have been me. Though now I planned to avoid it if I could.

My sister practically skipped down the road. A little white picket fence sat between tall, thick bushes. I hesitated as she let herself into the yard, falling back to the tall bushes lining the road and out of sight of the house. I clutched the small white bag I carried tightly. Closing my eyes, I reminded myself Kitteren would not have brought me along if I was not welcome, but it had been so long and I could not be sure I wanted to revisit this part of my life.

"Papa!" Kitteren called out. I never could bring myself to use her term for some reason even with just myself.

"You're here!" I heard Don's voice. It sounded older, but not like a man dying. A moment later, he asked sadly, "You weren't able to convince her to come again?"

I started to peek around the corner, not sure what to expect.

Kitteren turned around, "Where...? Ketayl, come on. You didn't fly all the way here to hide behind the bushes." She came back, grabbed my hand and pulled me through the open gate.

Don strode up to me, his walk not quite as strong, but still sure. Wrinkles were prominent on his face and hands, his hair had turned white, and even hunched over slightly, he still stood taller than me. "Oh, my brownie, how you've grown. Such a beautiful young lady." He placed his hands on mine. "And it's so nice to be able to see your face," he laughed, tucking my hair behind my ear.

"Don, who is...?" A Human woman who looked to be about Don's age came out of the house, drying her hands on her apron. "This is a most pleasant surprise to have both of our Elven girls."

I looked to Kitteren, confused. I had never met this woman before and she had not mentioned her.

Don moved and stood next to the new woman, putting his arm

around her. "This is my wife, Alice. We met not too long after Lindale took you two in."

I bowed formally unsure what else to do. Why had Kitteren not warned me about her ahead of time? Was there anyone else I should know about?

"None of that now," Alice chided. "I must have you at a disadvantage - between what Don, Kitteren, and Lindale have told me over the years, I almost feel like you're one of my children."

The statement put me on edge. What had they been saying?

"And she's still as talkative as ever," Don teased. Then I realized I had not spoken a word during the entire exchange. "Well, come on in. I'll get some tea going. You still like lavender with honey?"

I nodded shyly. Don originally introduced me to it. He said it was something he loved from his homeland. Lavender did not normally grow in this part of the Northern Isles, but he used to keep a small garden with some behind the house. It did, however, grow in Elven Territory where I lived so I had been able to get my hands on the flower easily before we left Great Tree. I clutched the small bag I carried tighter.

"Geez, Ket, I know you have a voice - you've been using it to give me grief lately," Kitteren said, tugging on my hair lightly.

"Sorry," I said softly and offered the bag to Don.

He took it, opening the bag to see what I brought and smiled. It contained a mix of pre-made bags of lavender tea as well as seeds for him to plant more. Kitteren suggested the seeds.

Don smiled at me as he held the door open for us. "You were always a child of few words. And thank you very much for the gift. I fear the two of us will be the only ones who will enjoy it. Never could get anyone else to drink it."

The interior had been updated: the wall between the front common room and the foyer removed, the flowery wallpaper replaced by soft white paint and much of the walls covered by picture frames of varying sizes and styles. The changes to the building did not throw me off as much as the perspective with my height differ-ence. I remembered having to climb on furniture to clean, but now I could reach those same areas easily.

The pictures were of him and Alice as well as who I could presume were their children and grandchildren from over the years.

Kitteren and both of our adopted parents showed up in some. I intruded upon the special connection they had.

I also started getting nervous about the fact there were all these people I did not know and would likely end up meeting. Mentally I cursed my sister in a manner I would never voice. I tried to justify my lack of knowledge as I had been removed from this life for so long.

"The only one we've ever been missing is you," Don said as he came up behind me. Patting my shoulder, he moved away toward the kitchen.

"And I intend to remedy that tonight," Alice said. "Provided your parent's travel plans haven't changed."

Kitteren smiled, plopping into a chair, "They arrive in a few hours - their flight here was delayed a little." Her movements made me notice the mismatched furniture I remembered also changed. My mind had overlaid the past on the present. I closed my eyes for a moment to try and clear the disorientation.

"Wonderful," Alice said as she took a seat. "We've planned to have everyone over for dinner this evening. Though I'm curious why you two came separately."

Kitteren looked at me. I stayed standing near the corner leading back to the kitchen. "You can sit down you know." Turning back to Alice without waiting for me to respond, she said, "Ketayl had business in Ocean's Edge yesterday and I wanted to get her here before she could change her mind. Mom needed to finish up with her students."

I debated my next course of action as I looked down the hall past the stairs and toward the open kitchen/dining area.

Both women looked at me expectantly when I turned back and it made me uneasy. I bowed and excused myself, "I'm going to go help with the tea."

I quickly made my way down the hall. I brushed my fingers along the decorated door on my right. Don used to keep his medical supplies in there. Well, the non-perishable items anyway.

I remembered Don getting an emergency patient one time while I had been in the house. I hid in the back corner behind some boxes to remain out of sight. I swore I had been in there for hours.

I stepped lightly, not wanting to interrupt him, but needing to know why Kitteren said he was dying. It made it harder to try and accept her words.

"Well, come in. No need to lurk," Don said. He never looked away from where he prepared a tray for tea. He had two different teapots ready.

"Do you need help?"

Don turned to smile at me. "We'll be in trouble the day I need help boiling water. So what is it that finally brought you back here?"

I looked down at my hands, moving further in so as not to be heard by the others. "Kitteren... she said you were dying."

The water started to boil. Don sighed in a resigned tone and set about making the tea as he spoke. "A little dramatic. I fear she may have been overzealous in her attempts to convince you to come visit. I'll speak with her later on the matter."

I tilted my head to the side, not sure what he meant.

"My dear brownie," Don started and I had a feeling I was not going to like what I heard. "I know you kept your distance for a reason. You have nothing to fear here now."

I shifted from one foot to the other, unsure of where he was heading with this.

"Now as for what your sister said," Don paused and there was tension in his body. "For a Human my age, I'm healthy, but I'm getting old. I don't have many years left and I fear this old man may have pestered your sister a little too much about being able to see both of my Elven girls again."

I thought about Kitteren's words. She specifically worded it as his time was limited, but not elaborating upon the statement would be a fault of both of us - her for not clarifying and me for not asking.

"Don't think too harshly about your sister, Ketayl. She means well. She only wishes to do whatever she can for you," Don said, picking up the tray and heading for the front room. "You probably don't know how much she missed you all those years you spent at the Arcane College and the joy she had when she got her sister back."

I decided to drop bringing up Kitteren's lack of clarification with her. It would not be worth the potential rift it could cause between us. The illusion of normalcy had become so powerful and it was all I wanted at this point. I just needed to get through this trip.

I followed him to the front room and we spent the rest of the morning catching up. By we, I meant I mostly remained silent while Kitteren spoke. I admitted to myself I had missed Don greatly, but it did not change the fact my sister's odd behavior concerned me.

And even more so when she occasionally excused herself to go take a phone call without a word as to who she spoke with or why she needed to take it. That said nothing of the text messages she seemed to be almost constantly responding to. Our parents would have messaged both of us. What was she hiding and why had she been so determined to get me here she would risk telling such a story?

5

WE MET our adopted parents at the airport and then got them settled at the hotel. I wondered why we had not waited and traveled together - even some extra time in Ocean's Edge would not have been an issue. Except for maybe my sister's strong dislike of Silver.

After a quick lunch, our parents left to meet some friends they had in the area, leaving us to our own devices. I thought it odd no one mentioned the plan prior, but I decided to use the time to my advantage.

I curled up on the couch in the suite with my tablet, intent on getting ahead on the reading in some of my classes for the next semester. Suddenly my tablet was gone from my hands.

Kitteren held it above me, giving me a look of annoyance. "You're not supposed to be working."

I missed when I reached up and she moved it farther away. I said, "It's not work, it's just some light reading."

Kitteren walked away, reading the title of the book, "'Advanced Theory on Elemental Influence in the Arcane.' Ket, this is not 'light reading.' This sounds like something for work." She tilted the device, trying to make sense of what was on the screen.

"It's for one of my classes for next semester," I corrected, getting up to try and reclaim my tablet.

"Guess I'm confiscating this then," Kitteren said, walking away with the device.

"Kih-tail..." I warned, emphasizing the name I used with her when it was only us. Why would she care what I was reading?

Kitteren turned around, her fists on her hips. "Don't you 'Kitayl' me, Keh-tal. You're on vacation. No work - it includes school work. Why are you even taking classes at the EAC again?"

Frowning, I crossed my arms - we had been over this, but I reminded her, "The Director wanted the EAC to re-evaluate me for rank, but they won't assign me one until I've taken enough classes to graduate." I found the situation tedious at best, but tried to make the most of the unexpected refresher.

"It's dumb you have to go through this again. What about all the time you spent there at the beginning of the year then?" Kitteren had not yet put down my tablet. I hoped to be able to snatch it. I could use my power to get it, but it would only serve to infuriate her. Dealing with an angry Kitteren was not on my list of things to do.

Sighing, I gave up. I dropped my arms to my sides and moved toward the window and took in the view of the harbor, not really seeing it. I had not talked about it, but then she never asked before either. "The Magus ran me through a battery of tests, but the Arch-mages wouldn't sign off on the results. Then I spent the next week testing out of classes, but they only let me do so many. At least they're letting me take the classes online except for the practicals." And even then, Magus Engelil convinced them to create a separate schedule for me because of the distance I would have to travel. Some even went so far as to allow Lockonis to do the testing in their place.

"I still think the whole thing is stupid. What rank do you think you are?" Kitteren inquired, which I found odd. She rarely ever wanted to talk about my arcane knowledge - she held a grudge against the Arcane College still which extended to my capabilities.

I eyed her for a moment, but answered honestly, "I don't know and I really don't care. Having a rank isn't going to change anything. Can I have my tablet back?" My knowledge and my actual capacity to use the information did not match up, which is what I assumed made it difficult for the Archmages at the EAC to sign off on the results. Lockonis' training sessions often focused on increasing my capacity because of it.

"No," Kitteren said. "Not until you tell me about the fairie."

I crossed my arms over my chest again and glared at her, trying to keep my rising anger at bay. "No means no. The fairie is dead - let her rest in peace." Please just drop this.

"Ketayl..." Kitteren whined, "Come on. What harm is there in telling me? They're just stories now."

Just like the story with the statue? To me it would likely never be "just a story" - I could not understand why this was so important to her.

I turned away from her so she could not see my face and grit my teeth. I closed my eyes and pushed back the memories - running, fighting, starving, being turned away at almost every turn. "I can't, Kitteren. Please don't ask me again." I could not tell her about the monster hidden just beneath the surface. That she saw an illusion even I started to believe until I encountered the necromancer's spell six months ago. It had been a strong reminder of how dangerous I was. The fact no one had been hurt by it was a miracle in and of itself.

"No, I'm not going to stop asking until you tell me. Ketayl, this isn't fair. You know everything about me, even my darkest time, but you won't share anything. Quit thinking you're protecting me!" Kitteren was fuming. My sister was definitely the more emotional of the two of us, but she was also free to let herself feel.

Apparently dealing with an angry Kitteren was on the agenda today.

Sighing, I gave a little, knowing she would not let this go other-wise, but only enough to give her a reason why. "I... I did things. Things I'm not proud of. I don't want to let it come between us. I just want to move forward."

"Ketayl..." she said. I could not turn around to look at her. "What happened? Come on, you can tell me. Please don't let me imagine the worst." Kitteren stood right behind me, her hands on my shoulders. Her touch normally did not bother me, but I forced myself not to move away this time.

I took a deep breath and found my escape. "Mother's version is better. I'm afraid I don't remember clearly," I lied. I only wanted her to give up on this hunt for information.

"And Mom won't tell me either. She tells me to come talk to you. Do you know how infuriating that is?!" Kitteren was getting worked up again and she was gone from being directly behind me.

Silence fell between us. I searched my mind for some kind of solution to the problem here. How could I convince her to stop asking?

The door opened and Kitteren said sharply, "I'm going for a walk." Then she left, taking my tablet with her. I did not even try to follow her. There was no point until she calmed herself down.

I sighed and laid down on the couch - there was much I needed to think about. I may be pushing her away more by not telling her, but I swore to myself to never let her find out. There must be a balance between the two. I just wish I knew why in the past few months she became so adamant about getting me to tell her. More than a few times she had come across as sounding desperate. It was a word I remember being used in her conversation with Lockonis recently.

AT SOME POINT I dozed off. Familiar violet eyes and wavy chocolate-colored brown hair greeted me when I woke. "Where's Kitteren?" Mother asked.

I rubbed my eyes and wondered what time it was. I said, "She went for a walk."

"Dayko, can you try reaching her again? We'll have to be going soon if we want to get to Don's on time," Mother spoke gently to her mate. Then she turned back to me and asked, "Is everything alright?"

Father fiddled with his phone, but kept the majority of his attention on us. His normally gentle expression hard - his jaw visibly locked and eyes narrowed. He ran a hand through his brown hair, mussing it up momentarily before it fell back in place and nearly back into his eyes with the exception of one piece which always tried to stick straight up.

I wrapped my arms around my knees when I sat up, making myself smaller. I admitted, "We got into an argument. She took my tablet." I was not sure why the last part would be important to anyone other than myself. The device belonged to the TIO and I started to worry about if something happened to it.

Mother nodded to Father, who then stepped into their bedroom and closed the door. She asked me, "What were you arguing about?"

I looked at those vibrant violet eyes which always seemed to know more than I thought. I looked away. "She asked about the fairie again."

Mother said nothing and simply rubbed my back. I buried my face, hoping this would simply blow over. If only she would drop the subject we could go back to normal.

"Kitteren said she would meet us at Don's house," Father said as he opened the door. His face still hard and he kept his brown eyes down at his phone.

"Thank you. Can you give us a minute?" Mother asked softly.

Father sighed loudly before he said, "You know how I feel about this, Lindale." Then the door closed once more.

I picked up my head at his statement and the use of her full name. It made no sense. Were they arguing about me? I did not want to be the cause of a rift in their relationship. It gave me something else to worry about. Maybe I was the actual problem.

"Don't worry about what Dad said," Mother spoke softly, rubbing my back. "I can't take sides in this disagreement. It needs to come from you, Ketayl. As you can tell, she already has a romanticized version of who the fairie is. I think now she just wants the facts to confirm her belief."

"And the truth will drive her away. I can't lose her," I whispered, refusing to meet Mother's gaze. Kitteren is the one who kept me going back then and still even now.

"I doubt there is anything you can say to do that. She loves you, Ketayl," Mother soothed. But she still pushed me to tell Kitteren what she wanted to know. Why did they not think I had a reason for my continued silence?

Getting up, I moved away from Mother quickly and told her firmly, "I swore I would never tell." I tried to smooth out my hair, still annoyed Kitteren forced me into wearing it down. "We should get going." My power was agitated and I paused to take a deep breath to try and calm myself.

Mother sighed and opened the door to their bedroom, letting Father know we were done. They began a conversation of a lighter topic while I paced to try and calm myself down. Now multiple people pressed me about the fairie. Why could they not just let the child remain dead?

WHEN WE ARRIVED at Don's house Kitteren was nowhere to be seen. Don assured me she arrived safely hours ago and I knew where I could find her.

Initially I thought his words cryptic, but quickly figured out it meant she went to the shack we once lived in. Or at least the area of it. Whether or not the shack still stood and in what condition, I did not know and I did not want to satisfy my curiosity. Instead, I found things to help with for the large dinner.

Don's dining area was too small to hold everyone so they planned to use the much larger area outside under a pavilion. Over the years his sons built him tables and benches as the family grew. I carried a load of plates out, setting the stack down on one end of the long table. Impressively I made it without dropping the heavy load.

Looking at the stack, I started to get apprehensive about how many people were going to be here. The phrase "too much too quickly" came to mind. I doubted my ability to remember their names alone.

A one-sided argument by the shed caught my attention. Turning, I saw Kitteren on the phone, obviously displeased with the person on the other end. Unfortunately, I stood too far away to clearly hear her side of the conversation.

I moved so I could watch Kitteren while I set the table. She paced, anger visible as she argued with the person. She ran a hand through her long bangs in frustration and then tugged on the ends. This would only make dealing with my sister harder. Or it could distract her - I could not guess which for certain.

Father strode over to her just as she hung up - exasperation plain on her face and her phone clenched tightly in her hand. He pulled her aside and she moved her hands while she spoke to him, waving a hand in the air at one point. I really wanted to know who she had just spoken to.

It took a few minutes, but he managed to calm her down, but not before his face turned hard again and I doubted his words were any more gentle. At one point he pointed sharply in my direction and I saw Kitteren shrink back before I looked away.

Despite the scene I knew they had a special connection. She had taken to Father's trade of being a tracker. I knew little else. I did not feel it was my place to pry further.

I hurried to finish and headed back in for the next load to bring out. In terms of the weather, it was a nice evening for a dinner, but Kitteren's mood might sully it. I assumed the blame would be mine since I set her off earlier, though the call seemed to be making this trip so far just as uncomfortable for her.

"Ketayl, dear, while you were outside, Jonathan and his wife, Elizabeth, arrived. They're in the front room if you would like to meet them," Alice said and smiled. I heard voices from the front room, but only recognized Mother's.

I bowed, and said, "I'll finish helping get dinner ready first." I was not yet prepared to meet the rest of Don's family. I was not sure why no one thought to tell me about all of the others - his children and grandchildren, in-laws. My head spun at the thought.

"You have a guest and you make her help with dinner?" A cocky male voice came from the doorway.

I saw Don, as he appeared 50 years ago. Then I realized this must be one of his sons. This overlaying the past on the present quickly wore my patience thin.

"Ketayl insisted on helping. Something you and your siblings could learn from," Alice chided him before she turned and smiled at me. "This is my son Jonathan."

Jonathan held his hand out to me, "Jon is fine. A pleasure to meet my long lost sister finally." He gave me a big grin. What had they told them about me? Why had I not been granted some notification of what I would be encountering? There was no way he could seriously consider me as a sibling unless he was just extending his view of Kitteren. Unfortunately, they would be disappointed if they were expecting me to have her personality.

Putting down the utensils I gathered, I slowly reached out and took his hand. I did not like being touched, but I did not want to be rude either.

Shaking my hand firmly, Jon then patted me on the shoulder as he moved farther into the kitchen, reaching into one of the dishes only to get his hand smacked with a wooden spoon. Alice admonished, "You can wait for dinner."

Jon walked away rubbing his wounded hand. He mouthed, "She's mean," to me.

I smiled, glad Don found this life after we left. He deserved happiness. Especially after the trouble he went through hiding Kitteren and myself from the authorities. He risked too much with the laws in place at the time.

"Alex said he was on his way to pick up Steph and the kids. I haven't heard from Joanna yet," Jon commented, taking a seat at the dining room table.

Alice stirred the pot for a moment. "We're also missing Kitteren, though she's somewhere on the property."

"She came back while I was putting the plates out," I said and suddenly had their attention again. "Please excuse me." I quickly hid my embarrassment by picking up my bundle and heading outside to set the table.

"Shy one, isn't she?" I heard Jon comment before I got out of earshot.

I did not see Kitteren outside and took a moment once I got to the table to take a deep breath. I could get through this. It was just dinner, right?

"Hey, Ket," Kitteren said softly.

I jumped, not expecting anyone. I tried to cover my surprise by getting the table set.

Kitteren put her hand over mine. "Ket, slow down."

I paused and looked up at her. I saw the opposite of what I witnessed by the shed. What did Father say to her? I clamped my mouth shut to keep from asking. She likely did not know I watched the interaction.

"Look, about earlier... I'm sorry." Kitteren locked me in place with her emerald green eyes. "I guess being here, together, has only made me more determined to know."

"It's fine," I said flatly. I was still aggravated with her, but I could understand where she was coming from to some extent. This place just dug up memories I would sooner have left buried and I was not certain if our roles were reversed I would be able to contain my curiosity.

"Let me help you at least." Kitteren took half of the pile and went to the other side of the table. She chatted lightly about inane things, but my mind wandered. It was not like her to not tell me exactly what her thoughts were. She never held anything back before, but I also had not seen Father get upset at her. There were simply too many questions and a more pressing issue of dealing with all these people I did not know.

6

AFTER DINNER, Jon and his twin brother Alex moved the tables and benches, rearranging them into a large circle and bringing the patio furniture back. Then they pulled me into taking pictures with all of them.

I hated having my picture taken. Even worse was being in the center. Alex and Steph's two young daughters took an instant desire to wanting to play with my hair. Joanna's son sat quietly where she placed him while they managed to convince the two girls to sit still and leave me be.

Mother produced a small brush from somewhere and worked out the messy braids the girls managed. The boy had remained mostly silent through dinner and seemed saddened by something. As Mother worked out a nasty tangle, I shot Kitteren a look, wanting at least a hair elastic back.

Kitteren stood to one side of me, not paying attention to me and smiling broadly, but it did not seem to meet her eyes. Don took to the other side and patted my arm in a calming manner. Elizabeth, belly swollen with child, tried her best to organize everyone. Jon kept telling her to relax and this was not work.

Joanna took an instant dislike to me and I could not figure out why. She seemed to have a good relationship with Kitteren. It bothered me little as Jon and Alex were all too happy to pester me with questions during dinner and after the chaos of taking pictures. I tried to keep my answers short or let my sister or Mother answer for me.

After pictures Don went into the house and came out with his violin. I forced myself to have a neutral expression despite my excitement. I missed hearing him play and I took up the violin once I transferred to the TIO in an attempt fill the void.

Don stood before me and held out the case. He said, "I'm afraid I don't play as well as I used to, but Lindale says you've gotten quite good at it."

Taking the case slowly, I looked around, nervous. Mother merely nodded, signaling for me to open it. Her grin was mischievous and I came to the conclusion she set me up. So far the evening had gone smoothly and in between asking me questions, they spent the time catching up with each other.

"I hope you don't mind I rosined up the bow when I pulled it out of storage this afternoon," Don said and grinned. "Made sure everything was in working order."

Carefully undoing the creaky gold-colored latches, I opened the worn brown leather case being held together by fraying brown tape in some places. The violin looked as good as it did over half a century ago with the golden tones reflecting in the finish. I checked the tune and tightened up the bow, trying to ignore the stares around me.

Don took a seat next to me, smiling broadly. This mattered for him and no one else. I figured I could push aside my fear of making a mistake in front of others for a little while.

I lifted the violin to my shoulder and played the song I knew he had a fondness for. Kitteren jumped in and provided the voice. It was a dialect of the common language which, well, did not sound like common. I used to sing it for Don and Kitteren, but I rarely sang anymore and did not think I could do it justice. Only Mother's tutoring me in private kept me in any sort of practice. Sometimes I thought she hoped I would take to her trade. Genetics forced me into the arcane.

I glanced at Don who merely leaned back in his chair with his eyes closed to listen. The smile on his face kept me going and I tried to ignore the others, not wanting to find a reason to stop. I rarely handled an acoustic violin and the rich sound was addicting. Even with the decent soundproofing between quarters at the main office, I had opted for the quieter electric version.

All too soon, I found the end of the song. Lowering the violin, I looked at Don who still kept his eyes closed. "Sir?" I asked softly, barely loud enough for him to hear me. I began to question if I had even spoken after a few moments.

Don smiled, opening his eyes. "Just remembering a different time. If you wouldn't mind continuing?" Perhaps he also saw both the past and the present. It made me question my being here again.

I looked to Mother and then to Kitteren who both signaled for me to play. Alex jumped up and said, "I'll be right back." He and his brother acted like grown children. They reminded me a little of Silver in that regard.

I sat still, unsure what to do. Joanna continued to glare at me. Was it a song she and Don made special? Then she remarked sharply, "I guess she only knows one song."

Her words caught me off guard. What did I do wrong?

"Don't be rude, Joanna," Alice chided before she stood up, looking at her watch. "If you'll excuse me, I need to get dessert out of the oven."

Kitteren jerked as if she just realized where she was and smiled, leaning back in her chair. "No, she knows more. Ket just doesn't often play for others. How about the one you were working on a while back?"

I sank back into my chair as the attention returned to me. "It's pretty hard." I knew the song Kitteren spoke of because she seemed to like it. It was fast paced and fun to listen to, but it was significantly more difficult than anything else I learned. I memorized the song before I had been able to play it fully.

"You sounded fine the last time I heard you," Kitteren smirked. She neglected to mention she only listened to me because she would let herself into my quarters. I kept asking her to stop and I still could not figure out how she bypassed the security.

I looked at the violin in my lap. I knew mine could take the almost abuse I would put it through, but this felt far more delicate. I ran my fingertips lightly over the finish.

Alex came back with a guitar and another case I did not immediately recognize. He handed it to Jon.

Jon said as he opened the small case, "Oh, don't wait for us."

I looked at Don who only reached over and patted my leg. "Go ahead. That old thing is tougher than it looks."

It seemed he had not lost his ability to somehow know what was on my mind. Not magic as far as I could tell - I had no explanation for it.

Taking a deep breath, I lifted the violin to my shoulder again and pulled the music up in my head. The fingers on my left hand moved quickly up and down the neck, creating the different notes. Most of the problems were in moving the bow for the more complicated parts, but I practiced this piece for so long, my muscles remembered what to do faster than my mind could direct them.

Alex bounced in his seat with a broad smile on his face once I finished. "Please tell me you know 'Dueling Strings' because I haven't played it with anyone else in ages."

I thought for a moment, recalling the piece in question. For some reason, Mother insisted I learn the piece. "I do, but I've only played it against a recorded track."

"Lead on my good woman," Alex smiled broadly, getting settled with his guitar. Jon blew something out of a metal tube and gave a thumbs up.

Joanna, however, glared at me and stood up quickly, "Well, I'm going to go help Mom."

I watched her go silently. I did not know what to make of her attitude. I glanced over at Kitteren who quietly watched her leave - it seemed as if her mind was elsewhere. She also continued to text sporadically through the gathering, but kept her phone down in her lap.

Steph leaned forward toward me, "Don't take it too much to heart. She treated me the same way for a few years even after Alex and I got married. She takes a while to warm up to people."

"Hey, don't leave me hanging here!" Alex cried. "I want to know if you can play it better than my old man."

Don smirked, "After the last song, my brownie has definitely bypassed me in skill." I thought he gave me too much credit.

"Why do you call her a 'brownie'?" Jon asked.

I shrank back slightly, not sure I wanted to hear Don's explanation. I vaguely understood the term, but he never spoke of it in any sort of detail before. Joanna's son quietly moved to a seat closer to me.

Don smiled gently, getting settled better in his chair before starting. "I didn't always know her name. Ketayl was surprisingly more quiet and shy back then. I think I might have heard her talk more today than ever before."

I fought the heat rising to my face. Not counting the times he had me sing while he played, his exaggeration was likely not far off.

Don continued, "So since she would help out around the property cleaning and whatnot and since most of the time I didn't see her doing it she became my brownie. Then you two came along and it was a disaster again."

Jon laughed loudly.

Alex bounced the guitar impatiently on his lap. I shrugged apologetically and lifted the violin back to my shoulder, settling in for another song, unsure about too many things.

What really worried me was Kitteren. It felt like she kept something from me - more than this. She remained silent, but distracted through the whole exchange. I knew her mind was elsewhere because she would have stepped in with Joanna before the others.

Not that I wanted her to stand up for me, but she always tried to anyway. Sometimes I think she forgot I was older and thus it was my job to look after her. Her behavior continued to baffle me.

———

THE SUN DISAPPEARED below the horizon by the time we got back to the hotel. My mind continued to run in circles about everything so far which meant rest would be elusive until I calmed it. Digging through my bag I found my normal swimsuit. If Kitteren had replaced it with a two-piece of any design I might have broken down and bought a replacement.

At this time of day, the pool downstairs would likely be free and since I was sans my reading material I needed to do something.

"You're going swimming?" Kitteren asked.

"I'm not ready to rest yet. I've gotten used to late hours," I said. The workload back at the main office demanded it and I could not sacrifice time in other areas except for downtime.

Kitteren sat on the edge of my bed, watching me. "More like all-nighters. There was one week I think you made it five or six days without rest. Just because you're Elven doesn't mean you should push those limits. You definitely made it easy to convince Vince and Lock-onis you needed a vacation."

Which now explained why the Director's second started doing an audit in the lab all of a sudden. I shot back at my sister, "And then Lockonis threatened to lock me out of the lab." The fact she blatantly admitted to being the one to report me angered me more than having been caught. I clenched my teeth and reminded myself Kitteren only looked out for my health and wellbeing.

"What happened anyway? It seems like every few months you get inundated." Kitteren sprawled out on one of the beds.

I took a deep breath. This time the problem had gotten worse than usual. "A few lab techs from branch offices have a problem with the fact I attended the Arcane College. I don't like getting Lockonis involved so I try to take care of the incoming work. I just fell behind with everything else I've been doing." I knew I should not let them dump the work they could handle in-house on me, but part of me continued to hope they would look past where I studied at some point and accept me as one of their peers.

"Geez, Ket, how come you never said anything? I know you had a rough time the first month or so after you transferred, but I thought that was as far as it went," Kitteren sat up and tried to get my attention, but I kept myself busy with rearranging my suitcase. If it had not been for her and Retanei, I might still be in the same situation.

"News travels," I replied, though wearing my Arcane College pin before had been the dead giveaway. At least as evidence, I did not have to worry about it. "It's not a big deal. I should have put more time in the lab and less in other things. Taken less time off."

"Uh, no. Ket, you rarely took any of your actual scheduled downtime. You've been juggling a seriously increased physical training regimen, working on getting those filters made and out to the branch offices, and schoolwork from the EAC on top of your lab work."

Kitteren forgot about the few hours I devoted to working on trying to figure out the cult of the Ancient Gods next move, but reminding her would only strengthen her point. I also squeezed in practice time, but took up swimming as a second option. I did not want to disturb my neighbors with the sound of my violin during those late hours, though I found the lab to be a good place to play at night while I waited for results from the various machines.

Then there were the video calls from Silver and the Ocean's Edge crew. Perhaps if I had tried to minimize those...

I crossed out the thought - I found I needed those. I started feeling isolated and alone before they began calling. I would hear from someone almost every night. Sometimes during the day if they called for an update.

Where was an over-sized shirt when I needed it?

"What are you looking for?" Kitteren asked after watching me for a minute.

"Something to use as a cover. Why did you have to repack my bag?"

Kitteren rolled over and looked at me upside-down. I was not sure if she was trying to be cute or not. "Because I love you and you need to have more confidence in yourself. Besides, those are all clothes you got as hand-me-downs from me and Mom. Well, with the exception of a few items. If you don't like what I packed you can always go buy some new ones."

"No," I said flatly. I could not afford to spend money frivolously. Bad enough occasionally I would sneak out for a small treat when I was in Great Tree. I needed to save my money for Kitteren...

I stopped that train of thought and looked at my sister. Why did I still feel the need to do that for her? So many times she and Mother told me to stop and use what little money I made at the Arcane College for myself. Now, obviously, both of them were doing well - living very comfortably, but I still felt obligated. I had not even helped pay for anything on this trip so far.

Kitteren rolled back onto her stomach. "You'll be fine. I'll walk you down there - they have towels available inside the pool room. Just change up."

I went to leave to go to the bathroom, but Kitteren gave me a look and I simply turned around. I did not want anyone to see my body, even my own sister. More importantly, I did not want anyone to see the scar which wrapped itself from a few inches under my left arm to the front of my left hip. Only Mother, Don, and a few doctors knew it existed. I tried to distract myself while I got the black and purple racing-style suit on. "You don't want to come?"

"Nah. I think I'll go for a run. I'm not ready to rest yet either." My sister sounded unsure about her idea.

Kitteren was not changing for a run. Maybe she forgot her clothes. Her athletic shoes would allow her to do so, but they were not her preferred ones for running. I wanted to justify her actions, but found I could not believe them.

And she knew I still did not like running as an activity of choice.

I wanted to question her. There were too many things which did not make sense, but I did not want her to start asking about the fairie again. Perhaps I just needed time to figure out how to craft a conversation around the information I wanted to get.

Once I finished, we exited our shared bedroom into the common room of the suite. The door was open and the lights were off in the bedroom for our adopted parents.

I tilted my head in confusion - they came back with us from Don's house and it had gotten late. I did not remember hearing them leave. "Where are Mother and Father?"

"*Mom and Dad* probably went to go visit some friends." Kitteren put emphasis on how she referred to our parents. It bothered her I was so formal. "Mom made a few in the area when we'd come back to visit. They probably went to go meet them at a bar or something."

Kitteren seemed annoyed at my taking so long to go for my swim. Which in turn, confused me more. Usually she would be more than happy to join me just to spend time together. Why did she not seem concerned about where our adopted parents had gone? Likely she would have made these same friends, right? Why did they not say anything before they left?

I shifted uncomfortably, double-checking to make sure I had my key for the suite.

"You look fine, Ket. Come on or the pool will get cold." Why did it feel like she was in a rush?

"Not likely," I shot back at her. I debated trying to follow her, but I did not have shoes on and while I could cloak myself, I would not be able to keep up with her on a run. I told myself tomorrow I would corner her and ask my questions. With everything earlier, I did not want to push the topic tonight.

7

———

I woke early to find the suite still as empty as when I returned from my swim. This worried me greatly and I paced in my night clothes, looking out the window, poking my head down the hall, finally caving and calling Kitteren.

"Well, good morning sleepyhead," Kitteren answered sounding overly chipper.

"Where are you? Where are Mother and Father?" I tried to keep the panic and worry out of my voice. There were no notes, no messages, nothing. I started biting my lower lip and then stopped as soon as I noticed the action.

"Slow down, Ket. Sorry, we decided to go out and get something to bring back for breakfast. I guess it took longer than we figured. Didn't mean to worry you," Kitteren apologized. Her voice sounded tired despite her attempt to cover it. And the background noise did not sound like a restaurant - I heard a heavy door close and what sounded like water lapping gently in the background.

I glanced in our room at her bed and it did not look like she rested in it last night. I could not recall having ever seen her bed made.

Taking a deep breath, I said, "Kitteren, we need to talk." I did not want to do this over the phone, but I needed to start somewhere.

"Can it wait? We'll be back in a bit." I could hear the worry in her voice.

"Fine." I hung up and set about getting ready for the day. My swim last night had not settled my mind like it normally did. Not with things not adding up. And with as much as Kitteren made me pack, I did not have room for my violin. My tablet also had not reappeared yet either.

Maybe I would find myself up at Don's today. I'm sure he and his wife could use help cleaning up after dinner yesterday. It would only be fair to show my gratitude for their hospitality.

I tried to stretch out the deep purple tank top which clung to me. At least a little longer would be nice. It barely came over my waistband. Kitteren had the figure and the confidence to wear this stuff. I would only wear it under a sweater in the spring or autumn.

I brushed my hair as Mother and Kitteren entered the suite. I bit my tongue, not wanting to involve either of our parents in the conversation I needed to have with my sister. Though I had become curious as to where they disappeared to so early. And why go out when there was breakfast being served downstairs?

I tugged on my shirt as I stood up from the couch, smelling eggs and meat. A little richer for breakfast than normal. I would have been fine with something simpler.

Mother directed me to the table, taking my brush from me. "Go eat and I'll finish your hair. It's the least I can do for making you worry."

The statement seemed weird to me, but I pushed it off. My stomach demanded food.

Only one container of food sat on the table. "You aren't eating?"

Kitteren immediately went to our room and Father had not returned with them. The picture before me made no sense.

"I'm sorry, my sweet girl. I didn't want to wake you and I had some business to take care of. Music is a demanding industry - I don't recommend it," Mother laughed. "Kitteren went with me and Dad so you could rest. She's been keeping me apprised of how much you've been working."

I rolled my eyes and popped a piece of sausage in my mouth, savoring the delightful mix of spices and meat. I guessed the business which served it back then was still going strong. I used to salvage the burnt ones sent back to the kitchen. They were never really burnt. I paused, considering the meal before me. Something felt very off about this.

"Would you like to go shopping with me today? Just the two of us," Mother proposed, gently brushing my hair. The tangles were long gone, but the motion soothed my frayed nerves.

I started to forget my aggravation and the conversation I wanted to have with Kitteren. I sighed, chewing on another bite of sausage. I swallowed and then said, "Okay." Maybe I would cave and buy some new clothes after all.

Shopping bored me. How Mother managed to talk me into this I still did not know. I stared at a white dress on a form. While I found it pretty, it was not something I would wear. I wondered if Kitteren would like something like this.

No, too soft and airy. She liked something a little on the sleeker side. Though she might like the single shoulder and the thin silver cording wrapped around the torso from just under the bust to the waist.

"Do you like this dress?" Mother asked, coming up behind me.

I jumped, not expecting her. I thought her occupied for a while speaking with one of the sales people. "Oh, I couldn't wear something like this. I was trying to figure out if I should tell Kitteren about it." Mother would not let me wander far from her, which limited where I could browse. She would request my attention on something to bring me back closer to her.

Mother looked at the dress for a few moments. "Knowing my girls like I do, I'd say this would look better on you. Why don't we find one in your size and try it on? Just for fun." She smiled at me and I knew there was no point arguing, though I rolled my eyes anyway.

We had been at this for hours so far and it was just after noon. It had been the same thing at multiple stores. Try this on, try that on. This was why I normally declined shopping trips.

Being prodded into the changing room with the dress, I took a moment to think without Mother distracting me. Why *had* I given in without much of a fight?

Then I remembered Mother had a way with people. It was a form of magic I did not understand and was difficult to combat - especially if you did not know what to look for. Getting food from one of my more favorite haunts from 50 years ago only helped her.

How had she known I used to frequent that place? Even Kitteren or Don would not have known. She always seemed good at finding out information, but this seemed inconsequential.

I thought about confronting her in regards to using her abilities on me, but what good would it do? Kitteren and I had been at odds most of this trip and likely she did not wish to see us fight.

Getting changed, I considered Kitteren when she returned. Mother tried to distract me so I would not pay attention to my sister, but I noticed she wore the same clothes she had on the night before. And she looked exhausted.

"How's it going in there?" Mother called. I had not spent as much time with all of them as I probably should have. Maybe this would be considered normal for a trip like this.

I struggled with the zipper. It was in an awkward position. "I don't think this is a good fit," I lied. It was a better alternative to begging for this to be over.

She stuck her head in through the curtain. "Nonsense, let me help you with that." Mother took over and I hung my head back, frustrated. "I know, this is not something you enjoy, but I needed to separate you and your sister for a bit. Besides, it's been a while since you last let me drag you around shopping. Despite what you may think, you're still one of my girls."

Mother kissed the top of my head and I wondered why she cared so much for someone who tried to steal from her in the first place. I had done nothing but cause problems for her. The most I had been able to care for Kitteren and keep both of them safe from me was to accept the Arcane College's proposal.

Her attention on my reflection in the mirror made me squirm. The dress alone made me uneasy, but those violet eyes of hers always felt like they saw deeper than I wanted them to.

I distracted myself with my surroundings. The spacious dressing room we both could stand in comfortably had little beyond the black curtains and mirrored walls. I looked at the black, cloth-covered stool wishing I could sit down and take this dress off.

"Absolutely beautiful. You should get it," Mother said and smiled. Then she made me turn around for her.

"It's uncomfortable and I wouldn't know when I would wear it," I whined. On the contrary, I would be content in the soft fabric, but I did not like showing this much or wearing such fitted outfits. Or dresses - I did not like dresses. They reminded me too much of the robes I had to wear before.

"Okay, okay. You're probably getting hungry anyway," Mother laughed and helped me undo the zipper. At least one of us found this amusing.

She must have heard my stomach, which might explain my crankiness. I looked at myself in the mirror one last time and started to think maybe I could make a change and this was a far cry from the well-worn gray robes.

One quick glance at the price tag and I happily put it back. There were other ways to make changes - ones not so expensive.

ALL THE TIME spent getting dragged around and I had yet to find a replacement shirt I liked. Or hair elastics. Mother stuck to the fancier shops, which did not carry what I preferred, though a few did catch my attention that were outside of my normal attire.

We sat out on the patio of a quiet cafe. I held a fried potato stick, nibbling on the end while I tried to think. We were in a newer part of the city. It felt like she avoided the areas I used to frequent. Not that I was complaining. I needed a break from seeing the past.

Mother sat back, which caught my attention. "You're pensive. This trip is still bothering you, isn't it?"

I nodded, unsure on how to word my thoughts.

"Listen, I may not agree with how Kitteren went about getting you to take a vacation, but I'm not going to argue you needed one. She just worries about you, Ketayl," Mother said gently.

I finished what I nibbled on and replied, "Too much. I'm fine."

"No, Ketayl, you weren't. I know she's been a pain in the ass to you in regards to finding out about what happened. You may not want her to know, but someday, you should tell someone. Even if it isn't me or Kitteren. Find someone you trust," Mother reached over to squeeze my hand.

I shook my head. It would mean admitting to someone what kind of monster I was. Had been. How did I even classify it now since I still had the potential?

Mother cocked her head to the side, studying me for a moment. "I only tell you this from experience. I never spoke to anyone about what I went through during the war. What I saw and even more so about what I did. It ate away at me until Dad finally got me to break down and let it all out. I still wish to spare my girls the details, but you need someone who will listen and understand. I'm here if you want and so are Kitteren and Dad. Don would probably be willing to lend an ear also."

"No, not him," I said quickly. I did not want to sully an old man's memories. Not to mention I truly did not want to bother him with more than I already had.

"Then how about that new partner of yours? Silver was it?" Mother suggested.

I eyed her for a moment, not sure why she would bring him up. Surely she had heard Kitteren's opinion of him by now. "Silver Blaise," I stated. "I can't burden him with more than he already has."

Should I mention he might be here soon? I did not even know what his schedule looked like or if he decided to turn Lockonis down or not. I had not spoken with him since I last saw him at Savanas' dinner. It felt wrong to not even get a general message from him asking how my day was or something along those lines.

Mother sighed in frustration. "I haven't had the pleasure of meeting him yet. I'm reluctant to take Kitteren's assessment at face value."

"She hates him," I stated flatly. "She still blames him for me getting hurt during my last field assignment."

"Your only field assignment so far," Mother corrected. "You haven't spoken much of what happened then either."

I started to retort she was wrong, but after having Kitteren lecture me for being careless, she avoided the topic whenever it came up. I guess I just assumed it went against some social norm to discuss such matters.

I broke off a piece of fish with my fork and took a bite, using the action to give myself time to think. I shifted, uncomfortable - still uneasy about wanting to discuss anything personal, but I did not deny the desire was there. If only to get it out.

Swallowing, I found myself out of time. "I don't know what to talk about." That series of events I could deal with a little easier.

Mother looked at me sadly. The forced gentle smile on her face told me it was not in sympathy, but in understanding. She took another bite, quietly waiting for me to continue.

I looked back down at my food, ashamed to admit, "I was scared. I thought I knew what was happening to me and I was wrong. And now..." I trailed off, still afraid of what lay just beneath the surface, barely kept in check.

"My little girl, so tough and fierce," Mother reached over and patted my hand. "You're going to have to explain a bit more - I wasn't there."

I bit my lower lip, debating my next words. I did not want to go into a lot of detail - the images of trapped souls still haunted me. "The spell the necromancer used. It affected people who were arcane or divine sensitive. I thought because I could see it I understood it. That it was just giving me a headache due to the amount of power in it. It actually broke down my control and I haven't been able to rebuild it. I feel like I'm barely able to keep my power in check."

Mother squeezed my hand before picking up her fork again. "Have you considered trying to work with what you have now instead of trying to go back? You've been adamant about not talking about your past here and moving forward, but you won't step beyond who you were six months ago."

I looked up at Mother, considering her words carefully. I simply wanted to go back to before I encountered Brown, but I could not. The case had not only given me problems with my power, but also new people in my life. Even Savanas called from time to time to check on me. So much happened since then because of the experience.

I munched on another potato stick, the smells before me reminding me my stomach still demanded food. Shopping with her had worked up an appetite.

"I don't know how," I finally admitted. I learned control to deal with what happened half a century ago, but now she implied I should give up on it.

"Neither do I, but sometimes you have to take a step forward. If you fall, get back up and try something else," Mother advised.

The thought made me more uneasy as making a mistake would likely come with dire consequences. I had no one else to look to for guidance as unlike other Arcanists, according to Magus Engelil, my ability to use my power was tied far more tightly to my emotional state. She did not think it permanent. I did not understand her words then or now and I did not know where to start.

I bit the tip of my thumb, trying to think of what I needed to do. What end result I needed. If I could at least see the end then I could plot a path there, right? But if I could not go back to what I had, then where did I need to be? I started tapping my fork lightly on my plate in contemplation.

Mother put her hand over mine to stop the motion. "Ketayl, easy. I can try to help. If you let Kitteren and Dad know, they'll be more than happy to do what they can. And I have a feeling you should trust your partner. If I know your sister, she's just being stubborn about him."

Mother did not understand I had already let her in too close. She knew more about what happened 50 years ago, but I needed to distance myself a certain amount from people to keep them safe. I was dangerous - that much I had always known.

"Shall we finish and continue our shopping trip?" Mother smiled broadly.

I groaned and ate slowly. I did not want to get dragged around to more shops. Mother continued trying to distract me and perhaps I needed it. To be able to step back so I could see the big picture.

8

THE NEXT DAY, Kitteren was once again missing as well as Mother. Father sat in the common area reading a magazine. "Good morning, honey." He smiled. Their pet names for me always felt awkward and I shifted uncomfortably from one foot to the other.

"Kitteren didn't come back again last night?" I asked, running my fingers through my hair in an attempt to get it into some semblance of order. Father and I were not close. Not like how Mother tried to connect with me, but he cared all the same and treated us as his daughters. I had not met him until one time a few years after I enrolled in the Arcane College and he came with them to visit. I guessed Mother met him soon after she returned to Elven Territory with Kitteren.

Father shrugged, turning the page. "She's had things on her mind. I've noticed she's been restless. Did something happen in Ocean's Edge?"

I frowned - I lost my chance to talk with her again. "She met someone. She wasn't at the ceremony with me so I don't know." I knew she went with Rathal after our lunch and likely joined with him. The two started flirting with each other the moment they met.

"Oh?"

I shook my head, turning back toward the room I should have been sharing with Kitteren. "I don't think there was any trouble." Not if her satisfied grin when she arrived with Rathal at Savanas' house was any indication.

"I'm going to help Don with some repairs he needs to get done on his property. Would you like to come with me?" Father asked before I closed the door.

While it seemed odd for Father to be helping out, I quickly gave up thinking about it too much since I had no plans for the day. Thinking about it would only frustrate me as the pieces I had would not fit. I nodded and excused myself to get ready.

Father and Kitteren were close and it bothered me he seemed unconcerned about her disappearances. Or maybe I just did not know my sister as well as I thought I did.

If only I could talk to her, but I missed my chances before because I did not think it the right time. I just wanted to sort all of this out. I bordered on offering to tell her everything just to clear the air. The fear of scaring her off held my tongue.

I STRETCHED, barely tall enough to reach where I needed to dust. Father disappeared somewhere on the property not long after we arrived. He returned at lunch, but then went off again. I had quickly gotten bored and started cleaning in an effort to stay occupied much to Alice's delight. Though at first she tried to convince me I did not need to help.

In the morning, I cleaned the guest rooms upstairs. Don had offered them to Kitteren, but she declined. Likely because I was with them this time and did not want to make me uncomfortable with the amount of time passed.

It annoyed me Kitteren could not have been bothered to inform me about any of them. I cared little for those types of surprises. That no one ever mentioned them to me felt wrong, but perhaps they deemed it unnecessary given the fact I had refused to return.

Alice left for the store late in the afternoon to get something to make for dinner. I had not seen Father since lunch. Don came into the front room with his violin in hand.

Smiling, he asked, "If I can get my fingers to work, would you sing for me again?"

I felt the heat rise in my face. Embarrassed, I admitted, "I haven't sung in a long time." Not counting the times Mother made me. They were almost always these songs - the ones I used to sing with Don, though there were others she occasionally snuck in during the rare practice times.

"Then you'll be in good company. It's been a while since I've played. Come sit with me on the front porch. If need be, I'm sure it could use a sweeping," Don said, waving me along with him.

Sighing, I put the duster down and grabbed the broom I left by the front door. I knew he only suggested sweeping so I would indulge him. Just me and Don, I reminded myself - no one else would hear this and I could not disappoint the old man.

I found it comfortingly familiar. Often, when Don was not expecting company, he would ask me to come sing for him. I could not refuse then and obviously not now.

I let him fuss with the violin, trying to get his fingers to remember what to play. It did not take long before he was playing the same melody - the one he crafted from a song I would sing to Kitteren while she slept.

The song was a story about a young boy going on a journey. He wanted to explore the world - experience everything. He threw away the customs of his clan to make his own path. Over time he came to appreciate his clan's traditions and made his way home. He had become a stranger to his clan - the child who left was gone.

I did not remember why I knew the song or why I sang it in the common dialect my sister and I spoke. I also spoke Elven at the time and understood normal common, even if it sounded funny to me. The details escaped me or perhaps I never knew the reason for it.

Don smiled at me from his rocking chair on the porch. "You sing it even better than before." He made a noise of effort as he stood. "I believe we have a guest."

My eyes went wide as I looked toward the gate. I saw no one there and wondered if he just wanted to tease me from when Mother hunted me down all those years ago.

Don walked to the gate, smiling at someone around the bushes. I followed him, the broom clutched tightly in my hands. Perhaps it was Mother again, sneaking up on me. It would be annoying, but some-thing I could deal with.

The person who came out from behind the tall, thick bushes, I did not expect. I took a couple of steps back, dropped the broom and ran, instinctively using my magic to cloak myself. I stopped just inside the front door, breathing hard and in a panic.

What on Terra was Silver doing here? Had he heard me? I tried to pull myself together as I listened to their conversation. I had forgotten he might show up. How had he managed to track me down all the way out here? I never told him about this place.

"You scared her off," I could almost hear the pout in Don's voice.

With my cloak in place, I twisted so I could watch them. I was suddenly grateful I spent the time figuring out how to get the energy consumption of this spell to a minimum allowing me to maintain it longer with little effort.

"I'm sorry, sir," Silver said. "I was told this was where I could find Ketayl. I did not expect her to run." Who told him?

Don smiled, allowing him in the gate. "She is very shy, you know. And you are?"

"Silver Blaise. Our Director's second asked me to come and help keep an eye on her and make sure she wasn't working." He bowed and then bent down to pick up the broom.

Don held out his hand in greeting once Silver stood up again, "Donald Blair. Once doctor and teacher, now just a retired old man. So you know at least one of my Elven girls."

Silver raised an eyebrow, probably at how Don referred to myself and Kitteren. "Yes, sir. Ketayl is my partner. I fear I haven't been much help to her recently though," he said sadly as he took Don's hand. I almost dropped my spell by accident.

I held my breath as they got closer, moving further into the house - trying to stay ahead of them. I knew I was being foolish and my taking off must only have confused Silver given the amount of time we spent talking over video calls. This had just been far too personal.

"Please come in and have some tea while you wait, though I don't think she took off as far as she did the last time someone spooked her, but it would be best to wait until she's ready," Don said, leading them to the kitchen.

I backed up the stairs leading to the bedrooms to get well out of the hallway. Silver turned toward me as if he sensed something, but continued a moment later.

Silver wore a dark blue dress shirt with the sleeves rolled up over his elbows and tucked into khaki-colored pants and black boots. His hair in its traditional braid, hanging over his right shoulder.

Stepping lightly down the stairs, I watched Silver settle at the table while Don busied himself in the kitchen. Don placed his violin on the counter separating the rooms.

"Did you teach her to play?" Silver asked. My mind screamed at him not to pry.

"Hm?" Don turned around, following Silver's gaze. "Oh, no, she learned long after Lindale took them in. Ketayl has always been attracted to the sound of my fiddle. It was lovely to hear her sing again. Her voice may have changed from when I last heard her 50 years ago, but it's still just as beautiful - at least to my ears."

Please stop.

"I didn't know she could sing," Silver said. He had a soft smile on his face. Something startled him and he hid his surprise behind stroking the small patch of hair on his chin.

I closed my eyes as I smelled the lavender Don prepared. Even from here the effect calmed my nerves. I dropped my cloak, realizing I would not be able to hide forever and stepped softly into the kitchen, startling Silver once again.

"Ketayl, I didn't mean to scare you earlier," Silver said. He stood and took my hand, kissing the back of it.

Rolling my eyes, I took my hand back and moved to help Don make the tea. I needed distance from him to figure out how to deal with this situation. Perhaps I should have remained hidden longer.

Don shooed me away. "I'm still able to make tea." He patted my cheek as I frowned. "Go sit. Let an old man have this."

"Yes, sir," I said softly, having little hope of not being overheard by Silver in the small room. My movements felt stiff to me as I waited for my partner to voice his judgment.

I sat quietly across from Silver, unsure why he was here in the Northern Isles when he should have been back at the main office getting settled in. Why would Lockonis want to send him here without it being an assignment? Or would it be an assignment for him only? I started to confuse myself despite the fact I had read the paperwork. I did not need to be babysat. Why did he have to accept the request?

Silver fiddled with his phone and then handed it to me. "This should answer most of your questions."

I read the orders, directing Silver here. They were less orders and more of a personal request from Lockonis to make sure I was not working. Exactly what Savanas told me.

Had it become so big of an issue they felt the need to send him?

"Savanas thinks it's just to give us a chance to get reacquainted since I've been away training for months. I guess it has happened before - having partners take time-off together to get to know each other. It's like how she has dinners regularly to stay connected with her agents," Silver offered as explanation. Again, similar to what Savanas told me.

I supposed I could understand the logic, but the whole situation still felt horribly wrong. There must to be something else. "Why didn't you tell me when you were coming? I could have met you at the airport," I managed to say evenly. I handed him back his phone and adjusted the black sleeveless wrap shirt.

Maybe I should have gone shopping by myself today to replace some clothes. Then I could have taken in some of the festivities as well. I would have felt less isolated.

On the same thought, I had needed the alone time with Don despite how short it was. I think we both needed to remember something good from the past.

A cup of steaming lavender tea with honey appeared in front of me and I took it immediately, drawing in a deep breath of the aroma, letting it calm and help bring balance.

"I was told someone was notified," Silver said, confused. "And with the time difference, I didn't want to chance disturbing you."

I thought about it for a moment and remembered the angry phone conversation Kitteren had the other evening. "Kitteren. I've barely seen her since dinner the other night." Her dislike of Silver went too far. I clenched the cup in my hands tightly.

Don smiled, "Perhaps she just wanted it to be a surprise." He always put a positive spin on things. Unfortunately, there were too many things not adding up.

Father entered in through the back door. "It looks like I'm going to need... Oh, hello there. I didn't know you had a guest, Don."

"This one is my brownie's," Don said.

Silver raised an eyebrow at me for the nickname.

I put my cup down and buried my face in my hands - I was not going to enjoy trying to deflect his curiosity after this. My hair fell around me and I wished I could hide completely.

"Dayko Eurlastiel," my adopted father said. His voice firm and I mentally tripped over the sound - I never heard him take such a tone. This was the second or I guess third time he surprised me. Father always seemed gentle and patient. "What business do you have with my daughter?"

The scraping of the chair on the floor told me the paladin across from me stood up. "Silver Blaise. I have been assigned as her partner and the Director's second thought I should come and help ensure she isn't working."

"I'm going to go back to work to take a vacation," I grumbled and Don patted my shoulder. This trip was turning into chaos. The pile of backlogged work started to sound much more fun than this. I would need to lock myself in the lab for a week just to let the dust settle.

"How good are you with repairing buildings?" Father asked, completely changing the topic and tone. I looked up at the Elven men standing over me, now confused. Father stood a few inches shorter than Silver, both of their postures relaxed. Though Father's eyes kept drifting down to the metal bracers and leather fingerless gloves Silver wore.

Silver seemed to also be confused be the sudden change in topic. He thought about it for a moment. "I would help maintain the buildings on the church's grounds, but there was never anything severe."

Father smiled down at me and asked, "Mind if I steal him for a bit? I could use a second set of eyes on a particular problem."

I waved them out the door. Please, allow me peace.

As soon as they were gone, Don sat down with his own cup of tea. "I take it you've told your partner little to nothing about your past."

I hesitated for a moment, unsure what his thoughts were and then nodded. "Silver doesn't need to know. He shouldn't be here."

"Maybe he does. Ketayl, you've always kept yourself closed off. You've put so much effort into making sure others are alive and happy. It's past time you let someone do the same for you," Don spoke softly.

What type of relationship did Don think I had with Silver? Talking about one's personal life seemed unnecessary for a working team. I thought over his words and figured he must know more about me than I assumed.

Taking a deep breath, I looked up at Don. The memories of six months ago were still a strong reminder. "I can't. With what I am - I'm too dangerous to let people close. Silver and the others nearly got hurt the last time."

"Tell me about it." I could not refuse Don's gentle voice, but I turned my eyes away in shame - preferring to stare into my cup. Soon enough I recounted what happened in Ocean's Edge. My emotions were close to the surface and all it did was prod me further into my story. My power pushed at me like a gentle tide, but did not fight to be free. Not yet anyway. I continued to fear it eventually would, but perhaps Mother was right and I could find another way.

I DRAINED my cup at least three times and felt exhausted. Don rubbed my back and said nothing. I had not planned on telling him anything. Now I felt broken. All the pieces I put back together came apart. I did not want to be seen like this, but damned if I could find the energy to move.

This reminded me of a time half a century ago when I came back from town beaten and barely having found enough food for Kitteren. I curled up on his couch, exhausted and hurting, and he offered me what he could for food and rubbed my back. It was shortly after he lost the other children he housed. The children were supposed to go to the orphanage before being sent to their respective territories, but were actually sold to slave traders by the people who rounded them up.

"Have you told Kitteren?" Don asked gently after a while. I laid my head down on the table and he stroked my hair.

I sat back and shook my head. "Kitteren doesn't want to talk about what happened and I've barely seen her the last couple of days."

"Odd for a family vacation," Don noted, only making my suspicions more pronounced. "Your sister isn't shy about telling people what's bothering her. While I know you don't want to talk about 50 years ago, perhaps sitting her down and telling her this much will help? She worries about you, my little brownie."

Father and Silver returned before I could decide. Father announced, "Don, I'm going to head into town to pick up some supplies to finish that project off. Silver can take my spot for dinner." He then thanked my partner for his help before leaving. I barely got a farewell. The exchange set me on edge again.

Something in Silver's face told me there had likely been more to their conversation than discussing repairs. I did not want to bring it up here. And especially not now where I still felt raw from telling Don my story.

Don and Silver began chatting lightly, trying to get to know each other, so I excused myself. I returned to the front room and picked up where I left off dusting. I needed to redouble my efforts. Why did Lockonis have to send him? Why did she and Vince have to agree to time off for me?

I had barely begun my mental questions when my phone dinged. Pulling it out of my pocket, I saw a message from Personnel about my vacation time. It was a standardized form, saying what paid out on this cycle, the dates used, days remaining, and what it was coded as.

I reread the message. The days remaining were not going down and I never saw the code "Vacation oo" before, but I never used my vacation time previously either. I did not remember it from the handbook I quizzed Silver off of during his training.

Before I noticed what I was doing, I dialed Lockonis. I had not even contemplated the time difference.

"Heya, Ket. This better not be about work," Lockonis answered cheerfully.

I cringed and admitted, "It is, but I just wondered if you could answer a question about a message I got from Personnel."

She paused as if not expecting it, but I rarely asked anything about other departments. I tried not to pry despite my curiosity. It was easier to keep to myself. "Oh, okay, I'll answer that."

"My days remaining aren't going down and it's coded as 'Vacation oo' - I don't remember it in the handbook." Granted, I did not know if she knew I found a copy just so I could help Silver.

Lockonis paused and I did not hear any typing in the background as if she needed to look something up. She never stopped working any other time I called unless it was serious. "Um..."

I walked outside while I waited, not wanting to be interrupted.

"Oh, now I remember," Lockonis said quickly. "It's a rarely used code. Kind of a we need to compensate you for time worked, which was why we also allowed Kitteren to book the flight out to Mystic Port for you. Didn't mean to under pay you for a bit there, Ket. When Kitteren came to us with the request and I looked into your actual time worked, we decided to do this rather than fight with Personnel to get an extra paycheck out. Hope you don't mind. At least you get to keep your vacation days, right?"

It felt like she covered something, but I let it slide just like I had been with a lot of people so far. I tried to justify it as she probably had something else important she needed to focus on. "Okay, sorry I bothered you."

"No problem. Enjoy your time off, Ket," Lockonis said cheerfully and hung up.

I looked at my phone to confirm the call ended. I had been certain she would be curious and bugging me about how things were going even if she was working on something. Lockonis always wanted to get me to talk. I told myself to just let it go and not to jump to conclusions. Everything had a reason, right?

"Something wrong?" Silver asked and I jumped, clutching my phone to my chest.

I put a smile on my face before I turned around. He leaned against a post on the porch with his shoulder. "Nothing. I was just confused about a message I got from Personnel. Lockonis cleared it up."

Alice pulled into the dirt driveway and I excused myself to go help her. Something told me I needed to break out my skills as a thief again to get more information. I only hoped I was wrong and making something out of nothing.

9

Dinner had been a relatively quiet affair compared to the last family gathering. Alice was quite charmed by Silver. He insisted on cleaning up afterward, shooing myself and Don off. Though Alice refused to leave him alone in the kitchen.

When Father had not returned, I declined Alice's offer for a ride back to the hotel and decided to walk. I briefly entertained the thought it would help me clear my head except Silver walked beside me.

The breeze picked up and I shivered - my outfit not providing enough warmth. My hair moved around me and I mentally cursed once more at Kitteren having taken my hair pins.

Silver gently grabbed my shoulders, making me pause for a minute. "Here, it's the least I can do after showing up unannounced and ruining your family time."

Warmth flowed over me before I could respond. "You didn't ruin anything. I just..."

"Didn't want me to see this? I don't know why not. It's a part of you, no matter how much time has passed. And it's nice to get to know my partner a little better," Silver said, his hands still on my shoulders.

I stepped away, uncomfortable. He seemed to like that word: partner. I guess I had not seen the previous arrangement as real until now. Before he was at a distance and busy with his own work and even now I did not think I understood the implications fully.

As he stood next to me I found I did not know what to make of this situation. How does one work with a partner? I had worked alone for so long. I only hoped his training better prepared him. But this was not work either. The situation had me confused.

"I didn't know you could sing," Silver said.

"I won't," I said flatly. Not again, not after this. I knew there were questions I wanted to ask, but embarrassment held my tongue. I felt my face getting warm thinking about it. I set back off at a quick pace.

Silver stayed quiet for a moment. "Ketayl, stop." He grabbed my shoulder and my momentum forced me to turn around and face him. "Why are you running from me? I'm your friend and I just want to be here for you. I want you to be able to trust me and if you're embarrassed, don't be. It was nice to see you outside of working for once and I didn't want to spoil the moment."

I glared at Silver for a few seconds before lowering my head and rubbing the bridge of my nose. "I'm sorry. This is just a bad time. I shouldn't even be here. And you would probably rather be getting settled in at the main office."

"No, I wouldn't," Silver said gently. "I was *asked* if I would come out here. I didn't have to, but here I am. Ketayl, I've been worried about you. Especially after you sent me those images." He brushed a lock of hair out of my face and I backed away.

"It's not like they were going to come to life and try to kill me," I responded. And truthfully they would not. Lockonis confiscated my student pin and then it, along with my Researcher and Brown's pins went to the EAC for research to make sure they would be safe for me to handle.

Silver ran a hand over his hair, letting out the breath of air he held. "No, and I'm not about to discuss my findings right now either. You need to step away from work and I'm here as a friend. You've been pushing yourself too hard. You could have asked me for help. You could have turned down helping me study so you could get some rest. I wouldn't have minded."

I turned away. "You had enough going on and I was waiting on test results anyway while I quizzed you." I started walking. I was never going to get back to the hotel at this rate. I did not like being cold and rude, but I had no patience left.

"Ketayl…" I heard the aggravated tone in his voice. Hurried footsteps caught up to me quickly. "If this is so bad, what kind of vacation would you rather take?"

I knew Silver was trying to change the topic and frankly, it was a good idea. "I don't know. Someplace quiet where I can read and be warm sounds good."

Silver laughed. "So I take it you wouldn't enjoy a skiing trip."

"Too cold." I wanted to shiver at the thought. Kitteren made me watch various sporting events with her from time to time and while it looked interesting, all of that snow made me cold.

"You wouldn't have to be outside the whole time. I'm sure there would be a spot by a fireplace where you could curl up and read."

I considered it. "Maybe." Sitting next to a fireplace sounded nice too. If I could be left in peace.

Silence fell between us and I felt calmer. It helped before to talk to him about inane things when I felt overworked.

"Silver, I'm sorry about earlier," I offered. "I didn't mean to be so…"

A finger appeared on my lips. "Don't worry about it."

I moved his hand away. Apparently he forgot I did not like being touched. I resumed walking.

We reached the end of the dirt road Don lived off of when a familiar black rental car pulled up and Father rolled the window down. "Sorry I'm so late. Come on you two, I'll give you a ride back. The repairs can wait."

Sighing, I could not decide whether to be relieved or annoyed at Father's appearance. I reached for the door when I thought to ask Silver, "Where are you staying?"

"The same hotel. Lockonis arranged for me to get a room there."

Shaking my head, I gestured for Silver to take the front seat and climbed into the back. Before I got in, I lifted Silver's phone off of him and tucked it under my shirt between me and my waistband. Just a test, I told myself, just to see if I still could. It took some magic, but mostly to make sure no one paid attention to me.

"Ketayl?" Father asked.

"I'm short, Father," I explained, "I'm fine back here."

Once we were off again, I settled behind Father, where it would be hard for him to see. While Silver focused on their conversation, I pulled out his phone to see what I could find. With the amount of times I forgot my own passcode, I had created an arcane solution for bypassing the lock screen. Feeling my way through the cast, I half-listened to Father and Silver talk about what needed to be repaired.

Silver received a similar message from Personnel with the same coding. I guess it made sense - he was basically here on assignment and did not have any vacation days built up yet. I really did not need a babysitter and cursed his task. I would have to lose him somehow and that was going to be through Kitteren. I just needed to get her to stay still long enough.

WHEN WE GOT BACK to the hotel, Father said he planned to turn in early and left me to deal with Silver who followed us to our suite. I had long since given Silver his phone back without his knowledge.

I stood in the doorway, blocking Silver from entering. "Thank you. Have a good evening."

"Ketayl, wait, would you like some company? It seemed like you wanted to talk earlier."

"No, I'm fine," I smiled and lied. I wanted to talk, but with Kitteren. My questions for Silver might be answered without having to involve him. "I think I'm just going to go for a swim."

"I can go with you if you want." Silver seemed nervous as he toyed with the end of his braid, tugging on it gently.

Crap, I had not thought my statement through. "No, I'll be fine. I just want to relax. It's been a long day."

"Are you sure?" Silver had me again questioning his orders.

I said calmly, "Yes, I prefer to swim alone."

"Can't you just leave?" a sharp voice came from down the hall. Kitteren strode over to us, Mother not far behind. "She doesn't want you bothering her."

"Kitteren..." I warned.

My sister's face showed a level of anger I could not remember witnessing before. "No, this jerk is bothering you and I won't stand for it."

Mother signaled to me she wanted to talk to Silver and I excused us, pulling Kitteren into the room. "*What is wrong with you?*" I hissed at her as soon as the door closed, keeping my voice low. I did not let her respond - my anger rising to the surface quickly. "*You drag me all the way out here and disappear. It feels like everyone is keeping secrets and treating me like I'm made of glass.*"

Kitteren's own anger changed to worry, or at least the way I interpreted it. "*Ketayl…*"

"*No, I've had enough! You knew about Silver being sent here, didn't you? You haven't been coming back at night to rest. You won't even talk to me these past couple of days. I should have stayed back at work at this rate,*" I stood inches from her face. As soon as I recognized the fear in her green eyes I backed away, pacing until I calmed down. Control, I needed control and balance. "*And you haven't told me why you had business in Ocean's Edge. You didn't even warn me about the rest of Don's family. None of this makes sense, Kitteren.*"

Kitteren got in front of me and pulled me into a hug. "*I'm so sorry, Ket. I didn't mean to. Gods, I'm an idiot. Look at what I'm doing to us. To you.*"

I did not fight her and rested my head on her shoulder. "*Not you, Kitteren. I… I have a problem.*" There, I admitted it.

"*What do you mean?*"

While I distracted her, I lifted her phone. It took a little more effort and magic given her form-fitting clothes. "*Ever since I encountered the necromancer's spell six months ago I feel like I can barely keep my power under control.*"

Changing the way I rested my head, I tried to quickly recall where all reflective surfaces were. I think Kitteren faced away from them. I used the hug to get into her phone and look for a message from Personnel. Sure enough, there it was with the same coding. Silver, I could write off. Kitteren made no sense.

Getting her phone back into her pocket was my next challenge. Silver had been easy because his pants were looser, but she liked tight clothes.

"*And I bet being here is making it harder,*" Kitteren said, pushing me away gently. I was about to lose my opening to return the phone. "*Why didn't you tell me sooner?*"

"*I was trying to fix it on my own because you kept avoiding the topic,*" I said and pulled my spell.

"Hey, what are you…?" Kitteren switched back to normal common and reached back, patting her empty pocket.

I waved the phone in front of her and grinned, "You took my tablet."

"Yeah, but I need that." She reached out quickly, trying to grab it, but I moved around to the other side of the coffee table.

I almost stopped at the worried expression on Kitteren's face. I tried to keep up the playful game. I wished I had more time to check her other messages - especially the text.

She jumped the coffee table and tackled me to the couch, grabbing her phone roughly from my hand. "You're not getting your tablet back until we leave." I cringed at her weight - she was heavier than I thought.

I rolled my eyes.

Kitteren got off me, sitting up and obviously spending time to think about what I said before I tried to lighten the mood and cover what I did. "Have you thought maybe you're just getting stronger?"

Getting myself back in order, I sat up on the other end of the couch. "No, but it feels like what control I do rebuild is made out of paper. In a storm, those walls don't hold up."

My sister sat silent for a moment and I gave her time to contemplate what I told her. Just as I needed time to start analyzing this confrontation. "I don't know, Ket. I wish I knew more about the arcane. Have you tried burning some of it off?"

I sighed, Lockonis scheduled me for training regularly. "It hasn't felt any different. It's my emotional control that's the problem."

Kitteren chewed on her lip. "I think you may just be getting stronger, seriously. Have you had any reactions beyond the weird eye-color changing thing?"

"No." And no headaches either. Those were the only two benefits.

She sat quiet for a moment before suggesting, "Then maybe it means you can let up on the emotional control."

"That's too dangerous," I reminded her. Why did I always seem to have to remind people I was dangerous? Maybe I just needed to remind myself.

"It wasn't when we were little," Kitteren pointed out.

I shifted, kicking my shoes off and sticking my toes between the cushions. She had a point, but then was not now. Then I had no training and used my abilities on an instinctual level. Now I knew how to wield that power with far more precision. "Yeah, but if your theory of I'm just getting stronger is right..."

Kitteren sighed. "Maybe not tonight, but we'll figure this out. I think I need a run after this to think. Do you mind?"

I shook my head. She knew I would not join her if asked. "I'm going to go to the market. If I can't have my tablet back, at least I can pick up a book to read. Maybe go see what some of the festivities are. Don't really feel like a swim anymore."

"You better not get a book for school," Kitteren warned, stretching for her run. Why was she not changing up? I would have to check her belongings later to see if maybe she had not brought anything for running.

I forced a smile and said, "I'll try to stay in fiction."

"Hey, what do you say we go into town and check out what's going on tomorrow? I heard there are some interesting events lined up."

We were still a few days off of the actual Summer Solstice, but it was going to be the start of the weekend. I nodded. I only hoped I could get more answers out of her then.

I WATCHED as Kitteren began her run. My shoes were not made for running so I did not try to follow her. It would be pointless - I would not be able to keep up. Not under my own physical power anyway.

I had no idea what to try next to find out more information. Kitteren said nothing when I brought up her behavior, instead taking blame for making me upset. I knew she used this run as a reason to get away from actually answering me.

And foolishly I let her go. Maybe I was hoping she would come to her senses and tell me what was going on. I kept trying to tell myself tomorrow I would get my answers, but something nagged at me that I would once again find myself disappointed. I needed to stop letting her go like this. I needed to be more forceful with her. I just could not bring myself to possibly cause a change in our relationship.

I leaned against the wall outside the hotel. This did me little good. I wished I knew how to track her phone. Perhaps I should spend more time with the cyber team or come up with an arcane solution.

"This is an odd place to think," Silver commented, coming up alongside me.

I almost forgot he was here. "Sorry about Kitteren's behavior earlier." Frankly it had been more embarrassing for me than Silver catching me singing for Don.

Silver waved it off. "I doubt she's going to come to tolerate me anytime soon. Not without some world-shattering event anyway."

"Well, I should leave you to your evening," I said, pushing myself off the wall and headed toward the market. I made a mental note to avoid the open market area.

"Hey, wait, why don't I come with you?" Silver caught up with me quickly. "I don't know this city and I wouldn't mind seeing more of it - I just got in this morning."

Sighing, I signaled him to follow. "Just... remember I don't like being touched."

"You let Don, Kitteren, and Dayko touch you," Silver observed.

I mentally cursed myself. "I'm used to them." A weak excuse, but it worked.

Silver took my hand and hooked it on his arm. "Then you can get used to me too." There was a broad smile on his face and I jerked my hand away, glaring at him. "Okay, so it may take half a century, but there's hope still."

I rolled my eyes and kept walking. My hair billowed behind me like a cloak when the breeze picked up. I took a moment to breathe in the salty air. I had missed that.

10

WHILE I BROWSED THE BOOKS, Silver looked thoroughly bored. Nothing caught my attention in terms of something I would like to read, but I figured if I kept this up, maybe he would leave. There was also the problem of I felt like someone had been following me. It went away while in the bookstore, but something told me it would continue once I left.

A half hour later and Silver still trailed behind me. I even wandered into the arcane section, hoping it would only increase his desire to leave.

I flipped through a book, a newer introduction to the arcane, when Silver finally spoke, "Aren't you past that now?"

"If you mean I spend most of my time in advanced arcane theory, then yes, but sometimes I like to browse the basic ones to see if someone has come up with a different idea. There's no one solid way to manipulate the arcane despite what the Arcane College may say." I looked up and pointed to a section not far away. "There are some divine books over there if you're bored."

Silver plucked the book from my hands and returned it to the shelf. "Maybe later. Let's go get something to eat, I'm getting hungry and the shops are going to start closing soon."

Mystic Port was in Neutral Territory - most places were staying open later to grab the Summer Solstice festival crowd, but they would be shutting down soon. And I could use a snack.

Silver grabbed my hand and practically dragged me out the door. I could not get my hand free and he did not stop until we were in the open market stalls. I looked around and shuddered. I spent way too much time here and kept seeing the past. These were the easier places to steal from and comprised of most of the market area back then.

"Are you okay?"

I tried to pull away and head back the way we came, but he had too good of a grasp on my hand. "Can we go back to one of the other shops? I don't want to be here." I wanted to get away from here.

"What's wrong with this place? There's plenty of choices without having to go far," Silver pointed out, completely oblivious. As he should be - he did not need to know of my thieving past.

"Fine," I ground out. It had been over half a century - surely no one would remember. Most of the vendors changed from what I remembered and I received no grief when I came on my own the first morning.

I browsed the stalls, trying to figure out what I wanted to eat and tried to ignore the wrongness of being here. I let my nose find the stall the sweet smells were coming from. They made different items from the same dough - some plain, some with salt, some with slices of meat, and others still with cinnamon and sugar.

Turning to look for Silver, I found him standing right over my shoulder. "This doesn't seem like a meal," he commented.

I returned my attention to the menu board, debating on what I wanted. "I just want a snack."

Silver seemed to consider it. "Okay, what do you want?"

I made a face at him. "I can buy my own food, thank you. I should be getting yours as well for having you come out here. Besides, do you have local currency?"

"We get paid in Units," Silver pointed out. "We're in Neutral Territory - they only take Units."

I sighed - I had forgotten that fact. I rarely went into Great Tree and bought anything. And even then, if I used my card, it automatically converted. With the TIO being an interterritorial organization, they did not mess with territory-specific currency.

"You can go somewhere else if you want. I'm going to get something here." I wish I could shake him, but he seemed adamant about staying with me. I continued to wonder about his orders. Especially with the lengthy conversation Mother seemed to have had with him. Should I ask? My thoughts sounded crazy even to myself. I was jumping at ghosts and shadows - none of it was real. Or at least I hoped not.

Silver looked at the board, debating. "Actually, this sounds good. I wasn't very hungry - we did have a large dinner earlier."

Alice went all out again on dinner and I wondered for a moment if they normally ate like that or only something she did for guests.

I ordered what I wanted - the small bite-sized pieces coated in cinnamon and sugar. I could find a drink elsewhere if I got thirsty. I waved Silver over to order while I got out money to pay for both of us. These places did not often take electronic forms of payment, though they were starting to more. At least that was how it was in Elven Territory.

Silver put his hand over mine as I dug through my wallet. He leaned down and whispered to me, "Put that away. I've caused you enough headaches."

The irony was I had not had a headache since I got hurt. "I will pay you back." Who I really wanted to try and pay back were the merchants, but I could not return to the past.

"I'd like to see you try," Silver smirked.

After we paid and got our food, he directed me toward the center of the market where benches and tables sat for people to enjoy. The market bustled with activity even at this time of day - the sun had nearly set. He led us over to a section of benches in front of the fairie statue.

"Not here, let's go where it isn't as busy," I tried to keep my voice neutral, but I knew I did not hide all of the unease.

Silver looked down at me like I lost my mind. Perhaps I had since I was scared of a statue. "What's wrong with here? It's not busy. We'll have the bench to ourselves. Besides, I like this statue."

He would. I averted my eyes from the bronze mass in front of me. "Why?" I found myself asking as I reluctantly took a seat. I had not meant to voice the question, but it was out. He said he arrived this morning, when did he have time to see this?

"Have you read the story?"

No, I lived it.

"It's a beautiful tale. Local folklore I guess."

One I somehow created.

"While I can't condone stealing, everyone needs to survive and I think the fairie more than paid back for what she stole," Silver's eyes were on the statue. I watched him - he seemed to have a deep appreciation for the tale, but it was not the whole story.

And I would never tell him the whole story.

"Fairie, brownie... these are terms I'm not familiar with. At least not in the context they are being used here. Can you explain?" Blue eyes turned to me and I turned away. My places to look were becoming limited.

"Fairies are mischief makers. Brownies are helpers. That's the short answer," I said quickly.

Silver took a bite of his braided bread with meat and cheese wrapped inside. I looked down at my own food, my appetite gone.

"It's a sweet thing Don called you then."

"A nickname, nothing else." Please drop this conversation.

"But something you earned."

And I earned other names as well. None I wished to keep. "I don't want to talk about this."

"Ketayl..." Silver said softly, then something drew his attention back to the statue. "It looks like the fairie is still an inspiration to other lost little ones."

Despite not wanting to see the statue again, I looked over to see what he spoke of. In the dying light of day the same Human girl from when I last came this direction stood before it. The girl sat down and put flowers at the base of the statue - ones she obviously picked herself. She tucked her dirty strawberry-blond hair behind her ear as she turned her face to figures above.

"The fairie isn't someone to look up to. The fairie is a monster," I said quietly.

"What do you mean?" Silver's voice sounded surprised. I needed to watch what I said better.

I popped one of the sugary bites in my mouth, using it to keep from having to reply.

Then another one disappeared from my small paper bag. "Hey!"

Silver smirked, tossing it in his mouth. "I didn't think you went for this really sweet stuff."

I shifted down the bench away from him and his thieving. "I thought you didn't condone stealing."

"I paid for it." His grin was broad and I knew I was likely doomed in having to deal with him on a regular basis.

I hated Silver's logic right then. I grumbled at him and better protected my food.

We ate in silence for a bit longer. Halfway through the bag I looked at it, unsure I could finish it. I had craved something sweet, but I did not expect so much when I ordered.

I also could not shake the feeling of being watched, but without it being through the arcane, I could not tell for certain. The sensation started shortly after I left the hotel with Silver. It let up in the bookstore, but now...

Something caught my attention and I reached down and grabbed a small wrist. The same little girl who had been at the statue now had a look of panic on her face. Silver got up to see the commotion.

Sighing, I said, "I'm the last person you want to try to steal from. You can have this." I gave her the rest of my bag of food.

The girl looked confused and then something made her incredibly happy. "You're the fairie, aren't you?"

I let go of her wrist as if it had suddenly become white hot. Regaining my composure, I asked, "Why would you say something like that? The fairie is a child." I waved in the direction of the statue, refusing to look at it.

"Yeah, but that's been there a long time and children grow. I learned the story well - I tell all the others in our gang."

"Gang?" Silver asked, kneeling down next to her.

"There's a bunch of us who don't live at the orphanage. We don't want to. The fairie lived on the streets. She has red hair like yours and eyes the color of an ocean storm. And you're an Elf. You've got to be her!"

I looked around to see what kind of attention we were drawing, but it appeared no one paid us any. People were busy milling about trying to get their shopping done. "There are others who probably share the same coloring I do." I did not want to outright lie to the girl, but I wanted to dissuade her of the notion.

"No one else knew I stole from them. No one else offered me food," the little girl said, puffing up her chest. "I've been coming here to pray for the fairie to help us. You've..." The girl looked up at something behind me. "Uh oh, I better go." Then she ran off, bag of treats tucked securely in her hands.

A Human man around my height and a much taller Elven man came into the center, searching. The Human ran a hand over his greasy dark hair and looked to be aggravated about something, muttering as he looked around. The Elf locked his gaze on me - a broad grin spread across his face slowly. It set me on edge and my first instinct was to run. I could not blame the girl for taking off after seeing these two.

Silver stood up fully, taking a stance in front of me.

The Elf then smacked the back of his hand against his companion's shoulder and signaled for him to follow - they left the same way they came.

I stood up, not sure what just happened. The sensation of being watched still had not left. I looked up at Silver who watched them go through the thinning crowd. With his jaw locked and eyes narrowed, he looked ready for a fight.

"Hey," I said softly.

Silver did not respond, still watching something.

I stood in front of him and crossed my arms. "Hey," I said a little louder.

Not getting a response, I gave up and walked away - my anger rising too quickly. I set off at a quick pace, needing to burn off some of the energy. My power swirled in agitation, but did not push at my limited control. I needed to get away before it chose to.

"Ketayl! Hey, wait!" Silver called and his longer legs let him catch up with me quickly. Now I ignored him. I got out of the open market before Silver stepped in front of me. I barely stopped in time to not run into him.

I glared up at him and then moved to go around. A strong hand grabbed my upper arm.

"No, we should stick together. I don't trust those two."

"Let go of me," I growled at him. "I can take care of myself." Too close to the surface. My power would not stay content much longer.

Silver looked like he wanted to start an angry tirade at me, but his face suddenly softened. "Ketayl, look, I'm sorry I didn't answer you before. You can't expect me not to take threats to you seriously. Tell me at least one of them didn't concern you."

My anger quickly deflated and I felt more stable. "The Elven man

- something wasn't right. And I've felt like I'm being watched for a while."

"I think we should head back to the hotel."

Sounds from down the street caught my attention. I wanted to go look at some of the cultural displays. I sighed, resigned to my fate for the evening. I could do it tomorrow.

Silver turned to see what caught my attention. "I guess as long as we stay together, we can spend some time wandering about."

KITTEREN LANDED HEAVILY on the bed. "Come on! Get up!"

I groaned and rolled over. I had a hard time resting last night after encountering those two men in the market. My mind would not stop trying to figure out what happened.

She did not take the hint and climbed on top of me to start shaking my shoulder. She repeated her desire for me to get up. I tried to shove her off with one arm, but she firmly planted herself on my hip.

"I can't get up with you on me," I said, my voice sounded tired even to my own ears.

Kitteren moved and took the covers with her. I curled up against the sudden cold. I put the pillow over my head in some attempt to get her to leave me be.

It lasted only a few seconds. "Geez, Ket. You're usually an early riser. What's wrong? I heard you tossing and turning."

"Had a lot on my mind." I had not spoken of what happened while at the market. I did not want people thinking I was jumping at ghosts, but even Silver had been put on guard. And then feeling like I was being watched...

Kitteren sat down on the edge of the bed far more sedately this time. "Ket, what's going on? What has you so worked up that you couldn't rest?"

I scooted over to the opposite edge of the bed and sat up. "Just encountered something weird last night. You know me, I can't let a puzzle go." I smiled back at her and hoped she would drop it.

"Okay," Kitteren said, but something told me she would not drop it so easily. "I'm going to take a quick shower - worked out a little too hard in the training area downstairs. But first..."

I watched my sister bounce over to the closet and dig through the few things hanging up. She pulled out a couple of hangers and stood there, holding them proudly.

I raised an eyebrow at the outfit she held. An airy, light gray skirt hung on one hanger - the other held a dark blue short-sleeve, v-neck shirt with a light gray, loosely-crocheted gray vest over it. The vest served little purpose other than to be decorative - it looked more like fisherman's netting - strands fell at regular intervals from the hem. "I think it will look good on you."

Kitteren rolled her eyes. "Not for me. This is for you. I saw it while on my run the other night."

I looked at the outfit more hesitantly. "I really don't care to wear skirts."

"Then wear your exercise shorts underneath it. Please, Ketayl? I have a similar outfit if it makes you feel better." Kitteren smiled sweetly.

Sighing, I strode over to her and took the garments. I could put up with it for the day. Perhaps doing this much would put her into a talkative mood and I could finally get some answers.

Once I laid them on the bed, she hugged me and then took off to go clean up. Shaking my head, I knelt down to dig out the last articles of clothing I needed out of my bag.

Kitteren left the door ajar and I heard her talking to our parents, but her tone of voice sounded serious. I got up and pressed myself against the wall next to the door, trying to listen.

"I don't know. It worries me," Kitteren said.

Father's voice was next. "I still don't like this. I'll let the two of you decide - I'm going downstairs."

The door to the suite opened and closed.

Mother sighed loud enough for me to hear from my position. "He has a point, but I'm reluctant to change things now. Go get ready - I'll make a few calls."

Why was I being left out? My emotions were too close to the surface - anger and curiosity clashed at each other hard. I closed my eyes and forced them back down. Patience - I needed patience. I would have access to Kitteren all day and it would just be a matter of getting her to slip something. But how?

I dressed quickly though I still could not figure out where the arm holes on the vest actually were when Kitteren came back into the room. She wrapped one of the big white towels around her torso and her hair still dripped water as she walked. "Let me help you."

I slid into the vest and let her fuss with it and my hair. I still needed to brush it. Then suddenly my skirt lifted and reflexively, I pushed it back down. The hem barely reached the top of my knees. "Hey!"

"I was just curious if you decided to wear the shorts," Kitteren said and patted me on the head. I grumbled at her and picked up my brush to start on my hair. I tried to ignore her as she took the towel off to start using it to dry her hair while she went looking for something in the closet.

"Hey, Ket, could I bother you to help me out here?"

I looked up to see what Kitteren wanted. She held a wet lock of hair in my direction. I sighed and opened my free hand toward her, using my still agitated power to dry her hair. The action settled it some and I felt more stable. Sometimes I felt she might be pushing it with these requests.

"You're the best, sis!" She smiled broadly over her shoulder.

"I've become a personal hair drier," I muttered.

I took a deep breath and fussed with my hair. I started wondering how much I needed give to get the answers I wanted. Was it even worth it? Just like I kept meaning to check Kitteren's bags for her usual running gear, but by the time I could, I let it slide again. My family would not outright lie to me, would they?

"Kitteren, you left these in our room," Mother said as she came in carrying a couple of shoe boxes.

I eyed them warily. Why could they not leave me be with what I had?

Kitteren had donned a similar outfit to mine, only the colors different - hers were more earthy tones: the vest and skirt a light tan while the shirt was a darker green.

"Oh don't look at me like that, Ketayl. You'll want to wear these today since you plan on walking around a lot. Your feet will be hurting if you wear your normal shoes," Mother said and set a box down on Kitteren's bed and then sat next to me with the other one. She opened the box to show a pair of gray sandals.

I sighed and shifted uncomfortably in my skirt. It did not matter I wore shorts underneath.

"You look fine. Put these on and I'll finish your hair." Mother took the brush from me and moved so she sat behind me on the bed. "The two of you look adorable actually."

I really wished I had been more firm in my resolve to not come here. Just the thought of trying to face down either Vince or Lockonis alone was enough to change my mind. Having to argue with both of them to reverse their decision would have been an outright nightmare.

"Did you have fun in town last night?" Mother's voice was as gentle as her hands. Immediately it set me on edge. No, I did not want to end up on another shopping trip.

"It was fine," I said flatly. I knew I needed to be on guard with her now.

Two strokes through my hair with the brush and then she asked, "What did you do?"

"Went to the bookstore. Didn't find anything I wanted to read. I still want my tablet back," I shot the last part at Kitteren. If I could drag her into this, I would. Maybe it would get the attention off of me.

Kitteren looked up from where she was putting her brown sandals on. "No. Ket, come on. Schoolwork on vacation?"

"I have other books on there." Granted, they were books I read to be better in the lab.

"I'm going to back Kitteren on this one - you need to disconnect," Mother chided softly.

I sighed. That attempt was shut down faster than I hoped.

By now there were no tangles in my hair, but Mother continued to brush it anyway. "Dad says he saw you leave with Silver."

"Wait, I told him to leave you alone," Kitteren jumped back into the conversation. "That good-for-nothing..."

"Enough," Mother's voice was sharp. Then she patted my shoulder and pointed at the box next to me.

I obediently put the sandals on. They felt comfortable, but I really did not like people buying things for me. I reminded myself that I was simply playing nice to try and hopefully get some information.

"What else did you do?" Mother asked, her voice gentle again.

I paused for a moment to think about how to avoid saying too much. "Just got a snack and browsed the cultural displays a little."

One, two strokes. "You seemed a little distracted when you got back."

Kitteren opened her mouth and looked in Mother's direction before she shut it again.

I could not claim I was simply tired. Kitteren would see through it in a heartbeat. "Just had stuff on my mind."

"Do you want to talk about it?" I fought against the gentle suggestion.

I shook my head. I knew I needed to be more alert today. I started to wish Kitteren and Silver got along better - I wanted him to have my back. Then I wondered where the thought came from. I never wanted to rely on anyone else. Bad enough I leaned on Kitteren so much after I first transferred to the TIO.

"Shit, Ket, what happened?" Kitteren broke her silence.

"It's nothing," I said quickly and immediately regretted it. Now it had become something. Before anyone could ask, I elaborated, done with the games, "I just ran into a couple of weird guys in the center of the market. They left - no incident."

"Was Silver with you?" Mother asked.

I rolled my eyes. "Yes. Can we be done talking about this? It was getting late and I probably shouldn't have had so much sugar right beforehand."

Mother ran her fingers through my hair. "You are more sensitive to things like that." She got off the bed. "Well, you two have fun. I'll message you when we're done so we can meet up."

Another meeting? On the weekend? I guess it would not be uncommon when the person you needed to talk to was only available for a short period of time. But still...

11

After a quick breakfast, Kitteren dragged me down toward the waterfront where most of the festivities were going on. We passed by vendors selling and promoting a wide variety of things from handmade crafts to health insurance. I wondered how many people got drunk and injured enough for the insurance company to have a booth.

The small canopies shading their workers and customers came in a variety of colors, though the majority of them seemed to be white.

I rubbed my arms as we walked, not able to shake the feeling of being watched. There were so many people here I must be imagining things. But I felt the sensation even before leaving the hotel. It seemed worse today.

Just overworked and still uneasy about being in Mystic Port, right?

"Over here," Kitteren said excitedly, taking my hand and dragging me toward a blue canopy.

Once we stopped, I glanced at what the merchant sold. "Jewelry?" Neither of us wore the stuff often by choice and this appeared to be all handmade. "Are you looking for a gift for Mother?"

My sister rolled her eyes. "No, us. A nice necklace will finish off these outfits, don't you think?" Kitteren made her way to a nearby display.

I shook my head. "I'm fine without."

Kitteren sighed and then shook her head. "You really need to lighten up and have some fun. Besides, your birthday is in a few days."

"We don't know when my birthday is. The date is just used for official documents," I reminded her. Why did my family insist on making a big deal out of it?

She stuck her tongue out at me. "We're going to celebrate it and you're going to like it." Kitteren's face turned sad. "We missed too many years."

I walked over quietly and looked at the necklaces on a stand next to hers. "You really don't need to do anything now. I don't like being the center of attention."

"I know, but I want to." Her words came out sounding a little whiny. I hated it when she pulled that tone because I usually ended up giving in to her. Granted it never took much - I always had a soft spot when it came to Kitteren.

I gently cupped a necklace to see how heavy it was. The largest of the silver leaves connected the black cording. Three smaller leaves hung from where one end of the large leaf met the cording - silver beads keeping the cords contained at various points. I found it an interesting design. A gold and brown one hung next to it.

"Oh, those would be good." Kitteren snatched up one of each and took them to the merchant.

I strode up next to her and asked the ridiculous question, "Do we have to look alike?"

She shrugged. "Why not? Mom has been dying to do this to us forever - you couldn't see her face while she was doing your hair, but she was so happy. She'll be thrilled when we meet her for lunch."

I rolled my eyes and walked away. I could deal with the necklace, but I wanted to escape before she found something else.

As I reached the edge of the canopy the sense of being watched jumped tenfold and I looked around trying to spot anyone. There were simply too many people here and the noise from the vendors as well as the rides operating not far off made it difficult.

Kitteren bounced around me happily, trying to get the necklace on me. Then she paused. "Ket, what's wrong?"

I shook my head. "I'm just not used to large crowds."

Something flashed across her face, but it disappeared too quickly to make out. "Well I'm here so you don't have to worry." She finished getting the leaves around my neck. "You look great, see!" Kitteren dragged me over to a mirror hanging near the entrance to the vendor.

Kitteren looked bubbly and happy. My expression had not changed from my normal one. Maybe I was still too tired to try - I did not get a full night's rest. I guessed the necklace added something, but I was never good with these things. I held the pendant leaves in my hand and looked down at them - they were just pieces of metal. These did not hide secrets like the Arcane College pins did. Just like my badge did not either.

I shifted uncomfortably, knowing the badge resided in my wallet in the small black pouch on my hip. I still felt undeserving of it.

"Let's keep checking out the vendors until it's time for lunch." Kitteren grabbed my hand and dragged me along. "Then this afternoon, we can go to the concerts. You're going to love it."

I told her I disliked shopping on more than one occasion, but listening to music sounded good. I just wanted to shake this feeling of being watched.

She paused as we passed a food vendor. "Are you hungry?"

"Not really," I said.

Next thing I knew, I found myself in line with Kitteren.

"I said I wasn't hungry," I reiterated.

"No, you said 'not really' which means you could do with a snack. Besides, you have to try the shortbread from this place - the ones with the fruit filling are fantastic." Kitteren had already dug out money from her wallet. "Don't make me choose a flavor for you."

"I really don't want anything." A last ditch effort, but I browsed the board anyway. There were only a few options, but they sold drinks as well. A bottle of water would be nice, though the price here made me reconsider. I mentally compared it to the other vendors we passed. Why did festival food have to cost so much? And especially a bottle of water?

"Two raspberry shortbread buns and two bottles of water," Kitteren ordered. She stood ahead of me, talking to the Dwarven woman at the counter.

Obviously, she would not listen to me. I quickly moved up with her. "Can I at least get this to try and make up for not having helped out on this trip?"

Kitteren looked at me like I was crazy. "No. And I'll tell you why as soon as we find a place to eat."

My sister chatted up the woman serving us as we waited. Bored, I looked around again and saw a familiar head of silver hair on a tall form. Maybe that's where the sensation came from, but Silver seemed interested in the ongoings of the festival itself.

I took the opportunity to look around more, but again, there were simply too many people. Too many would glance my way as they also took in their surroundings.

As soon as she paid and handed me my half, Kitteren took off for a side area. She found a quiet corner to sit under the shade of a large canopy.

"So why won't you let me pay for things?" I asked quietly.

Kitteren sighed and took a bite of her bun. Once she finished, she answered, "Because it's the only way I can try to pay you back."

I raised an eyebrow at her as I adjusted my grip on my food. "Pay me back? You don't owe me anything."

"Yes, I do. Shit, Ket, it's not just the money you would give to Mom to help care for me. But everything you've done for me my whole life. I want to show you how grateful I am and... I don't know. It's the only thing I can think of to do. I've screwed up pretty bad this trip so far." Her eyes were down. I fought the urge to just forget everything.

I found my opening to start asking questions. "Like when you didn't come back to rest at night?"

"You noticed, huh?" Kitteren seemed embarrassed at having been caught.

I sighed and pointed out, "It's not hard - you hate cleaning and making the bed falls under that." Her quarters often had clothes hung on the backs of furniture and on the floor in her closet instead of on hangers.

My sister looked down at her food. "Sorry."

Taking a deep breath, I explained, "Kitteren, I don't want apologies, I just want to know what is going on."

My words caught her off-guard and she fidgeted. "Well, you remember Joanna, right?"

I nodded.

Kitteren shifted in her chair as she elaborated, "She's caught up in a pretty nasty divorce right now. She's afraid her soon-to-be ex-husband will try to forcibly take her son away. I spent the night with her a couple of times to help."

I cocked my head to the side. "Why didn't you say something before?"

"I didn't know how you felt after how she treated you. Joanna grew up knowing me and she's pretty abrasive under normal circumstances, but I think meeting you in person was a bit much for her right now. She's actually sorry for how she acted." Kitteren's explanation for not telling me seemed trivial, but I could follow her logic.

I shrugged. I had gotten used to people not liking me for trivial reasons.

Concerned green eyes were suddenly in my line of vision. "Ket, I can't read minds. What's going on?"

I shrugged again. How do I bring up that I felt like everyone kept secrets which somehow involved me?

"Is that idiot partner of yours bothering you? I mean, he's got the stalker thing going right now." So Kitteren noticed him as well.

I shook my head. "But you knew he was coming and didn't tell me."

Kitteren sighed and sat back in her chair. "Yeah, but the stupid paladin being here makes no sense. I just wanted you to have a quiet vacation. Him being here is like having work follow you."

Again, I could not argue with her logic. Everything had a reason, right? "The big brother act does get old quite quickly, but I'm certain we'll figure out a compromise."

There was a long pause before Kitteren said, "I still don't like him."

I sighed and said, "I know."

Kitteren smirked. "Can I ask you a question now?"

I eyed Kitteren warily. "I reserve the right to not answer."

She rolled her eyes. "Fine. Why did you decide to pick Mom's pocket?"

I had been expecting a different question. I sat back and thought about it, thinking answering this would be alright. "I'm really not certain what I was thinking at the time. I might have just wanted to try my abilities against someone more aware." I needed the test to go after the others taken by the slave traders. I just did not need to tell her the last part.

"Worked out for us, didn't it?" Kitteren sat back and took a bite of her bun.

"I suppose it did. Mother has been kind when she had every right not to be." In more ways than one. I don't think I would have made it off of the pier alive that night if Mother had not insisted on helping me get those children freed.

Kitteren rolled her eyes. "Why can't you just call them Mom and Dad? They'd like it better. You're too formal and it makes it sound like you don't like them." It was something she got on my case about every so often.

I took a moment to explain, "I'm just trying to be respectful. I haven't been around them for as long as you have. I don't want to make things more awkward with a familiarity that isn't there."

"Gods, Ket, you know how infuriating you are sometimes?" I was starting to. "It'll be fine - I promise."

"Mom! Dad!" Kitteren called and waved to them, pulling me along behind her. I tripped over something and stumbled to catch myself. Why was she in such a rush?

Kitteren stopped to help me, but I had steadied again. "Can we slow down?"

"Sorry. I just want to make sure we have enough time after lunch to be able to grab good seats."

"Oh, look at you two," Mother gushed. She came over and picked up the pendants on my necklace to look at them. "These are a nice touch."

Father came over and put his arm around Kitteren's shoulders, smiling. "Let's get in line so we can catch up."

I followed at the back, still uneasy. I looked back over my shoulder in time to catch Silver's gaze. I had not seen him since Kitteren insisted on buying those buns.

I waved to him and then returned to the rest of my family. This must be awful for him to be alone - his own family lost to the necromancer.

"What's wrong, Ketayl?" Mother fell back to walk next to me.

I shook my head. Bringing Silver up within earshot of Kitteren would only result in an argument. The day had been fairly nice so far and I did not want to ruin it.

Kitteren again ordered for me when we reached our turn in line. I walked away, frustrated I could not even make my own decisions.

Mother quickly caught up and prodded me to an open table near the back corner of the large tent. "Just relax and let your sister introduce you to the things she likes here."

I sighed and sat down, staring out of the tent at the festival goers mingling about.

"I noticed a certain someone following you," Mother said. Kitteren and Father were still waiting on the order.

"This isn't fair to him." I knew how it felt to watch others with their families and being alone. Now with my role reversed it hurt to watch him be alone.

Mother took a deep breath before she said, "You do remember I spoke with him, right? He said he told you this was his choice."

"But he lost his family..." I could still see the images of all of those people clearly.

"Ketayl," Mother said gently. "You are his family now and in time he'll find others. I'm afraid my business has kept me away from being able to spend as much time as I would like with you and I'm grateful he's here to try and fill the gap."

"Mom..." I paused and covered my mouth. Damn Kitteren for putting the thought in my head. "I'm so sorry, I didn't mean to..."

Before I finished my apology, Mother pulled me into a tight hug. "You have no idea how long I have wanted to hear you call me that."

"What's going on?" Father asked, setting one of the trays down on the table.

Mother's voice sounded off as she told him and my sister what I said. Almost as if she had been crying.

Kitteren sat down across from me with another tray. "See, I told you."

"I didn't mean to be disrespectful," I said quietly, looking down at the plate of seafood placed in front of me. Did they honestly expect me to eat all of this? Even half of this would be on the large side for a meal. I was hungry from being dragged all over, but not this much.

"Ketayl," Father said softly, which caught my attention. "We've been hoping you would eventually be comfortable enough to not be so formal."

I felt the heat rising to my face and looked back down at my food. I did not wish to continue this conversation.

"What else do you two have planned for the day?" Mother asked, thankfully changing topics.

Kitteren had a mouthful of food and swallowed quickly. Her manners were not the best under normal circumstances. "We're going to go to the concerts this afternoon. Haven't planned anything afterward."

I thanked whatever God would listen that she had not planned the whole day out. I might be done after these concerts. My legs were already complaining.

The smells from the plate in front of me reminded me I should eat - I worked up an appetite getting dragged around the festival grounds.

"Perhaps we can spare some time to go as well?" Mother asked, looking at Father.

He shrugged. "I don't see why not. Unless they call back needing something else from us."

I vaguely wondered who "they" were, but I was not privy to Mother's business. They put so much emphasis on how much I had been working and here they were getting pulled into meetings and whatnot.

The conversation between the three of them carried on over mundane topics. I answered when necessary. I finished eating first and excused myself to go throw my plate out after dumping the rest of my fried potato sticks on Kitteren's plate.

Unfortunately, the trash bin was on the other side of the tent. As I made my way over, I noticed Silver sitting not far away by himself. I made my way over once I got rid of my plate.

"Hey," I said.

Silver looked up from what he had been reading on his phone. "Hey. You look nice."

I looked down at my outfit and then shifted uncomfortably. "Thank you, but I don't like wearing this stuff."

He opened a hand to the empty seat next to him and I took the invitation.

"Are you enjoying the festival?" I asked. This was a public event - he had every right to be here.

"It's interesting and different," Silver said, putting his phone away.

"Though it feels similar to the small fairs we held on the church grounds."

I tried not to cringe at the fact this had to be making things worse for him. "What were you reading?"

"A new novel Brad suggested to me. I'm still not used to reading on a device like this, but it's far more convenient. And I've had a hard time putting it down."

I started to stand. "I'm sorry, I shouldn't have interrupted you."

Silver put his hand on my arm. "Ketayl, don't worry about it. It's just a book. Please don't feel you need to leave."

I moved my arm away from his hand and sat back down.

"What are you doing for the rest of the day?" Silver asked.

"It's none of your business," Kitteren's voice came from behind me.

I looked up at her. Stopping to talk to Silver had been a bad idea. "Kitteren..." I warned.

"Yeah, yeah. We're going," she said and left.

I stood quickly, knowing I needed to follow. "I'm sorry. I'll catch up with you later." I grew tired of having to apologize for Kitteren's behavior.

"Have fun," Silver smiled. I wondered if it was real or just to mask how he felt.

I bowed and left, catching up to Kitteren and our parents. While I still found annoyance at my sister's attitude toward him, I did not want to start an argument right now. Would it even be worth having words with her over? My sister would not simply change her mind because I did not like it. If it started interfering with work then I would definitely have to address it.

I did not know what to do before that scenario became reality. I felt a certain loyalty to my sister and did not want to cause further issues, but at the same time I disliked how she treated Silver. I had started to consider him a friend and wanted her to stop. How was I supposed to protect her and protect someone else from her?

I remained silent as I followed and looked around, trying to spot anyone who would be watching me.

"Is something wrong?" Father asked quietly - he fell back beside me, letting Mother and Kitteren get ahead.

I shook my head. I did not want to be viewed as crazy, though I started to feel that way. "Too big of a crowd."

"Are you sure it's just that?" Father asked.

I looked up at him skeptically. What could he be getting at?

"I ran into Silver this morning. He told me about yesterday. You could have come to us." Father placed his hand gently on my shoulder.

Silver would. I faced forward and chose my next words carefully. "I made more out of it than it actually was."

Father continued, "He said you mentioned feeling like you were being watched. And I'm guessing you're feeling it again now."

I had to remind myself Father trained as a tracker. Trackers were notoriously observant. "I think it's just the size of the crowd and that I keep running into Silver."

"The latter would be my fault," Father admitted. "I asked if he wouldn't mind keeping an eye out for you two. I know Kitteren and she can get easily distracted."

I stayed silent. Had he expected trouble? The thought of secrets still being kept came back to the forefront of my mind.

"Ketayl," Father said softly and pulled me to the side. "Don't ignore this feeling. How long today?"

Those brown eyes stared down at me, concern plain on his face. I shrank back slightly and admitted, "Since before we left the hotel this morning."

I thought I heard a growl come from him as he looked in the direction Kitteren and Mother had gone and crossed his arms over his chest. With the noise of the festival, I could have heard wrong, but he definitely did not look happy at what I said. "Just know you can come to me with this. I'll try to help keep an eye out while we're here, but I'm afraid our meeting later this afternoon will take us away from you two again."

"What's going on?" I asked, desperate for some piece of information.

Father smiled. "Hopefully nothing, but I take my children's concerns seriously." He patted me on the head and I glared up at him.

I hated being short.

Father tugged me in the direction Kitteren and Mother went. "We better catch up before they come looking for us."

I still felt like I missed something. The reasons for their disappearances all made sense. I just hoped they were not lies.

12

WE SAT five rows back in the center section of the large amphitheater. How had Mother and Kitteren managed to secure such prime spots given how quickly the seats were filling?

I shifted uncomfortably on the stone bench, but could not move too much being stuck between Kitteren and Father. Father whispered something to Mother, and I only hoped it was not about me. The noise around us kept me from being able to hear anything he said.

Kitteren elbowed me gently - just enough to get my attention. I turned to her and she pointed at the stage where musicians started to take their seats. They were not organized like the orchestras I occasionally watched videos of.

I turned and looked around to see how many people had filed in. I caught a glimpse of Silver a section over and maybe a row or two back - it was hard to tell with the way the seating curved. His attention pointed toward the stage. Now that I knew what Father asked of him, I expected to keep seeing him pop up. Surely it would have ended the feeling of being watched.

Kitteren sat on the end, but being surrounded by so many people still bothered me and I searched for who might be watching. It appeared as if most of the festival goers were coming this way.

"You okay?" Kitteren asked, concern on her face.

"Big crowd," I answered and returned my attention to the stage.

"Well, yeah. This is one of the biggest events of the festival," Kitteren said. "Don't worry about everyone else - they'll be too engrossed in the concert soon."

I glanced down at my watch. It had just hit 1500. Was it really so late? I knew it took us a while to walk over here, but not so long as to explain the time discrepancy. I guess we left the hotel later this morning than I estimated and it threw me off.

A drum beat caught my attention and I looked up at the stage. A Human man walked on, playing a handheld drum. Even with all of the other musicians on the stage, he alone produced the sound so far.

We were close enough so when he flicked his small drumstick in the air and still heard a beat, I could see the confused and curious expression on his face. The large screen above the stage helped by focusing in. He played with the stick in his hand, twirling it back and forth while sound continued being produced.

He turned to talk to a musician behind him - enough to show the audience his other hand inside the small drum making the sounds with the bands around the upper parts of his fingers. I smiled at the small comedy routine. The man grinned and returned to playing. The other musicians on the stage started joining him.

The music took on the flavor of the region. A female Human fiddler came on, taking over leading the song. I found myself clapping along rhythmically with the rest of the audience.

Kitteren nudged me with her shoulder. She greeted me with a broad grin and then pointed back. I turned to see male dancers of mixed races coming down the aisles. Only a couple per aisle.

They found their spots and began fast-paced, energetic footwork. Though originally native to only Humans, all races in this part of the Northern Isles adopted it. I remembered watching children learning it one summer. It had not mattered what race they were as long as they wanted to learn. Given the circumstances at the time, I kept to the shadows and watched silently.

Women dressed similarly to the men dancing entered the aisles and took up their dance partner. The music continued for another minute or so before it suddenly stopped. Even the dancers looked confused.

Three woman in brightly colored dresses took the stage. One started singing slowly and I recognized the language. The words close enough to my own native dialect of common that I roughly understood what they sang.

The song switched back and forth between this language and normal common. I found myself becoming absorbed by the performance as they actively engaged the audience, telling one story after another with each song they sung.

The sun moved noticeably by the time all of the different performers finished and the crowd began departing the amphitheater.

I felt lighter - like my worries from earlier washed away. Mother and Father smiled broadly and Kitteren obviously could barely contain her excitement. My sister grabbed my arm and tugged me toward tables set up at the back of the amphitheater. If not for the crowd still clearing out, I would have been half-dragged.

The tables displayed merchandise from the various groups - shirts, posters, small trinkets, and copies of their music. What did Kitteren want here?

Our parents stood behind us, easily seeing over our heads and I wanted nothing more than to be out of this crowd. I looked up at them, silently pleading to let me out.

"If you want to take Ketayl, I'll stay with Kitteren," Father suggested to Mother.

She managed to pry me out of the crowd and we found an empty bench not far away. Mother glanced at her watch as she commented, "You seemed to have enjoyed the show."

I nodded. I had, but the feeling of being watched came back too quickly now that I was parted from the crowd. At least I had a slight reprieve from it.

"Unfortunately, Dad and I will have to get going. Are you and Kitteren okay on your own?"

I tried to keep the unease out of my voice. "Yeah."

Mother turned her violet eyes to me with concern. "Ketayl, what is going on?"

I shrugged and offered my usual answer: "Too many people."

Silence fell between us before she found something else to talk about. "Did you understand what they were singing?"

I stopped at the question - it had been so different from the others. "Mostly. It's close enough to what I know to get a rough understanding."

Mother admitted, "I've been trying to figure out where you two actually come from, but it's a large area to try and narrow down. Kitteren unfortunately doesn't remember anything."

I stiffened. Vague memories flashed quickly and I shoved them back. "I couldn't find it again if I wanted to," I said. When I had been told to take Kitteren and run, I did not pay attention to the path I took.

She cocked her head slightly, probably trying to determine the amount of truth to my answer. "Nothing to help me narrow it down?"

I shook my head. "Don says he thinks we're from the Highlands region, but it's all I know." You could put a map in front of me and I would still not be able to give more information.

Mother sighed. "I'll figure out something. I never did get an answer of what made you leave your original home in the first place."

I glanced at her before returning to watching Kitteren and Father in the crowd. They were discussing something. I supposed there was no harm in telling Mother why. Before I just never wanted to share anything and the question had not come up for some time. "The village was attacked."

"Hm." Mother paused and seemed to contemplate the information for a moment. "I wonder if it's still in existence then."

It did not matter. At least not to me, but perhaps Kitteren wanted to find it. I thought it better we both forget. Kitteren did not need to know certain things and I only wanted to see her happy.

Father approached, a plastic bag in his hands. "I'll take this with us so you two don't have to carry it around." It looked like a mix of music discs and a thin book or two. "Think we have time to grab a light dinner?" He looked at Mother expectantly.

She glanced at her watch again and nodded. "They can wait after taking up so much of our time this trip."

I found myself once again being dragged along. It was what this trip really had been so far - me just being toted from one place to the next, not really taking part. I only felt free enough to explore alone or with Silver.

I chewed on the thought for a while, wondering why.

We finished eating and Kitteren spoke of finding something for dessert when her phone rang. Mother and Father were still with us - Mother seemingly too happy to let the people she had business with wait.

Kitteren moved away from us to take the call privately, but there was a look of shock on her face and she spoke quickly and quietly to whoever was on the other end. She ended the call and came back over. Her hands shook as she quickly typed up a message. "I need to get to Joanna's house. There's been a problem." Obviously it was not Mother or Father she messaged.

"It's on our way, we can give you a ride," Father said before turning to me. "Do you want to go back to the hotel?"

Given how Joanna felt about me so far, I guess it made sense to not even ask if I wanted to go as well. It still did not feel right though. I shook my head. "I can make my way back. Unless you want help, Kitteren."

My sister shook her head, her hands still shaking as she continued to type on her phone.

I stayed and waved to them as they left. Alone finally. I took a deep breath as soon as they were out of sight. Now I could try to do something about the sensation of being followed.

"Is everything okay?"

The sound of Silver's voice from behind startled me. I kept my back to him and said, "I'm not sure." So much for being alone.

Silence fell between us and I debated what I should do next. I could stay and try to enjoy the remainder of the festival for the evening. Though even with Silver next to me, I could not shake the continuing sensation of being watched.

He came around in front of me and offered me his elbow. "A lovely lady shouldn't be left alone. Especially not on such a beautiful evening as this."

I glared at him and he laughed. "Why are you here?"

Silver sighed and lowered his arm. "Because Dayko asked me to follow you after hearing about last night."

At least the stories matched. I was still annoyed he told Father about yesterday.

"Look, Ketayl, I've been watching you all day. The only time you relaxed was at the amphitheater and it didn't look like you got much of a say in what you did. I'd be happy to keep you company if there's something you want to do."

"I..." This was the first time I had been to this festival. This area had not been built like this half a century ago. "I don't know. I've never been to this before."

Silver seemed surprised by my admission. "Well, it looks like we're together on that. I think I saw some games and other interesting things over by the rides."

As good of an idea as any. "Okay."

"If there's something that catches your attention, please say something." I raised an eyebrow at him, but Silver seemed genuine in his statement.

I nodded and began heading toward where the rides were. I just hoped Silver did not want to try and talk me into going on any of them.

"Can I ask you something?"

I glanced up at Silver as he walked beside me. I shrugged. Asking did not mean I would answer.

"Why do you let Kitteren push you around?"

"What?" I thought about his question. Is that what it looked like?

Silver toyed with his braid for a moment. "She..." he paused. "It's like she didn't acknowledge when you said something to her about what you were doing."

I bit my lower lip. I guess I could see where he got the notion. "I know I let her get away with more than I probably should, but..."

"But?"

I fidgeted with the hem of my vest for a moment. How much should I tell him? "Kitteren was really sick all the time when we were little. I guess I just want to see her happy. I hadn't thought about it that way."

"I'm also seeing it from a different perspective. Ketayl, you need to think about yourself also. Don't let her, me, or anyone else push you around."

I paused and Silver turned to see why I stopped. "I'm truly sorry for how she's treated you. I just can't seem to convince her to stop."

Silver gave me a lopsided grin. "I think I can handle a few insults."

I bit my bottom lip and wrapped my arms around my waist, keeping my eyes forward before I continued walking in silence.

Perhaps I should simply step back and let the two of them work it out.

Silver kept his word when I caught sight of the cultural displays lining the small street between the vendors and the rides. He quietly followed me, occasionally asking a question which often times I did not have the answer to.

He tried his hand at a few games. Some he won without much effort and others he failed at and I could not help but hide my amusement behind my hand at his antics. I still tried to understand why I began doing the motion of covering my mouth with my hand - why I felt the need to hide my genuine feelings.

Perhaps simply to help keep my distance.

While he busied himself with a game involving tossing rings onto various pegs, I wandered to a nearby food vendor. The sun had gotten low on the horizon and I needed a snack. I purchased two small bags of popped corn by the time he had started heading my way. I finished my transaction before he could intervene.

I held out one of the bags. "Thanks for being my shadow all day."

"It's important to have your partner's back," Silver said and smiled, accepting the bag.

As we moved away from the crowd, I admitted quietly, "I still feel like I'm being watched."

Silver stopped in front of me, his voice concerned, "Even now that I'm not poorly following you around?"

I nodded.

"Ketayl, why didn't you say something sooner?" The aggravation in his voice had me debating if I should have remained silent on the matter.

I took a deep breath and admitted, "Because I'm not sure if it's just the crowd or not."

Silver looked around for a moment before he asked, "Do you want to head back? I know there are still events going on for a few more hours."

"I think I will, but don't feel like you have to leave too." I did not want to ruin the remainder of his day. "I'm kind of tired anyway."

Silver shook his head. "I'm done for the day. Maybe we can come back tomorrow?"

I nodded and started to head in the direction of the hotel. We made it to the regular streets when I caught glimpse of a familiar little face peeking out of an alleyway.

I knelt down and held out the remainder of my bag of popped corn to the homeless girl. She slowly stepped out and eyed Silver warily. Odd, she had not been scared of us last night. Well, not after I initially stopped her from picking my pocket.

"You're offering me food again?" Her voice shook.

I nodded and put the bag on the ground for her.

She snatched up the bag and stepped back. "Are you here to help us?"

"Help you?" Silver asked. Her question confused me as well.

The girl burst into tears. "The others are gone. I can't find any of them."

"Maybe they're down at the festival?" I offered. If it ran during my time, I certainly would have found it to be a prime place to get food and money.

She shook her head. "You don't understand. There were a lot of us. Then the others started disappearing one or two at a time."

I stood up and looked at Silver to see if he heard of anything, but he shrugged. The article from the first day nagged at my mind, but I pushed it back.

The little girl got mad. "I thought you were back to help us!" She took off into the alleyway.

Immediately I chased after her and stopped short at the entry. The two men from last night were there and the Elf held the child. Her eyes were wide with fear and pain from the way he gripped her arm.

Upon realizing I had seen them, the Elf threw a menacing grin at me and put the now thrashing girl over his shoulder. The two men ran.

"We should call the... wait!"

I took off before Silver could finish. This could not be happening again. I ran as fast as I could, following the trail of popped corn down narrow alleys I once navigated with far more ease when I was smaller. A few times I used a quick burst of my power to help jump over toppled trashcans and other debris.

The trail died and I kept going anyway, having a feeling I knew where they were headed. After a few turns they abandoned the tight alleys for more open streets and I could see them again. The closed businesses around me would not be of any aid in stopping them.

Silver ran close behind me and I felt as if I kept falling farther behind. My lungs were burning and I tried to ignore the pain in my side. I would not be able to concentrate enough now to use my power effectively. I could not even think of what to use.

I saw the girl struggling, reaching out to me. They were headed toward the docks. If they took her to a warehouse, I could do something. If they took to the water…

My worst fears came true as they jumped into a boat, its engines already running and waiting for them. It seemed in an instant, they were gone. The glare from the sun off the water made it impossible for me to track them.

I fell to my knees at the edge of the dock, breathing hard. I slammed my fists into the wood, cursing myself for letting them get away.

"Can you teleport us?" Silver asked.

I could not focus enough to teleport myself let alone attempt to bring someone else with me.

"Where?!" I asked sharply in between deep intakes of air. "Even if I could see the boat, I couldn't get myself on it while it's moving."

Silver said something, rubbing my back, but I did not hear it. I put my head down on the dock and thought about screaming in frustration, but had not caught my breath enough to put forth the effort.

This could not be happening. Not again.

13

KITTEREN SAT NEXT to me in the common room of our suite. Silver spoke quietly with the Highlands Office TIO agents. I had gone numb. My mind did not want to accept that history appeared to be repeating itself.

I already gave my statement and Kitteren just kept her arm around my shoulders.

Mother and Father argued quietly on the other side of the room. Somehow quietly enough I could not hear them in the small area.

Father gestured in my direction at one point and Mother put her hand on his arm, gently pushing it down. What had I done? All I wanted to do was save the girl.

"Ket, talk to me. Please," Kitteren begged. I had not spoken beyond giving my statement.

I held my tongue. My legs still ached and I rubbed my calves, trying to get the soreness out.

Silver had called Father. Father then called the Highlands TIO Office. Somehow they got here in record time. Kitteren gave Silver a hard time about what happened until I stepped in and informed her it had been my decision.

At this rate I was bound to get a headache. I enjoyed not having them.

"You should probably stretch," Kitteren suggested quietly.

"If I'm not needed, I'm going for a swim," I said, getting up and heading for the room I shared with my sister. I remembered seeing a changing area at the pool itself so I would not have to walk past them in my swimsuit.

I heard Kitteren start to argue and then one of the agents saying they were done here for now.

I managed to get my suit and brushed past everyone before anyone could stop me. I needed time to think and there were too many people around. I knew the agents would not be able to stop these people in time. No one knew about this better than I did and likely no one would take me seriously if I tried to explain.

I mourned the loss I likely would have to take to do this. The fairie was a monster - I would do everything I could to maintain myself, but I started to wonder how high the cost would be this time. Likely I would lose Kitteren if she found out.

***

DESPITE THE SIGNS saying not to, I dove in. I was alone in the pool room and I needed to get wet fast or I would find the water too cold to get in all the way.

Turning over, I floated on my back, staring at the ceiling. I had not actually wanted to swim, but I needed to get away from the others.

The slave traders changed their method from 50 years ago. Was it even the same crew? Something told me yes, at least at the top. It felt like someone was baiting me to go after them.

The last time they held the children in one of the warehouses. Would they have doubled-back after we left? But why have a boat waiting in the first place? I marked the idea as highly unlikely.

Now they were being held in the harbor, but where? With such a busy port there were many trade vessels in and out daily. I did not know where to start. Then I needed to take into account the local fishing industry also.

I needed to shake off my escorts and go down to the waterfront and investigate. There had to be some clue. I just hoped it would not be too late by the time I found the child. With any luck, they were still collecting the children to sell and were not ready to meet with a buyer.

The water flowed around me quietly while I contemplated the

actions of the two men. I think they knew somehow, but I did not remember them from the last time. Why wait for me to see them take the girl? This trip had been a horrible mistake, but I could not let this go even with the potential of it being a trap.

I sensed someone enter the pool room and folded up, swimming under the water until I got to the side near the door. I peeked over the edge of the pool.

"I didn't mean to scare you," Silver said, taking a seat in one of the chairs. He had not changed from earlier and it did not look like he planned on swimming.

"I came here to be alone," I said flatly.

Silver toyed with his braid once he settled. "Too bad. Dayko asked me to come down and make sure you were okay. You could just pretend I'm not here."

I raised an eyebrow at him, not moving from where I was hiding most of my body. "Why you and not Kitteren?" Him being sent made little sense to me, but most things this trip had.

"Because I was with you when it happened. And he and Lindale were having what looked like was going to be a lengthy conversation with her when I left," Silver said. "I take it you didn't bring your violin this time."

"No..." Silver had become more observant than I remembered. I floated along the wall, still holding on so I could keep my head up and keep track of him.

Silver sighed loudly. "I'm sorry, I didn't mean to interrupt you. You can go back to what you were doing. You looked peaceful."

Not the word I would have used. And it irritated me I needed to be watched by people I trusted. And now I had to have a babysitter inside the hotel. How in the Hells could I move to go find the children when I could not even be free to think?

"You're planning on going after them, aren't you?"

"What does it matter to you?" I snapped and immediately regretted it. I sank back into the water in shame.

Silver got up and came over to kneel next to where I floated. "You're my partner and more importantly my friend. I don't want to see you get hurt."

I glared at him and debated moving away, but I had pulled myself against the wall to try and hide as much of my thin frame as I could.

Silver stood up, "Look, the Highlands agents have things under control. They'll find the girl."

"It'll be too late," I whispered, not having planned to speak aloud.

Silver sat back on his heels and watched me for a minute. I disliked the feeling of being sized up. "Ketayl, what is it? I've never seen you so agitated. Not even when you were balancing quizzing me while pulling late nights in the lab and answering my thousands of questions while trying to study yourself. You can tell me - I want to help where I can."

I shivered - I needed to get out. It overrode my need to hide my small form from Silver and I swam to the end of the pool near the towels.

I dropped down under the water, holding onto the wall and pulled myself up quickly, bringing up a shower of water. I sat on the edge for a moment before rolling to my feet and grabbing a towel.

After wrapping myself in a large, fluffy towel, I grabbed a smaller one to start drying my face and hair. "What matters is I know what is going on better than anyone else. I'll be able to find her. There are probably others as well, but I have to do this alone."

"No way that's happening," Silver said, coming over to where I stood. I'd use my power to dry off when I went to change, but I enjoyed the luxury of wrapping up in a large towel. "What about working with the Highlands agents?"

I leveled a look at him which I hope conveyed the fact no one would let me work a case while on vacation.

"Right," Silver said, taking the smaller towel from me and helping soak the excess water out of my hair. I thought about pulling away, but it might hurt. "Then let me help you. An extra set of eyes and ears couldn't hurt. But you have to promise me if we find them, we let the Highlands agents handle it."

I pried my hair out of his hands. This was the problem with having it down - it became too easy of a leash. "Fine, but I make no promises." I would have to somehow lose him in this endeavor. I did not want him to get hurt. This was my fight.

Come morning, my family had taken off again. Mother left a note saying she had a meeting with some manager and Kitteren returned to Joanna's house. Father went up to Don's to finish the repairs.

A knock on the door to the suite kept me from giving it much more thought. Fixing the strap on my top, I peeked through the small lens to see who it could be. Silver stood there, his arms crossed.

Opening the door, I commented, "You're up early." I still wore my night clothes and I had hit the point of I did not care how I looked in front of him.

"Paladin of the Holy Church of the Sun - kind of means I'm up before dawn," Silver replied sarcastically. "Did I wake you?"

I shook my head, running a hand through my hair. "I probably would have been up a while ago, but I couldn't calm my mind enough to rest."

"Well, get dressed. There's breakfast downstairs and I'm famished," Silver gently directed me toward my room.

"Pushy," I commented before closing the door. Thinking about it, I could get used to this. Having a partner might not be so bad. It was a comfortable, but not too close of a relationship.

Too bad it would end before it really started. I felt guilty about my plans to ditch Silver at some point so I could move freely. I supposed I could see how the morning went and maybe reconsider. There might be a small chance this could end much more peacefully.

I started to think maybe my biggest problem right now had become finding something comfortable to wear.

As I pulled up my short jeans I frowned at the length or rather lack thereof. Silver called through the door, "Where is the rest of your family?"

"They already went their separate ways this morning. It has been like this most of the time I've been here." I did not know why I told Silver so much, but I felt like I needed to explain.

"And here I was thinking it was going to be hard spending time with you," Silver said and I rolled my eyes.

Once I finished, I opened the door so I would not have to speak loudly to be heard. Sitting down on the bed, I started brushing my mass of hair.

"Here, let me," Silver said, sitting on the bed behind me and taking my brush.

"I'm quite capable of doing my hair," I argued, twisting to take it back.

Silver hid my brush behind him and turned me back around. "Humor me."

Crossing my arms I sat still. What was his thing with my hair anyway? Or anyone's this trip I wondered. Why did Kitteren insist on having me wear it down?

"I noticed you haven't been wearing your hair in a bun lately. Trying something new?" Silver asked.

I sighed and told him, "No, Kitteren took my hair pins and anything else to tie it back. I haven't been anywhere to pick up more."

"Seems a bit excessive." His fingers were sure but gentle. "Mind if I try something? It'll help keep it out of your face."

I waved my hand for him to do whatever. I was not overly picky and if it contained the mass, the happier I would be. I again briefly entertained the idea of cutting it.

Silver started a weave at the top of my head, pulling more hair into it with each twist until he ran out of hair to gather and then braided it down. He dug a hair elastic out of his pocket.

"Not too bad considering it has been a long time since I've done one of these," Silver said. He tapped me on the shoulder with my brush and I took it.

I paused a moment to process his comment. "You used to do hair for other people?"

Silver waved the end of his own braid at me. "When there were more families at the church, we'd rotate who cared for the children. I found myself doing hair a lot when I wasn't teaching classes. And getting my own hair done."

I smiled at the mental image, though I had a hard time imagining Silver sitting still while children played with his hair. "I'm sorry you left that."

Silver stood up and guided me toward the bathroom so I could better see what he had done. "There haven't been many families there for almost a decade and most insisted on teaching their own children. Besides, if it wasn't for the request from the TIO, we likely wouldn't be having this conversation."

I paused to consider what he said and wondered if he meant when we requested a divine consultant. A little morbid to think about this early.

"Still, you could have stayed and helped them rebuild." I picked up the hand mirror Mother kept and turned my back to the large mirror so I could see. The braid was pretty and it worked well to keep my mass of hair contained. Maybe he would let me keep the elastic afterward - at least until I retrieved my own items.

Silver's face went neutral and I feared I said the wrong thing. "That may be a discussion for another time. The short version is despite the fact we follow the same doctrine, the new members were very different from my family."

"Why not now?" I asked. Silver had been adamant in knowing about me, why deny me answers?

He took a deep breath, looking at his own reflection in the mirror. "Because I still don't truly understand it myself. At least not enough to explain it."

I supposed it was fair enough.

"Why do you call the fairie a monster?" Silver asked. I nearly dropped the mirror. "And you react oddly every time the fairie is brought up."

I put the mirror down gently. In here with the large mirror, I could not hide from him. I closed my eyes for a moment to try and find a way out of this. Kitteren and Mother, I could tell no all I wanted. For some reason I could not do the same to Silver. What about this Elven man made me feel like I could tell my darkest secrets to him?

My mind answered with because as a paladin he probably often listened to people's problems.

"I know the full story. It's not just a myth or legend - time just turned the events into that along with a helpful amount of embellishment. I'd rather not retell it if you don't mind." My words sounded hollow to my ears. I knew the odds - I would likely need my full power and end up becoming the monster again to end the girl's terror. How would I be able to do that while still afraid of my own abilities?

"You were there? Were you one of the rescued children?"

Apparently I now had his full attention and I hoped he would drop it. I looked up at Silver in the mirror and kept my mouth shut. It would be better for him to believe that.

"But the girl seemed to think you were the fairie."

"Things change over time," I said and managed to get around him and left the bathroom.

"Ketayl, stop. Which is it?" Silver grabbed my shoulder.

I turned and smiled at him, pushing how uncomfortable our conversation made me feel to the back. "You said you were famished - we should get going."

SILVER PESTERED me all the way down to the dining area. There were a couple of tables set up serving various items for breakfast. He stopped when there were others around, but his theories started becoming more wild. He had even asked if it could be another sister or other relation who shared my coloring.

I refused to answer anymore and served myself before sitting down at an open table near the window. It had a nice view out over the harbor.

"Ketayl..." His voice bordered on whining. What intrigued everyone about this story?

Sighing, I signaled him to wait while I finished. "All that matters right now is freeing the girl and any others who may have been taken. That story won't help us."

Silver made a face at me. "Someday will you tell it to me?"

"Not likely," I answered. I had to be honest with him - it would not be fair otherwise.

He made a face of frustration at me before continuing, "Does your family know?"

I sighed, he was not going to give this up and my hold on not wanting to tell anyone was loosening. "About as much as anyone else does." I assumed the extent of Mother's knowledge stopped about there as well.

Silver remained silent. Finally I could eat in peace. But back then I never ate this well. Food like this was a luxury I stole from the open back doors of restaurants. I did it rarely and often something off a plate of someone working. I would not take a lot - just enough to hush my stomach so I could continue to find food and money to care for Kitteren.

"Ketayl?" Silver's voice startled me and I realized I had been staring at my plate.

I kept seeing the past overlaying the present and it worried me. I could not afford the distraction. "Sorry, just thinking."

He raised an eyebrow at me and said nothing further.

I knew Silver would not let this go. I just did not want him to know what kind of monster I truly was. The illusion I created over the years had only ever been for the safety of others.

"KETAYL, we've been at this for hours and have nothing. Let's take a break for dinner. We can compare notes and come back fresh," Silver said, stretching.

He did have a point. I had not been able to shake him all day. As soon as I started to get a distance away, Silver would close the gap. We started where the children had last been held, which only confused him because I would not explain my reasoning. From there, we searched along the docks, but we could find no sign of the boat or anything else to give some sort of direction.

What confused me was his initial reluctance to go near the warehouses. He caved when I suggested we split up and I would search near the warehouses.

I signaled for him to lead the way. I followed Silver through the market and put up with letting him buy dinner again. Sitting on the outside patio of one of the restaurants, I considered a new option. I knew the city a lot better than he did, despite the time away. It would not take much to lose him in the open market at this time of day with the festival crowd milling about.

"What are you thinking?" Silver asked, eying me cautiously.

I started to worry I said something - no way in the short amount of time we were together could he have gotten to know me well enough.

I decided to try something neutral, "Just frustrated."

"You seemed pretty interested in that one warehouse. I thought you were going to fall off of the crates at one point," Silver said.

"The windows were covered, but I thought I heard something inside."

"Probably just a cat or something. It didn't look like it was in use." Silver seemed nervous. "Likely abandoned. It looked like it had seen better days."

I took a moment to watch him toy with the end of his braid. The table blocked much of the movement, but after many video conversations, I knew he had different ways he expressed how he felt. Nervous without a doubt - the tension on the rest of his braid as he tugged on it being the tell-tale sign.

Then I realized if I knew this much about him from just the fairly frequent video conversations then he also learned my habits. I needed to be more careful to conceal my thoughts.

But I also wondered what made him nervous so I dropped some information as bait, "It was the warehouse the children were kept in the last time."

My statement caught Silver off-guard and it gave him something to think about. "You really don't think they would return there, do you?"

"Familiar ground." Or it would be if they still owned the property, though it had likely been seized.

Silver stroked the patch of hair on his chin. "True, but if the TIO caught wind of this happening again, wouldn't they go there first and check it out?"

"The TIO wasn't involved the last time. Plus, it burned down. The layout is different than what I remember. Before they didn't have a dock inside of the building." I might have tried to swim inside if Silver had not been with me. Though I did not know what kind of security they had in place to keep people from doing just that.

He eyed me again. "You know far more than even I figured. How do you know it burned down?"

"Public record," I said quickly to hide the fact I dropped more information than I intended.

Most of the warehouses also bore some kind of sign designating what company it belonged to, but the one in question did not. Though it did have a skywalk to another warehouse behind it.

Silence fell between us and I finished my meal quickly, not wanting to miss my window of opportunity. Silver decided to voice his thoughts, "It wasn't far from where they took off in their boat. Do you really think they would have basically doubled-back to the warehouse? Wouldn't it make more sense for them to stay out in the harbor?"

I pointed in the direction of the closest tower down by the water. "They would have to deal with the Harbor Master watching."

Silver followed where I pointed and considered it before saying, "If the Harbor Master saw everything, wouldn't they have caught them as they escaped?"

I had to give Silver credit there. With a harbor this large, no way the Harbor Master would be able to see everything. Especially smaller boats. Or they could be bribed to turn a blind eye to something.

I stopped myself there. I did not want to consider conspiracy at the moment - I needed to focus on finding the girl.

I sat silently while he finished. Silver tried to change the topic of conversation, but I retreated too far inside my head trying to piece together what I did know.

As we left, Silver walked ahead of me as we would not have been able to walk side-by-side. He started talking about where we should head next and while it had him distracted, I slipped into the opposite traffic, turning at the first available stall to break line-of-sight. I reached into my pouch and turned off my phone as I moved. I did not think he could track me through the phone's GPS, but I did not want to be heard if he called or messaged me.

I quickly left the open market and maneuvered myself into the alleyways. I paused every so often in the shadows to make sure I had not been followed.

It must have been a good half an hour before I wove my way down to the warehouses. I stayed away from the ones I wanted a better look at. Silver would likely start there once he noticed my absence.

It did not stop me from feeling guilty about losing him, but at the same time, I also lost what felt like a tail again somewhere about the time I entered the alleys.

I used a quick flight spell to get myself up to the roof of a warehouse, trying to get a better vantage point to look out over the harbor. It would not be noticed here unless someone nearby could see the small arcane remnant I left behind.

Business hours were over and most of the cargo had already been loaded or would be loaded early in the morning. But they took the girl by boat.

Quietly laying down on my stomach, I watched the boats in the harbor. Fishing trolleys headed in and out, typical for them to be moving at all hours. Could they be using one of them?

I considered the idea for a minute. Not likely - a decent cargo hold, but one which could easily be seen into. One quick view from the Harbor Master's Tower and they would be shut down immediately.

There were of course the larger cargo vessels containing grains and other food stuffs. Lots of rooms - plenty of places to hide children. But they would have to submit to inspections.

A smaller boat caught my attention. It was still a decent sized vessel, but it was a harbor cruise boat. There were no lights on in the enclosed area and it moved around the harbor slowly. Candlelit dinner? I would not be able to see that much detail from here.

This train of thought was getting me nowhere. For every reason to use a particular ship, there were equal reasons not to.

Activity below caught my attention. Silver ran down the docks in a panic - his braid trailing behind him. He paused every so often to stop and look around.

I felt bad about disappearing on him, but I had no other option. I could not have him mixed up in this.

I used my power to get myself back down to the ground quietly.

Then I noticed he spoke on the phone with someone while he ran and searched.

I pulled back into the shadows, casting an invisibility spell before he could spot me and followed him. I had a feeling even Silver held back and following him might just give me some answers.

15

SILVER CONTINUED for another couple of piers before joining a group using crates to hide in front of the warehouse I planned on investigating again later. I was not overly surprised this group included Kitteren, Mother, and Father. I had not expected to see Rathal, Brad, and Darius. I also recognized the two who interviewed me from the Highlands office and there were a couple more who I did not know, but who looked vaguely like people Mother and Kitteren had spoken to while we were out.

Mother looked up in my direction and I ducked back around the side of the building. I almost forgot she could sense my presence. Peeking back around, I must be at the edge of her perception because she went back to talking quietly with Father. She had a worried expression plain on her face.

I used the noise Kitteren made to cover my approach while trying to maintain my distance from Mother. It was stupid to move in closer, but I needed to know what was going on. I could not make out what upset her as she took to cursing in multiple languages - all of it directed at Silver who took the onslaught stoically. Nothing useful of what I could understand.

Mother stopped her and said calmly, "We both knew it was a long shot to get her to talk. Bringing Ketayl here was not going to change her mind very easily. Now she's taken off and has managed to slip even the added security. I should have known better."

I bit my lower lip to keep from making any noise. There was another reason they brought me here? Why could no one have just said something? What did they want from me?

"Does she know about this assignment?" Silver asked, folding his arms. His face was hard and he briefly turned to look in my direction as I inched closer. I paused and he returned to the conversation.

"No, and Ket can't know. She's been working herself into the ground and I'm not about to put her in harm's way more than I already have," Kitteren quickly answered. "It's my turn this time. I just wish she would talk to me about what happened back then."

Mother made a face and said, "I hope you know what you're getting into. Let's get everyone inside and talk specifics since our window of opportunity is limited. We need a plan to make sure Ketayl is safe and then we can move."

As they filed into the warehouse, Kitteren grabbed Silver and pulled him aside. She demanded, "What in the Hells are you really doing here?"

"As Ketayl's partner, Lockonis thought it best I come. What is your problem with me?" I had not seen Silver take this kind of tone with anyone. "I know you wouldn't have told me, but why couldn't you have told your own sister about this?!"

I felt my heart racing and my power begin to push against my control as I started to piece together the truth. I held my breath and tried to force my control back into place. I needed more information.

"My problem?! You nearly got my sister killed! For all your vaunted talk about being a protector, you sure couldn't keep her from doing something so stupid," Kitteren yelled at him.

"I could not have stopped her!" Silver matched Kitteren for level.

Kitteren's voice dropped, "Yeah, that's what Ket says too. I don't know why she defends you." She brushed past him and I did not pay attention to the fact she headed in my direction until she ran into me. "What the...?"

The bump made me take a few steps back to regain my balance and I accidentally dropped my spell, having lost concentration.

"Ketayl..." Silver said, surprised.

"Ket, what are you doing here?" Kitteren reached out for me and I batted her hand away, getting out of her reach.

I backed up slowly, shaking my head, not able to believe the evidence in front of me. No one trusted me enough to tell me they were here on assignment. All the lies I had been told. Turning, I ran.

I heard hurried footsteps behind me along with shouts of my name. Using my arcane abilities, I put forth all the speed I could manage. I could not afford to lose control at this stage. I quickly cast a thick fog around me so I could disappear. I did not want to be found right now.

Eventually I made my way back to the hotel after I wandered for a while - long enough to recharge my arcane energy levels. My mind finally stopped running itself in circles and I was worn out. My family could easily find me here, but I felt like I could deal with them. I trusted them, how could they...

I did not trust them enough to tell them the whole story. Too afraid they would see only the monster and to them I was as fragile as glass. In trying to reconcile what I heard, I completely forgot my self-proclaimed mission.

Mother stood out front waiting. "Ketayl, thank the Gods you're safe. Where have you been? Why is your phone off?" She moved to pull me into a hug, but I backed away. The thought of having been lied to this whole time still stung.

Even Mother had not trusted me enough to tell me about this. I answered sharply, "Down by the warehouses."

"Down by..." Mother looked at me and realized how much I knew. "I thought I sensed another presence. My ever inquisitive little girl," she reached out to touch my face and I stepped out of her reach.

Rubbing my arms, I turned away, not sure if I had enough physical energy for another run.

"We decided to leave you out so you could enjoy your time here. It wasn't for a lack of trust," Mother said softly. "Dad wanted you on the team, but both your sister and I knew how much you went through before. I know my words are hard to believe." She paused for a moment. "I'll admit I'm impressed with how you slipped the entire security detail on you."

I turned, not understanding what Mother referred to. I opened my mouth to ask, but my voice left me.

"I take it you didn't hear everything. Will you come with me so I can show you? I fear we may need your help," Mother asked, putting her hand on my shoulder.

I nodded. I needed to know the truth.

WHEN WE ARRIVED BACK at the warehouse, there were far more people than I saw previously. A boat sat in the water inside and the place looked like a command center.

"What are you doing?" Father said as he approached, "I thought you didn't want Ketayl involved. No offense, sweetie." He gently put his hand on my head and I moved away. I hated being short.

My curiosity overrode much else at the moment and I folded my arms while I waited for more information. Though Mother's earlier comment about Father wanting me involved came to mind. Could that have been the reason for his previous harsh words to Kitteren and other cryptic statements?

Was this what even Savanas had been trying to warn me about?

Mother looked at me a moment before responding, "I didn't, but circumstances have changed. I forgot how good Ketayl was at finding out things she shouldn't."

Father sighed. "We've got a situation - I can't reach Kitteren or Silver."

I knew my eyes went wide, which caught their attention. Fidgeting a moment, I said, "Kitteren bumped into me outside. I... I ran. They chased after me."

Others milled about us, curious, but kept their distance. My braid fell over my shoulder and I started toying with it. I pushed it back, not wanting to think Silver managed to rub off on me already.

I heard someone comment about how they should have called it in.

Mother put her arm around my shoulders and pulled me away from the others.

Father followed and assured, "It's okay. They're probably busy having a shouting match with each other. Those two are like fire and ice. I don't envy the headache you're going to have back home."

"We can't afford to delay at this juncture," Mother said, biting the tip of her thumb. "We'll lose our target and the children."

"Children?" I asked, lost. Was all of this the same mission I deemed for myself?

Mother took a deep breath. "Your sister took over what you and I started 50 years ago. What happened back then severely crippled them - halted their operations for a few decades. Much of this team has been working on hunting these slave traders for years, but it's been slow as they rebuilt under an organized crime group - it took us a long time to dismantle them this far."

I thought back - a chunk of the waterfront businesses burned that night. I rubbed my arms, remembering what actually caused the fire. That was when I learned just how dangerous I was.

"Ketayl, there was a reason Kitteren kept pestering you to tell her about the fairie. She just couldn't tell you why because this is classified as a Dark Op," Mother said, breaking me out of my thoughts. "She wanted to take your place - to be bait for them. The captain has wanted revenge on you specifically. We hoped it would be enough to draw him out. We've managed to get most of his buyers, but not him or his crew."

All thoughts of keeping my control were gone and I panicked. "No! She can't! She's not an Arcanist!" I quieted as I gained the attention of all present. "She's not me," I said softly.

"Do you think you can help us?" Father asked.

I searched my thoughts. I could say no and walk away feeling burned by the betrayal or finish what I started and keep the people I cared about safe. I glanced around at all of the people here and the whole operation going on. Kitteren was missing at this important juncture because of me. Silver had been sent here because of me. Unintentionally I had caused them these problems.

I stood up straight and looked Father in the eye and asked, "What do you need?"

Father signaled for me to follow him. We went over to where a bank of screens sat. Rathal leaned against a stack of boxes, watching us. He winked at me as we passed.

"We need someone to get in and do a quick reconnaissance on the boat where we think the children are being held," Mother said, pulling up a satellite image of the harbor. "This boat here." She pointed at the gray image.

I remembered the harbor cruise boat. It struck me as odd, but there were too many possibilities.

I managed to lock my emotions in place. Crossing my arms over my chest, I listened patiently.

"Their operation is small. Whoever they sell the children to has to come to them. This boat moves around the harbor as if taking a cruise, but there is no record of the boat as part of a business. If you inquire, they'll tell you it's privately owned and under renovation."

Father stepped in, "We've done what we could for long range surveillance, but we don't know what the layout on the lower decks is like. Whatever is going on is primarily down there and because they aren't a business and don't leave the harbor, they don't have to submit to regular inspections. There's also an armed guard patrolling at night. The part of the harbor they anchor in is dark and well out of the sight of the Harbor Master's Towers. We've previously tried to get someone in undercover within their operation, but it didn't end well. The most intelligence we received pointed toward this boat."

Mother finished, "Kitteren was supposed to go tonight and do this - both of us had been hoping you held some crucial piece of information we needed, but at this stage it's irrelevant. All I need is for someone to move around, give us a rough layout, and locate the children. We'll have boats positioned waiting to move in and handle the rest."

A hand fell on my shoulder. Father spoke to me softly, "You don't have to do this, Ketayl. We can figure out..."

"I'm going," I said firmly.

Rathal approached, a soft, black bundle in his hands. "Time to suit up then." He grinned broadly. "I've always wanted to say that."

16

I SHIFTED UNCOMFORTABLY. The suit had been made for Kitteren and while she stood a couple of inches taller than me and had more muscle I still found the suit rather tight. I could only imagine how uncomfortable it would be for her.

She and Silver should have returned by now. I bit my lower lip with worry that something happened to them.

I sat and listened to the specific details while I put the soft boots on - their tread meant for silent movement, but would be deadly on slick surfaces.

They argued back and forth shortly after I agreed to help. Many did not want to chance sending in someone untrained, but Father reminded them I escaped not only Silver, but also Darius and Brad who had been following me on foot and Rathal who tracked me through the security camera network. And that I remained elusive until I finally stopped trying to hide. Mother only looked at me during the discussion and I turned away.

My mind drifted and I could not afford to miss details. I had a hard time keeping up with what the others went over - they used terms unfamiliar to me. My task would be as straightforward as it could get. The Ocean's Edge crew occasionally chimed in with a change they thought should be made to accommodate my different skill set, such as suggesting I could teleport over instead of needing to get in the water.

One of the Highlands agents, a Human woman whose name I had to be reminded was Mackie, put together an equipment bag. The small black pouch would easily attach to my thigh - Kitteren planned on carrying a knife, a flashlight, and a few other small items. The headset I needed to wear would have a camera on it with a live feed. I kept reminding myself it was just in and out. The others would handle the rest.

Mother stepped in when she finished. "This is all I want you to do. When you find the children, we'll know. Just keep moving. I am not putting you at any more risk. Do not engage anyone unless you absolutely have to."

Father paced in the background, getting more and more agitated. He had still been unable to contact Kitteren or Silver. With their phones off, he could not track them. Just as they were unable to track me when I took off. At the most I thought I would be giving Silver grief.

Mother knelt in front of me, adjusting the zipper and the collar snap of the suit I wore. She said softly so only I could hear her, "Ketayl, you don't have to do this. No one will think less of you if you decide you want to back down. The Gods only know how much I destroyed your trust by not telling you. Dark Ops be damned."

Mackie strode over and started fitting the headset to my ear. I looked at Mother and told her, "I can do this." I could do this and not become the monster again. I would not have to fight this time. There were teams ready just for that possibility. "Have you tried scrying on Silver?"

Brad caught my question. "Ket, you know as well as the rest of us he blocks scrying somehow."

"That's my point," I said quickly and then slowed down, not sure my idea would actually work. "He'll create some kind of void, won't he? Something we can use to get a rough area."

A female Dwarf whose name escaped me leaned over the railing. "Would need to try an' cast as if from a bird's eye view. It'd be worth a shot. If you can give me a few minutes, I'll give it a go."

Mother looked up and ordered, "Make it quick."

"Good idea, kid," one of the Highland's agents said.

I nodded shyly - I only hoped it worked.

I fidgeted in the tight outfit and clenched my hands a few times trying to get used to the gloves. The fabric barely made any noise, but I would still have to exercise extreme caution.

The Dwarven woman came back a few minutes later as promised and shook her head. "Sorry ma'am. He might be in the harbor, but it's a bloody big area to try and guess - too many blockin' scryin'. Though it may make huntin' for other scum a bit more fun."

Father spoke up, "Thank you for trying."

Mother patted my face in her motherly fashion and stood up. "Let's roll out!" she ordered.

I took the boat with Darius and Brad. As soon as we got close to the target boat, I could teleport - they wanted to try and keep how much arcane energy I needed to expend to a minimum. It was a slight change of plan from what they originally set up with Kitteren. At least I did not need to get wet.

We were to get close in a small boat with the two of them using a couple of guys night fishing as their cover. Their fishing vests disguised the armor they wore. Brad had jokingly asked if he could keep whatever he caught.

The others would split up on opposite sides of the harbor from the dinner boat and board their own watercraft. Many of the agents moved onto the one inside of the warehouse, so they could have mobile surveillance. I overheard Mother ordering her crew to keep my feed active on the main monitor.

I did not enjoy having to lay down on the floor of the boat between Brad and Darius, but I could not risk being seen. At least a plastic cover lay over me so they were not staring at me curled up. Their rifles were wedged in on either side of me.

"I'm sure glad you don't need to stand to cast, that might make this difficult," Brad said.

"Are we close?" I asked. This was uncomfortable.

Darius spoke next, "Not yet, kid. We need to look like we're searching for a good fishing spot."

"Why are you here?" I finally asked after a few moments. It bothered me since I first saw them, but it had been the least of my concerns at the time.

Brad spoke this time, "We volunteered. Kitteren stopped in Ocean's Edge to try to recruit more agents for this mission. We're all cleared for Dark Ops."

Darius continued, "Savanas is holding down the fort with a couple of new agents and some help from the main office so she could spare us for a few days. Besides, we were getting bored. It's been a slow spring. Even Rathal hasn't managed to get into a fight."

"He was too busy running from Holly." Brad laughed.

Rathal's voice came through the headset, "You guys know I can hear you, right?"

"I'd still say it if you were in this boat," Brad tossed back.

"Okay, enough, boys," Mother kept her voice calm, but a low warning tone rang in it.

Silence fell and I just listened to the sound of the water, letting it calm me.

Darius whined, "Man, why can't I have a beer?"

"Outside of you're on-duty?" Brad asked. "You need better taste in drinks."

"This coming from the wine lover. I don't know how you can tell the difference between grapes." Darius sounded utterly bored.

Brad laughed at him. "I have a far more refined taste my friend."

"Wine doesn't go with fishing."

"You win this one," Brad conceded.

Both men laughed. I heard lines being cast from their fishing poles once Brad cut the engine. They repeated the process multiple times - the conversation turned to their cover. I started to cramp up being tucked away like this and I hoped they had not forgotten about me.

Finally Darius nudged me with his foot. "This is a good spot."

I poked my head up over the edge of the boat and thought the plastic cover still in my way at first, but it was just so dark in this part of the harbor. I kept myself low, barely spying the target boat over the edge.

As they trolled slowly around the stern of the harbor cruise boat, I saw my opening. "Got it, I just need the guard to pass."

"Good luck, kid," Darius whispered.

As soon as the opening became available, I teleported, my body able to stretch out now. I felt stiff as the deck of the boat formed beneath my feet.

I chanced a glance back at them before casting my spell to cloak myself. I hoped no one on board could see teleport lines.

"Well, shit, if things could run this smooth all the time..." I heard someone say over the headset. Their thick accent told me one of the Highland's agents had spoken.

The above decks were in the direction the guard went. Below sounded like a better option to start. Besides, they wanted a better look there anyway. I heard the guard start yelling at Brad and Darius to go find a different fishing spot.

A gun shot rang out and I started to back track to see what happened.

Mother's voice stopped me, "They're fine, keep going."

Taking a deep breath, I quietly padded my way down the narrow stairs.

HOW WAS THIS SHIP ORGANIZED? It did not seem like a large ship from the outside, but I started to become concerned I might get lost as I took in the general layout. I had not even gone into any of the rooms yet - someone would always show up about the time I considered it.

The doorway at the end of the hall opened and I rushed for it, sneaking in after a Dwarven man came walking out with the two I encountered in town.

I had to hold my breath as I recognized the Dwarf and my hand went to the scar on my left side. He gave me it to me 50 years ago. He now bore a burn scar on much of the right side of his face. I forced myself not to think about fighting or running and focused on the task at hand long enough to get myself into the room.

Finding myself alone, I let out the breath I held and wrapped my arms around my waist to try and control my shaking. "Ketayl. Ketayl, keep it together." Mother's voice cut through the memories of the Dwarven man wielding a knife standing over me.

I heard a few people I did not recognized start talking about aborting the mission and getting me out of there.

I took a deep breath and forced myself back into the present. Just keep going.

I stood in an office of some sort and figured I must have made it all the way to the bow given the shape of the room. With no one here, I dropped my spell to conserve energy.

Ledgers lined the wall next to the desk. What looked like

surveillance pictures were pinned to the wall behind it. I stepped closer to get a better look in the dim lighting.

I appeared in every picture, but I knew not all of them were me. There were some with recent date stamps in places I had not been at the time of day they were taken. My hair was also up in a bun and I wore the clothes I normally would. Those were all crossed out with a black marker. The one which caught my attention showed the time Silver grabbed my arm when I went to walk away from him at the open market on the same night we first encountered the two men. The stubbornness in my face surprised me, but my evaluation got cut short.

"Ketayl, you need to hurry and get out of there," Father came through the headset.

I wanted to ask who the other me was and then I figured out Kitteren played the role. I never considered the fact we were close enough in appearance she could pass as me with little effort.

Tearing my eyes away from the pictures, I glanced down at the ledger open on the desk. The numbers and shorthand meant little to me, but hopefully it meant something to one of the others.

I heard the door start to open and immediately recast my invisibility spell.

"The buyer will be here tomorrow, captain," the Elven man said calmly.

The Dwarven man from before strode in and took a seat. "Aye, I remember. We'll have our prize soon - that harpy of a woman can wait. For now, I want our *guests* to have a chance to consider my offer."

I could not get stuck in here and took the opportunity to leave through the slowly closing door. I cringed as the end of my braid softly thumped the door as I passed. I flattened myself against the wall and listened to hear if the men noticed. The Human man strode down the hall and I held my breath, certain he would hear my heart pounding in my chest.

I should have said no. I was not trained for this.

"Ketayl, if you need to abort, we can get a boat close enough," Mother said gently. I must not have moved for a length of time.

No, I was going to finish this. I steadied my resolve to find the children if they were here and then started to move.

Seeing the hall finally empty, I started peeking in doors as I passed and someone noted the purpose of the room. I wished I knew who spoke to me, but at least the calm male voice helped settle my nerves.

I managed to make my way back to where I started, but at the end sat a set of double doors still being guarded by a Human man. Suddenly he turned and banged on the door. "Knock it off in there."

Then the cries of children became loud enough for me to hear from halfway down the hallway.

He grumbled and rolled his eyes, anger plain on his face. He yanked open the door and pointed his gun inside. "I said to be quiet before I silence one of you permanently!"

I started to move by the time the others began discussing if I should stop him or not. Pulling his gun arm up, I opened my other hand near the side of his head and released the electricity spell I hastily conjured.

"Now that was nice," a female voice said in an appreciative tone through the headset as I struggled to get the slumped over form into the room.

I managed to get the dead weight into the room and set him down just inside dropping my invisibility spell in the process. I saw the children huddled together on the far side of the cargo hold.

"Fairie?" the same little girl from the streets came up to me. "You did come."

"The rescue boat is less than a quarter of a mile from you, Ketayl," Mother said. "They'll be coming toward the stern. They're moving slowly so we don't alert the slave traders."

"You'll all be safe soon," I tried to assure them. Looking out over the scared crowd, I could not leave them here. I spotted the boy from the news article and Joanna's son in the group. Why was her son here? Then I remembered the urgent phone call Kitteren had gotten. Why hadn't she said anything?

Why had they started taking children with homes and families as well? I would have thought it too large of a risk.

I turned to reach for the door, but paused as Joanna's son made his way forward. "Ketayl, are you taking us home?" He clung to my hand. "Please don't leave us here." I barely knew this child, but his face had gone from despair to hope when he saw me.

"The boat to take you back isn't here yet," I tried to explain, but so many small faces turned to me silently pleading for help.

Taking a deep breath, I held up my free hand for them to wait. There were around 20 children here and I never teleported more than just myself before.

I could do it - I knew how, I just never tried it. If the rescue boat got close enough I might even have enough left to teleport myself back afterward. There could be more children elsewhere, though unlikely - they kept them all together before. The way the captain talked about his guests, I did not think them here willingly. They could be in danger, but I could also be wrong.

I took a moment to peek out the door and check the hallway. I needed to clear the remainder of the distance to the back patio-like area I arrived on. Then I just needed line-of-sight to the boat. If they were moving as slowly as Mother suggested, I could make an educated enough guess to get us all there safely.

"Ketayl, what are you planning?" Mother asked, worry clear in her voice.

I closed the door again and moved away from it so I could speak without someone passing by hearing me, though the missing guard might be enough to start an alert. "I need to know which boat they need to go to."

Only silence came from the other end for a few moments. Then Mother asked, "You can teleport all of them?"

"I can't leave them here," I did not want to voice my uncertainty. The small faces surrounding me looked up in silent hope.

Silence again until I heard Darius come through. "We can cause a distraction and try to pull their attention to the other side."

"On my mark," Mother ordered. "I want the rescue boat closer so Ketayl doesn't have to teleport far. Once it's in position, I'll have them cut their engines and set up a signal light."

I took a deep breath and smiled down at the children around me. "We'll be going soon."

"I'll keep eyes on the stern, but you're on your own for getting them that far, kid," a male voice said.

I knelt down while they continued to organize the various boats and spoke to the children. "I'm going to need all of you to hold hands and stay with me, okay? We don't have very far to go."

I waited for Darius and Brad to begin their distraction before I checked the hallway again and stepped out fully into it once I saw it clear. I signaled for the children to follow. I silently prayed to whoever might be listening to let me get them to safety without incident. As soon as the last child left the room, I closed the doors and hoped it would be enough.

A few long seconds later I stood on the back patio, hearing shouting from the bow of the boat, surrounded by frightened children, and searching for whichever boat I needed to get them to.

"Ketayl, the blue side lights. I'll flash them as if we're having electrical issues," a female voice came through. What was that supposed to look like?

Despite my concern, I easily spotted the outline of the small barge with the lights flashing. It stopped closer than I anticipated with a wide open deck. I calculated the distance and told the children to gather as close as they could to me. I touched two different heads, too focused on trying to weave together the spell quickly and build the bridge to take us over to pay attention to who I touched. I closed my eyes to work my way through making sure I kept everyone else with me.

"Hurry, kid, the distraction isn't going to last much longer."

I finished building the arcane bridge to take us all across and in a flash, we appeared on the rescue boat. I sank to my knees and took deep breaths, ignoring the chatter in my ear. The intensity of taking so many with me felt as draining as the energy required. My head spun from the effort. I had a few small arms clench themselves around me with cheers and thanks. The agents on board pried them off gently and started trying to organize them.

"Is everyone okay?" Mother called as her boat came up between us and the slave trading boat.

"Your girl did it, ma'am," the Elven woman on board told her.

Rathal leaned on the railing next to Mother and whistled. I tried to watch them, but the world kept spinning, though it began slowing down.

They were close enough the boats bumped into each other. "Ketayl, can you come over here?" Mother asked.

Putting my hands on my knees, I managed to get up. The little girl from the streets tugged on my braid. "Please don't leave us."

I knelt down and pulled the hair elastic out of the end of my braid. I gathered her hair over her shoulder and put it in loosely. "I have to go. My job isn't done yet, but here's a promise I'll come back, okay?"

"How is that a promise?" a Dwarven boy asked.

I smirked. "I need to give it back to the person who lent it to me. You're safe here with them."

My hair unraveled as I stood up again. This was going to make the remainder of the recon mission harder, but the main deck was mostly just a large dining hall from what I could tell - I did not think it would be an issue. I needed some time to recharge though. I only hoped the glowing golden arcs from the teleports would go unnoticed by everyone else. I could dissipate them, but I did not have the energy required at the moment.

Mother reached down a hand as I tried to climb up to the higher deck. I staggered, though unsure if it came from the experience of teleporting so many or the rocking of the boat. Likely both.

Once we separated from the rescue boat, she asked, "Are you okay to go back?"

I glanced over as the slave trading boat came into view again and quickly calculated the arcane energy needed to return. Rathal handed me another cup of water while I tried to figure out if I had enough left. I drained it before I answered, "I think so, but I need a few minutes to gather enough arcane energy to get there."

"Yeah, let's not have a repeat of six months ago," Rathal said and stepped too close to me for comfort, trapping me between him and the railing. "Forgive me for being forward, but I think I'd rather head off the problem."

Rathal placed both of his hands on the sides of my head and pulled me in closer. I could feel the rush of arcane energy being transferred and it felt as much like a cooling breeze as did the wind off of the water.

I sank back into the railing once Rathal finished and let go. "Thank you, but you didn't have to..." I knew he was arcane sensitive, but I did not know he also had capacity. I supposed it made sense seeing as he once told me he studied at the EAC for a time.

He shrugged, looking a little drained for the experience. "It's not like I was using it anyway."

"I loathe to send you back into enemy territory, but we need to find out who the captain's guests are," Mother said softly.

I already assumed I needed to go back to finish the job. Looking for some people did not seem like much more trouble. I absorbed as much arcane energy naturally as I could in preparation - I would rather have as much as I could get than possibly run short.

I MADE myself invisible again as soon as I hit the deck of the boat. With Rathal transferring his arcane energy, I would have enough to teleport myself back when I needed to with some to spare. I just needed to make this quick or I'd run myself low again. I wanted to avoid anymore hospital visits if I could help it.

I had not yet left the back patio when I heard a man from below ask, "Where in the Hells is Ron?"

"Damned if I care," a second man said. "He probably went to go take a piss. The kids are too scared shitless to try any daring heroics. Besides, where are they going to go in the middle of the harbor?"

I kept myself plastered against the wall leading downstairs to listen. I should have done more than simply shut the doors after getting the children out.

The second man spoke again. "Leave the brats be. We don't want to scare them to death - it's bad for business." After a few moments, I heard boots echoing down the hall.

Only silence came from my headset. I found I wanted the chatter to help keep me grounded. I just needed to finish this job and then I could have all the words I wanted with the people who lied to me.

I fully understood this was classified as a Dark Op and I technically did not have clearance. The truth silenced by red tape. It did not mean I could not be upset about it.

As I made my way up the stairs toward the dining hall, I rushed to balance precariously on the railing to let a guard by. I scooted in the door he came out of, finding myself in the back part of the large room. A smaller room sat in the center - it blocked my view of the front part of the dining hall. A bar sat along the side facing the stern of the ship and looking down the small hallway, I could see the corner of another bar on the other side.

Well, nothing of note here. I took a moment to look at the faded and worn woodwork of merfolk and other sea creatures which must have been impressive at one time. The guards appeared to be staying outside of this room. Good for me they directed their attention on outside threats.

I quickly padded over to the other side of this half of the dining hall to see what was down the other hallway and made my way back, needing to be able to view one of the friendly boats I knew. Maybe these guests were on the other side or in the center room. Another open deck sat above me, but no one said they saw anyone of interest up there.

I walked slowly and as quietly as I could down the short hallway on the worn carpet. I heard low voices as I traveled, but the sounds of the boat around me made them indistinct.

As the room came into view, I saw no one in here either. A sound somewhere between laughing and sobbing coming from the floor on the patron's side of the bar. I moved faster, how could I have missed...

Kitteren and Silver sat tied to barstools bolted to the floor. Why were they here? Were they the guests the captain referred to?

Father's voice rang through my headset, "Ketayl, abort. Get yourself out of there. Everyone else move in now."

Blood smeared the side of Silver's face, but he held himself as upright as he could. Kitteren sat slumped over making the noise I heard.

"Dammit, Ketayl, get out of there," Mother ordered, her voice bordering on panicked.

"You need to keep it together," Silver said, his voice low.

Kitteren sat up more and I could see she had taken not quite as much of a beating as Silver had, but the split lip alone made me cringe. I brought this on them when I ran instead of listening.

My sister spoke softly, "It's going to be my fault. I'm never going to be able to live with myself after what I did to her."

I finally broke out of my daze at having found them here and moved to get between the two to start analyzing their restraints.

"What in the Hells?" Kitteren said, tucking her legs up. My hair had fallen over her legs when I stepped over her.

In my ear I heard a number of people yelling at me to get out. As I heard the guards moving into action against the coming boats, I dropped my spell, becoming visible mostly behind Kitteren, trying to figure out how to get her free.

"Ketayl, what are you doing here?" Silver asked in a hushed voice.

Kitteren twisted so she could see. "Dammit, Ket, can't you see this is a trap?"

"Yeah, and I'm still here. I'm not leaving." Getting annoyed with the constant yelling in my ear, I took the headset off and put it on Kitteren. I figured she could put up with it so I could concentrate. I did not have enough arcane energy to teleport three of us. Not to mention all of the boats were now moving far too quickly for me to try and target.

"Knife, Ket," Kitteren said softly. I stopped, confused. She quickly elaborated, "Give me the knife in your pouch and go. I'll get us out of here."

I forgot about the knife. I fumbled to dig it out of the pouch attached to my thigh. The velcro echoed loudly in the room as I tore the small bag off in frustration.

"You make a horrible infiltrator," Kitteren joked lightly. It sounded empty.

Silver spoke, "Ketayl, please just go. I can protect us until help arrives."

With the gunfire being exchanged outside, where could I go? I got the knife out and tried to figure out how best to get the plastic ties off without cutting her.

"It looks like I didn't have to wait long at all."

I froze at the new voice in the room. I did not need to turn around to know it belonged to the captain. I slipped the knife into Kitteren's hands before turning to face him.

The men I had seen in the city flanked him. The Human looked downright blood thirsty as he grinned madly, toying with the dagger in his hands.

"Are you responsible for the noise outside? Of course you are. That bitch there may have been a thorn in my side over the years, but she still hasn't come close to causing me the problems you have." The Dwarf smiled despite the fact I already heard a couple of splashes from his men falling overboard.

The captain moved, making his way behind the bar while his men remained where they were. He pulled a glass and a bottle of amber liquid out from under the counter and started pouring himself a drink. How was he not at least showing concern for the fight going on outside?

"Now, I'm a reasonable man and I do need to make a profit. Capturing you alive is the bigger gain here, though I'll still make a fairly good amount if you're dead. I'd like to keep this as clean as possible so if you surrender, I won't order my men to kill the brats in my cargo hold and you get to choose which of these two gets to leave." The captain took a drink. "Also, you'll want to call the people outside off. That's part of the deal."

The gun fire slowed and stopped.

"That's pretty impressive given you haven't spoken a word," the captain noted. "So, do we have a deal?"

I clenched my fists and thought through my options. I could not choose who would leave and he never said he would let them leave alive or what would happen to the other. And given they had not yet realized the children were gone put me into a far more precarious position.

"Fine then, I'll choose. Kill the lad," the captain ordered.

I reacted reflexively and unleashed pure force to knock back the Human man who strode forward with his dagger raised. He hit the windows near the bow with a sickening thud and the glass cracked. The Elven man would have also fallen back if he had not leaned up against a post.

"I'll take that as a no then. Deal with her," the captain ordered his man standing.

The Human had not gotten up and stayed slumped against the wall. The Elf, however, strode forward confidently and I moved toward the right side of the room, wanting to put distance between myself and the two on the floor.

I chanced a quick glance at the two. "I'm sorry," I whispered. I turned back to my opponent and tried to quickly gather what little arcane energy I could from around me in preparation.

The captain advised his subordinate, "Careful, mate. It looks like the rumors about her power fading might have been wrong."

No fire. I could not use fire. I would put everyone in jeopardy if I did.

The Elf sneered at me, cracking his knuckles as he strode forward. He stopped a couple of yards away before launching himself at me. I barely had time to get out of the way and let him run into the wall.

It did not stop him for long and I found myself trying to keep up blocking or deflecting attacks. He kept me too busy to try and focus my power where I needed it for offense. The hexagonal pattern of my shield spell flashed brightly with each strike landed. Maintaining it took more energy than I anticipated.

I found an opening and rammed my shoulder into his stomach, using the momentary reprieve to step away and double-check everyone's location.

Kitteren and Silver still sat where they were tied. Silver stared at me like I was someone he did not recognize. Kitteren kept pleading with me to run - worry plain on her face as her shoulders moved slightly. I assumed she continued trying to free herself, but there were a lot of plastic ties to get through.

The captain leaned against the wall behind the bar with his hand on the doorknob to the center room. He treated our fight like a show. His attitude only angered me and I rode the wave instead of trying to force it back.

The Human got himself up with the dagger back in his hand. He tossed it and caught the blade, moving as if he planned to throw it.

The captain spoke again, "Remember boys - she's worth Hells of a lot more to us alive. Though do make the little bitch suffer. She set me back a long time the last time we crossed paths and I'd like a chance to thank her for this scar."

I concerned myself with the Human wielding the dagger and did not pay enough attention to the Elf. I took a hard punch to the jaw, staggering back several steps. I tasted blood in my mouth, but ignored it for the immediate danger.

The dagger flew in my direction and I used my power to deflect it - sending it to sink deep in the ceiling. With the weapon out of the equation I still had these two. I also did not know when the captain would stop sitting back and join in the fray or call for reinforcements. I hoped his other men were too busy staring down the TIO agents outside.

I also needed to get on the offensive. If these people wanted the fairie, then they could have her. I let instinct take over and launched my own attack, bowling over the Elf, allowing me to get on the other side of him. Now both of my opponents were in front of me.

The Human jumped over his companion and I cast a wind-based spell to knock him back, sending him across the room again. He hit the port-side wall with a sickening thud. Part of my mind told me to control the amount of force I used so I did not kill someone, but instinct overrode rationality.

All that mattered now was getting Kitteren and Silver out of here.

If I had to kill every last enemy on board, then so be it. I could deal with the consequences later.

I heard people moving outside of the dining hall, but I could not spare time to find out what was going on. I managed to get on the offensive and it took everything I had to keep the Elf on his toes.

Dropping to one knee, I swung my leg out and tripped the Elf. He landed on his back with a loud thud, but rolled out of the way before I could touch him with the hastily conjured electricity. Hitting the floor with it instead which caused the lights to flicker violently for a few seconds.

Conjuring pure arcane into my hands, I kept after him even before the lights stabilized - my feet kicking out to try and hit him physically, looking for an opening.

He got in a hard kick to my left hip and I fell to my knee, turning my power to defensive until I could get back on my feet. Feeling the pain shooting through my leg as I stood up, I knew I would not be able to just walk it off.

I held his attacks back as best I could and found my opening. Quickly concentrating electricity in my hands, I dropped my shield and grabbed his arm as he threw a punch, slamming my open palm into his chest. His body convulsed as it hit and he dropped to the floor. The only one left was the captain.

I walked forward slowly with my arms crossed and my palms open to the outside, preparing to bring my full power to bear on the remaining enemy in the room.

The captain twisted the knob on the door behind the bar. With a smile, he opened it, allowing a Troll to come in. I felt the blood drain from my face as I looked up at the hunched, towering figure. It leveled a tooth-missing, menacing grin at me as he approached slowly. The gray-skinned creature obviously savoring the upcoming confrontation. I took a limping step back.

The Troll moved fast and with my hip injured, I barely made it out of the way in time for him to charge past. I could not think of what to use to combat this creature.

By the time the Troll got himself off of the wall and turned around, I had begun putting up an ice barrier between us. With any luck, I could get it thick enough to keep him contained for a minute or so. At least long enough to think of something else.

My ice wall shattered like glass before I could finish.

I tried to block the first swing from the Troll with my power, but I barely noted my feet left the ground before I hit the wall hard. I did not remember falling to the floor and the pain in my right shoulder made it hard to focus.

Struggling to get up, a large hand wrapped around my throat and I felt the ground disappear once more. How did I not know they had a Troll with them? How did no one know? There were also more people on board than the previous intel provided. This time they took better care to hide their activities.

The Troll gave me a wicked grin and I knew the captain directed him, but I could only hear my heart beating wildly. I swung my legs, despite the pain, trying to find something to get a hold on. I clawed at his hand with my left arm - my right useless.

I could see the faces of those I cared about out of the corner of my eye shouting. Kitteren and Silver struggled hard against their restraints. The barstool holding Silver sat at an odd angle, or perhaps the lack of oxygen made it look that way.

All rational thought left as panic completely took over. I could not breathe and felt like I was on fire. I only hoped I bought enough time for the rest of the team to get here.

Suddenly I felt the floor beneath me again and coughed hard to get air back into my lungs. It took a couple of painful deep breaths to clear my vision. The Troll fell back, clawing at his chest. By the smell, he burned from the inside out. It had happened again. Within seconds, he became little more than a charred corpse.

I covered my mouth at the sight and looked around, but flames did not dance around me.

"I'd suggest you stop or this one is gone," the captain said. He held a gun pointed at my sister's head. He now stood above his captives on top of the bar. A few red dots danced on his chest, but he seemed unconcerned. He had a crazed look on his face.

"Ket, get out of here," Kitteren said with tears in her eyes, "Please. Don't worry about me."

Anger took over and my left hand was out in front and my hair floated about me. I used my power to hold the captain in the air and forced his gun arm up and away from the two on the floor. Managing to work the fingers on my right hand, I pried the gun from him, using my power to dismantle it before him, letting the pieces fall between his guests.

Struggling, I managed to get to my feet. "*You couldn't let me rest in peace.*" My voice sounded strange to my ears. My power wrapped around his throat, squeezing slowly as the Troll had done.

"Ketayl, stand down!" Mother shouted from the port-side doorway.

Her voice jarred me from my thought of killing the captain and I dropped him. Agents were on him and quickly took him into custody. Others started freeing Kitteren and Silver or securing the captain's men. I could not bear to look in the direction of anyone and see the disgust. Now they knew the monster. The illusion I had carefully crafted over so many years shattered by my own hand.

Father stood before me, asking me something, but I could not hear him over the pounding in my ears - the pain I managed to ignore came back full force. I clutched my right arm to my body, swaying on my feet. It was the last thing I remembered.

17

COLORS SWIRLED AND DANCED. I was surrounded by iridescent bands and with no defined walls, ceiling, or floor, I floated, knowing peace.

I had been here once before, but then the colors were all shades of purple. Something forced me to retreat to within my own power. I could not remember why I would be here, but it did not matter - I was safe.

For too long I viewed my power from the outside, watching it push against me as I tried to keep it contained. I held my hand up and let the strands of changing colors weave through my fingers. Why did this seem dangerous before?

It nagged at the back of my mind someone else needed to be safe. That I needed to make sure they were safe. Memories started to filter in - Kitteren and Silver. But the others had shown up. They were safe now.

The colors swirled about me. I twirled and danced with the iridescent bands coming to play. The sound of my laughter surprised me.

Then I noticed the outer colors starting to fade. Black took over and all too soon I found myself alone in the dark. Where had the colors gone? Where was my safe haven? I curled up against the dark. I felt cold and alone.

Angry, pulsing red began to show up above, pulling me toward it and I tried to move away. I swam against the strong current. It over took faster than I could retreat and I got ripped backwards.

I felt, more than heard myself scream. Pain at a level I had not previously known originated from my right shoulder. Other areas hurt also, but none felt like pieces being slowly and painfully moved.

"Lin, her eyes," I heard Father say.

I tried to look around for the source of his voice, but only black greeted me. I clamped down on my jaw, not wanting to repeat the sound. I would only be able to hold it for so long. Why was it dark here? I heard other voices: most of them too far and indistinct.

My breath came far too fast and I could not form words to beg for it to stop. I needed to tell them to let me go back to my safe place.

"I know, but it can't be helped," Mother said, her voice strained. A hand stroked my head. Too many other hands held me still and I tried to move away from all of them. Especially whatever caused me pain in my right shoulder. "I'm going to try and put her back under. I don't know how long I can hold her there."

The words I could make out made no sense to me and those speaking might as well have been in a language I did not know. I tried to latch onto the familiar voices, but the pain and darkness overrode the attempt.

I heard voices but saw nothing. I looked around frantically, trying to find some source of light. The pain made it hard to focus.

Somehow, despite feeling like someone tore into my shoulder, I started feeling drowsy. I pushed back against it, but found myself literally powerless against the gentle tug. Then the world faded completely from my senses.

"THESE WERE the dead zones you saw when you tried to search before?" Father spoke softly, though his voice still carried through the room.

I could only hear the sound equipment beeping besides him. My mind felt cloudy and struggled to analyze my situation. My power slumbered still far out of my reach. I tried to ignore it for the moment, grateful for one less thing to worry about.

"Aye. The little lass had a good idea, though it will take some time to weed out the legitimate businesses usin' anti-scryin' magic. I intend to get started once we're done with this operation." The woman's voice sounded familiar. I could not place it though.

"That's good work, Fan. I'll leave it to you and your team. I think I'm going to need some family time once we're done here," Father said.

I cracked open my eyes and saw nothing. Perhaps a dream? But I should be able to see something. I rested in a reclined position and it was warm.

"That you will. Ketayl especially will need time to recover. Both physically an' emotionally," Fan said. "Speakin' of, someone is awake."

I heard people coming closer and tried to move, but could not. I found myself bound up in something and started to panic. I could not feel my right arm either.

"Easy, Ketayl, easy. I'm right here," Father said. "Fan, can you go get Lin?"

"Aye, an' I'll check on the boy too. The numbin' agent will wear off in about a half hour," Fan said and left - the door making little sound.

"Let me get you out of those restraints. You kept trying to roll over onto your injured shoulder." Father's soothing voice kept me anchored.

My voice barely made it above a whisper when I admitted, "I'm scared." I could not contain the emotions rushing through my mind. With my power gone, they were free to run. I did not even realize until now I had used my power to keep it all contained.

A strong hand touched my forehead. "I know, honey, I know. Just stay focused on me. Fan went to get Mom and she's checking on Silver."

"Kitteren? Silver?" Were they safe? Did I fail my mission?

"They're fine, Ketayl. I promise. We need to focus on you." While Father spoke, I felt straps being released, but I could not move much still. The room heated up fast.

"Why is it dark and hot in here?" I could not hide the fear in my voice.

Whatever kept me bound quickly loosened. "We needed to keep you warm to try and keep you from going into healing shock. Silver's energy was mostly spent by the time he finished getting your shoulder pieced back together. You still need time to heal completely, though I expect he'll be helping the process along as soon as he has enough energy."

"Please turn on a light." I needed to see. I needed to know where I was.

"Ketayl, I need you to remain calm. Do you remember the prototype arcane restraint you and Lockonis have been working on?" Father's voice continued to be calm yet firm. He rubbed my uninjured shoulder comfortingly.

I nodded uselessly in the dark. "Lockonis said it was too overpowered when she tested it on herself." What did the prototype have anything to do with it being dark?

Father took a deep breath before saying, "We borrowed it on the off-chance we needed to restrain a mage. Ketayl, trust me we had absolutely no intention of using it on you, but we didn't want to chance Silver's safety while he was trying to restore your shoulder."

My power slumbered out of reach because of the prototype restraint?

"Your vision should come back when we take the arcane restraint off. Do you think you can put up with it for just a little longer? Silver will want to make sure nothing shifted while we were transporting you and help speed along your healing."

I nodded. Lockonis had not said why she deemed the prototype overpowered and I had been too concerned with the backlog and other tasks to ask. "Where are we?"

The tension in Father's voice noticeably left. "Remember the warehouse the team gathered in? You're in the infirmary. This was closer and less public than the hospital."

"Public?" Why did that matter?

Mother spoke, "Our operation isn't finished yet. We need to keep you safe and hidden until we can get the last buyer."

"Lin..." Father's voice rang with a warning tone.

Mother sighed, her voice resigned, "I know, Dayko, but after all of this, she deserves to know."

Father said sharply, "It can wait until she's recovered more."

"No it can't," I said quickly. I was blind, I was scared, and I was confused. I needed to clear out at least one of those.

Father sighed and patted my left shoulder as he got up. "Where's Kitteren?"

"I sent her on errands. She's too feisty to let in here." Mother sounded drained. What happened? How long had I been out?

I heard the door softly open and close once more.

"My fierce little girl. I should be angry you disobeyed orders, but..." Mother trailed off and ran a hand over my hair. "According to the schedule, this buyer is being accompanied by someone who put a bounty out on you."

"Bounty?" What bounty? There had been no mention of this before, but the captain kept mentioning I was worth more alive.

Mother continued to stroke my hair. "It's complicated, Ketayl, and we have little information. So far, it seems limited only to these slave traders and the final buyer we're after."

I looked down at my lap, or at least where I thought my lap should be.

The door opened sharply.

"Silver, is everything alright?" Mother asked, concern in her voice.

He sounded out of breath when he spoke, "Yes, ma'am. May I speak with my partner privately?"

I refused to bring my eyes up. Even if I could not see him, I could not face Silver. He had seen the monster. They all had. Why had Mother or Father not brought it up? Perhaps because the part which could do damage had been restrained.

I shifted uncomfortably during the long pause before Mother spoke, "Of course. I'll be downstairs checking on how the team is progressing if you need me."

The door once again closed with a quiet click.

Silence filled the room and I resisted the urge to lift my head.

I heard Silver start to pace - boots landing heavily on the floor. After a few turns, he suddenly growled at me, "What in the Hells were you thinking, Ketayl?!"

I kept my mouth shut and my head down letting my hair hide me. I tried to pull my knees up to my chest, but could not quite manage it with my arm bound down across my waist.

"No, don't you dare run away from me." Silver pushed my knees back down. A weight landed on the side of the bed. "I want to know what made you think you could take on those slave traders. Look at me, dammit!"

"I can't," I said quietly, raising my head toward where I guessed he sat.

"Your eyes - they're completely black," Silver breathed. "What caused this?"

"Doesn't matter," I muttered and turned away. It embarrassed me to be caught in such a vulnerable stage. As much as I had been in revealing the monster.

Silver's hand touched the side of my face, firm, but not hurting. He forced me to look back in his direction. "Don't pull that with me." His breath hot on my face.

Fear kept me from moving. My panic quickly built and my breath sped up. It felt like I could not get enough air. I gripped the bedding with my one free hand and kicked, trying to push myself away, but getting nowhere. While my movements made no sense, neither did the situation I found myself in.

Silver backed away and I could feel him shift on the side of the bed. "Gods forgive me. Ketayl, please, calm down. I didn't mean to scare you."

I felt myself pulled against a hard chest. A hand stroked my hair. I gave into the instinct to circle my free arm around the warm body and hold on tightly to the back of his shirt. I buried my face and fought against the surge of emotions.

I became the monster of legend again. They spoke of my safety, but what of their safety from me? I had to remain blind to not hurt anyone.

We stayed like that for a while. At one point after I calmed down, I started to doze and I did not care I remained curled against Silver. I felt tired and likely this would be the last time I would be able to remain close to someone.

"I can't let you sleep yet," Silver said as he pushed me away from him. I let go, not looking up at him out of embarrassment. "I need to take a look at your shoulder and maybe we can find you something more comfortable than how we have your arm bound."

While I had been curled up against him, I began to feel my arm again and the deep ache that came with it. I crossed my legs and looked at my lap. There was a dull throb in my hip as well, but easily ignored at the moment.

I quickly backed away from calloused fingers that tried to tuck my hair behind my ear. Scared, unsure of who the hand belonged to. I thought only Silver was in the room, but I had not been paying attention to the sound of the door.

"This has to be absolutely terrifying for you," Silver said softly, brushing my hair out of my face. "Will you tell me now what is causing your blindness?" I held still only because Silver's hand reached under my hair to rub the back of my neck.

I did not trust my voice and searched with my free hand for the device. The leather band had been designed to wrap around a wrist or ankle. I tapped it when I found it on my left ankle.

"I'm sorry. I was so focused on restoring your shoulder I paid little attention to anything else going on. I only know what it's supposed to do. Ketayl, I am so sorry, I never wanted to hurt you, but I couldn't leave your shoulder in that condition."

I sat quietly, still unsure of exactly what happened.

"I don't know how you're going to forgive any of us," he said, and I wondered if he meant to say it aloud.

That was my breaking point. "Forgive?! I'm the monster here. I..." I killed the Troll when I panicked. I did not know the status of the others I hurt either.

Silver's hand at the back of my neck paused. "Ketayl, do you really believe that? You risked everything to protect us and you think yourself a monster?"

"I killed..."

"I wanted to," Silver cut me off. "Badly enough I almost pulled the damnable barstool out of the floor. If our positions had been reversed, the body count would have been far higher. I will not stand for the crimes these people committed, but it's not up to me. They will now be held accountable for their actions."

"Ketayl," Mother's voice joined in the conversation. When had she returned?

I remained silent. Her presence only reminded me of worse things I had done.

"Silver, if you wouldn't mind tending to her shoulder before the numbing agent wears off too much," Mother said. "I think she's already starting to feel the pain return."

Silence fell in the room and I sat there, staring blindly. I could sense Silver's hands hovering around my shoulder.

It felt like a long time before Silver spoke again. "Everything stayed in place, but I'm afraid I won't be able to push the healing along too far. It's too soon to do much more than lock the pieces in."

"Understood," Mother said, all business. "Kitteren should be here shortly with something more secure for her arm and a change of clothes."

Silver's voice sounded tense, "I'd like a chance to actually look at her shoulder. My spell can only tell me so much."

I did not like being ignored, but held my tongue. I clenched my teeth tightly when Silver began using his magic to push along the healing. It hurt and for some reason I had not expected it to.

"It'll be over soon, Ketayl," Silver soothed as he worked. "Just bear with me."

"This is you getting even for me taking off, isn't it?" I quipped. I had to do something to stop my mind from its downward spiral.

The pain from healing stopped for a moment. "I..." Silver said and paused. "I'm sorry, I guess my sense of humor is out right now." He resumed his tending.

Silence fell again.

The pain started to get to me - both the physical and emotional. I could not get past the fact I so easily fell back into being that person again. "I didn't want to..."

A more delicate hand touched my hair. "Didn't want to what?" Mother asked, her voice gentle.

"I didn't want to hurt anyone. I just..." Why was I so stuck on this?

She continued to stroke my hair. "I know and again I wasn't fast enough."

Her statement confused me, but the pain had a good chunk of my attention. I grit my teeth.

Kitteren burst into the room. "I've got what you requested, though I had Hells of a time explaining why we needed the sling."

The worst of the pain from healing eased up, but it still ached deep in my shoulder.

"That's as much as I can do for now. It still needs to stay as immobilized as possible," Silver said. "Can we get the arcane restraint off now? I didn't know it blinded her and it wasn't right to have put it on her before."

"We'll have this discussion later, Silver," Mother said quietly. "But for now, I don't see why not. Are you ready, Ketayl?"

I nodded. Being able to see was not as important as being able to feel my power - find comfort in it as much as I feared it.

Hands pushed me back against the bed. Mother spoke gently,

"Are you sure? I don't know what will happen. Lockonis didn't give us much information."

I thought of one problem I needed to voice. "Yes, but you won't be safe from me."

"Safe from you?" Kitteren's voice sounded confused.

Silver said sharply, "Ketayl, knock it off. You could have easily taken out the whole room and us with it, but you didn't. Even in a blind panic, you only attacked the enemy. And trust me, I was there."

"Enough," Mother said sharply. Her voice softened when she continued, "Kitteren, can you take the arcane restraint off? I can't stand seeing one of my girls like this."

I turned my head toward Mother, letting her stroke my hair. I should fight the touch, but I needed to stay grounded.

I could feel Kitteren's hands on my ankle, undoing the buckle. As soon as she pulled away, I curled up against the rush of my power coming back, breathing hard. I felt nauseous. It felt like all of my nerve endings were on fire and the sounds in the room were cranked far beyond their highest levels. The soft beeping of the machines might as well have been sirens going off directly in my ears.

As I became re-accustomed to my power again, the world began to right itself. I stayed curled up, breathing more normally. I felt exhausted. Maybe now they would just let me sleep.

"No, Ketayl, not until we get you changed," Mother soothed. "We left you in Kitteren's suit because we were pretty sure it was the only thing holding your shoulder together."

I cracked open my eyes, not remembering having closed them. I needed to squint against the light, but at least now there was light. I needed to remember to have a conversation with Lockonis about the arcane restraint.

"This isn't going to be fun getting it off of her. We're probably going to have to cut at least the right sleeve so we don't move her shoulder too much," Kitteren said. Someone tugged at the boots on my feet. "I'm a bit jealous - you got to wear it."

"You can have it back - it's too tight," I said, my voice weak. "I can mend it later."

Kitteren laughed lightly though it sounded strained.

Mother took my free hand and squeezed before tugging the glove off. Once gone, she went to work on the other one, trying to move my arm as little as possible.

Someone worked at my elbow. I looked up and saw Silver intent on getting the knot out on the rope they used to secure my arm. I could not read his face.

Mother prodded me to sit up. "Come on, Silver wants to take a look at your shoulder."

I grabbed the collar when she tried to unzip it. It meant they wanted at least the top part off.

"Ket, I know what this outfit entails. All your girlie parts will be covered," Kitteren chided.

That was the least of my worries.

Mother pried my hand off of the collar. "It's past time I checked that too. It's nothing to be ashamed of."

I closed my eyes and sat still. I could cover the scar between both of my hands probably.

I sat quietly while they cut the right sleeve open after Silver finished getting the rope off of me. Cool air hit my overly warmed skin and I shivered.

"That looks really bad still," Kitteren said as soon as they got my shoulder freed.

"The bruising is expected," Silver said flatly. "The swelling should go down in the next day or so, but I'm sure an ice pack will help. Can we get the other side off? I want to make sure there isn't more bruising from injuries we might have missed."

Mother initially left that side alone and I dealt with as much as I had exposed. The sports bra kept things modest.

"I'm fine," I shot at them, holding the remaining half of the top in place. I would not look at anyone. I could not. I did not want to see what their expressions were.

"You'd say that if you had just been thrown almost completely through a wall by a Troll. Oh, right, you just were," Silver said, his voice clipped.

Mother scolded sharply, "Enough. I let you have your words with her before against my better judgment. Ketayl has always been diffi-cult to deal with when she's hurt."

"That's putting it mildly," Kitteren said quietly. "More like next to impossible. I'm impressed she's cooperated this much. There's this weird quotient of how badly she's hurt to how difficult she is."

I felt anger begin to rise and I tried to push it back down, but not before I said, "I'm sitting right here."

Mother ran her hand through my hair again. "You don't have much choice here either. You're outnumbered."

"I brought some of your usual clothes. I'm sure you want out of the suit," Kitteren offered.

Sighing, I let go of the top. I'm sure I could manage to hide the scar with my arm or my hair. Thinking further on it, I reached behind me and pulled my hair over my left shoulder. Problem solved.

"Good to see you mellowing out," Kitteren quipped.

I turned to glare at her and stopped. She looked like she had been crying. What happened while I was out?

Mother and Silver took my distraction as a chance to get started peeling the suit off. I looked away from Kitteren and did not fight the other two. I felt Silver's fingers touch my back and flinched.

"That wasn't pain, Silver," Mother said. "I think Ketayl's at her limit of being poked and prodded. Just a little longer. Kitteren and I will help you get cleaned up, dressed, and then you can rest. I'll have Fan find you something for the pain."

I mentally cursed at the idea - I still hated medication.

Silver continued to move, lightly touching me and I shifted uncomfortably. He finished with my left arm and went to move my hair. I brought my arm down quickly to try and keep it covered.

"Ketayl..." Silver sounded more tired than angry now.

"Let me," Mother said and pried my hair out from under my arm with some effort. "I need to check on it anyway. It was my fault it happened."

I looked at Mother confused. She would privately check the scar over the years, but it had been quite a while since the last time. How was it her fault?

In my confusion, she managed to move my arm away. "Oh, it's barely there anymore. It should easily fade completely before you reach your first century." Mother traced the scar from under my left arm to where it ended at the front of my left hip and I squirmed between being uncomfortable with the scar showing and because it tickled a little.

"When did that happen?" Kitteren sounded angry and I could not understand why.

"The last time she crossed those slave traders," Mother said calmly. "I wasn't fast enough to keep her from getting hurt. And at that time, my healing abilities were very limited. Thinking back, I should have gotten her to Don first before exacting revenge on their operation."

"Wait, wait." Even from my peripheral vision, I could see Kitteren getting overly animated. "You're telling me she *actually* took them on? At the age of eight? I always thought you were exaggerating."

"Ketayl is obviously not going to tell you the story, so I will. Besides, I have a feeling she needs to hear my side," Mother said. I looked to where she still knelt, staring at the scar. "She somehow knew what happened to all of the non-Human orphaned children who the people in the outskirts of town, including Don, had taken in. She just couldn't get them out with the sheer number of guards and I doubt anyone would have listened to her if she told them. Not that she spoke much."

Even Silver stilled to listen. No, he should not be here for this. "Please don't," I begged.

Mother stood up and stroked my hair. She continued anyway. "I had arrived in town, not even a full day when this little brat had the gall and the skills to actually steal from me. Well, I couldn't let that go and managed to track her down with quite a bit of effort. Certainly more than the wallet was worth."

"Stop," I whispered. I looked away from everyone and hugged myself with my good arm. Why did she have to choose now of all times to talk about this?

"Somewhere along the line, while talking to Don and seeing both of my girls, my thought of teaching her a lesson changed. I had gotten too curious about these other children and what Ketayl knew. So I followed her that night."

"No more, please." I started to think I had actually not spoken.

"Why not just ask?" Kitteren's voice broke Mother's story.

"Because she spoke even less back then if you think it even possible," Mother answered. "Kitteren, the only one she ever really talked to was you. It forced me to quickly learn to read her. But getting back, it turned out we would need to team up. The children were being held in a warehouse at the time. Same place as where this one sits."

At least I remembered that much right. I still kept my eyes away and silently prayed for Mother to stop. Divine intervention seemed to be the only thing that could stop her. Neither of the other two in the room were acting on my pleas.

"She decided to distract the guards so I could get well over 40 children out which also gave me the opportunity to look through their ledgers. By the time they were out and running for a safe place, Ketayl had made it to the pier where the boat the slave traders used to conduct business transactions was moored. You had a trail of at least a dozen of those guards behind you I believe."

I shrugged and immediately regretted the decision as pain shot through my right shoulder.

"Ketayl, you can't move it yet," Silver said softly and he put his hand on my shoulder, barely touching, and the pain began to dissipate. I wanted to tell him to leave - that he heard enough. I could not form the words and sat silently in my personal Hell.

"I tried to catch up. I figured I could get the attention of most of them at the very least. I don't know if she meant to head onto the ship, but thinking on it, the tighter turns would have been easier to lose most of them. I'm not sure what happened until I reached the ship myself."

There was a pause, but I refused to speak. I could feel myself getting worked up again as my mind decided to fill-in her story with my own memories. I thought I could lose a few of them on board.

"I remember seeing this little Elven girl taking on these big thugs in an all-out fight and holding her own. I think I might have been too awestruck at the sight to react the way I should have," Mother continued.

Silver moved away and I sat still. I hid all of this for so long, but I did not remember Mother being on-board the ship. I wanted to cry at the torture, but held back.

"Our now captain decided to bring a knife into the fight, which I'm thinking is what threw you into a panic when you first came across him near his office," Mother commented. She stroked my hair. "She was hurt badly and cornered while I was trying to figure out how to get her out of there. Then something spectacular happened." She moved away and then began using her hands to help tell her story.

I cringed and looked away. Spectacular would not have been the word I would have chosen.

"This wave of power knocked everyone back, and I should have been too, but it brushed right by me like a breeze. I believe the same as the two of you experienced." Mother laughed, "And it would have been bad if it hit me. I had been pretty precariously balanced and would've ended up in the water."

How had my power not hit her like the others? And I did it again as well as burned the Troll? I racked my brain for a reason. My eyes darted back and forth on the information my mind laid out before me.

"Ketayl, hold the analysis until I'm done," Mother chided. "In knocking these guys back, a few oil lanterns also got knocked over and started a fire on the deck. Those old ships were so laden with oil it didn't take much."

I had not meant to. I kept my eyes averted from everyone and wrapped my uninjured arm around myself again.

"And then this little thing takes off while the crew is still trying to get up. I caught up with her in an alleyway where she collapsed. I managed to get the bleeding stopped, even at the risk of healing shock, wrapped her up in some sail cloth I found and tucked her into a safe place. Then I went back to the ship."

What? Why had Mother not spoke of this before? I looked up at her, not sure I knew the truth anymore.

She smiled sadly at me. "I had a feeling even you didn't have the whole story. Not after what you said." Mother petted my hair. "By the time I returned they had gotten the fire under control. I decided it shouldn't be and spread the fire as far and fast to their holdings as I could. I'm the one responsible for the port fire, Ketayl, not you."

I just stared at her. Silver returned and placed something cold against my injured shoulder making me stiffen up.

"For some reason, I always thought you knew. Anyone who died that night was by my hand, not yours. And even in a blind panic, you can still tell friend from foe. While I knew, we didn't want to chance you could in your state and elected to put the arcane restraint on you."

"Especially when Silver explained what he had to do," Kitteren said, her voice sounded strained.

"I am truly sorry for the pain I caused you," Silver said softly.

I wanted to be alone right then. I needed to try and process everything. "I'd like to rest."

Mother and Kitteren made Silver leave and helped me clean up and change. He came back in with Fan when they could not figure out the sling. Thankfully Kitteren brought a baggy gray short sleeve shirt which covered the bruising on my shoulder. The stretchy black calf-length pants were soft and comfortable.

"Silver, if you don't mind staying with her? Kitteren and I need to get back to preparing for the next stage," Mother said.

He nodded and then turned back to me just as Fan tried to hand me a couple of pills and water.

I shook my head at the medication.

"Take it, Ketayl. You won't get decent rest otherwise," Silver said, his voice tired. "Just know we're not done discussing this."

"Easy, lad. No need to get testy," Fan said as I took the medication. "I don't have anythin' on hand that is listed as okay in yer file, but this should at least work enough to let you get some rest."

I nodded and laid down at her insistence - the bed had been set flat somewhere along the line.

Silver came over and put the blanket I had been wrapped in back over me. "Thank you, Fan. I've got it from here."

"There's a cot in the closet. I don't think Ketayl is the only one who needs some rest. I won't be far if you need me," Fan smiled and patted my foot.

I rolled onto my left side and closed my eyes. I only hoped when I woke up again, I would find this had all been a dream.

I listened to Silver digging around in the closet. I said, "You don't have to stay here. I'll be fine on my own."

Silver sighed loudly, coming back over to the bed. Something pushed up against my back and I turned to see what. He positioned the pillow behind me. "I don't want you to roll over onto your bad shoulder. And Ketayl, I need to stay. Not because of orders. Not because I'm the one handling your recovery. Because you're my partner - my friend." He opened his mouth to say more and shut it.

Silence fell between us and as he started getting the cot out, I curled back up.

Silver pulled the cot around to the side I faced and set it up.

I yawned. A thought went through my head I decided to share out loud, "I'm never taking a vacation again."

Silver stopped short in the middle of sitting down on the cot. Then he plopped down and started laughing. "This one doesn't count. Mixing business and pleasure rarely works from my under-standing."

I just made a noise at him. I did not even know what kind of noise I made - I felt sleepy which made it hard to concentrate.

"Sleep, Ketayl. You've walked through the Hells enough for at least one day," Silver stroked my hair and I tried to bat his hand away, but missed wildly.

He needed to stop fussing over me. "Not glass," was the most I could get out and my voice sounded slurred.

"I didn't think what Fan gave you would kick in this quickly," Silver sounded amused. "And no, you are not glass. Though you're going to give me a complex if you keep this up. Now get some rest."

I briefly thought about trying to stay awake just to defy him, but the draw of sleep became too strong. *"I'm sorry,"* I said before falling into the world of dreams.

18

No one else occupied the room when I woke next - even the cot had been put away. I quickly dismissed the notion of it all being a dream with the dull ache in my shoulder and my arm bound to my side.

I disliked still feeling tired after resting and dragged myself off the bed. The medication had not worn off fully and I stumbled, holding onto the bed with my unbound arm for support. I knew I initially turned it down for a reason.

Having my right arm tied to me did not help matters any. I was still working my way back to my feet when Father came in. He rushed over to help me up. "You shouldn't be trying to move on your own yet."

"I'm fine," I said, trying to get my feet to cooperate. At least my speech cleared.

Father picked me up easily and sat me on the bed. Now I was back where I started. "I'm sure you feel fine." He touched a button on his headset. "Fan, can you come to the infirmary?"

"I'm fine," I reiterated.

I received a look of annoyance. "Just humor me and let Fan take a look at you. Then we'll see about finding you something to do to keep you out of trouble."

A face I did not expect popped in the door. "Hey, I heard you call for Fan. Something wrong?"

A battered and disheveled copy of myself stood in the doorway. I remembered seeing that reflection in the mirror when I changed up earlier - a dark bruise on the left side of her jaw and I could see the strangulation marks. She dressed in clothes I remembered originally packing and her hair had started coming out of its bun.

"Kitteren, you shouldn't be in here dressed like that," Father admonished.

She looked down at herself. "Oh, sorry, I forgot. Guess it doesn't matter anymore anyway. I was a damned fool for not listening to the advice I was given."

The look on Father's face confused me, but I still had far too much missing information. At the very least, I could try to get up and move around. I needed to ignore the face which looked too much like my own.

I scooted myself to the edge of the bed, intent on taking this attempt slower when Father moved me back to my previous position. "You need to wait since you nearly fell the last time."

"I'm fine."

"You keep saying that," he sighed.

Kitteren bounced over and sat at the foot of the bed. "I don't know how you can say you're fine when you shattered your shoulder. That's not counting all of the other injuries you sustained." Her energetic self sounded forced.

Fan came in and set about gathering things and bringing them over to where I sat. I did my best to fold my arms and stare at a wall away from everyone.

"Ket, look at me." I refused - I could not look at my reflection. She got into my field of vision and I looked away again. "Okay, so this is probably very strange, but I could use your help when the buyer shows up. I'm obviously not very good at pretending to be you so maybe you can talk me through it?"

"Let me go instead."

"No!" both Kitteren and Father said at the same time.

Fan decided to step in as the voice of reason, "Lass, how do you expect to deal with basically one arm tied behind yer back? Don't you worry none - yer sister will be completely safe. Just need to let the bastard think he's gettin' you."

"And Hells if I'll let them near you," Father said. It surprised me for some reason.

Fan started packing up her things. "You seem to be fine, lass. Anythin' you want to tell me about?"

"She nearly fell getting out of bed," Father said quickly.

I ran my free hand through my hair, pushing it out of my face. "It's only because the medication from earlier hadn't fully worn off yet."

"Aye, that was somethin' strong - wanted you to get some sleep. That'll help you heal faster. I'd give you somethin' more mild, but it likely won't do you any good," Fan said, moving about the infirmary.

I shook my head, "I'll be fine."

"You need to stop saying that," Father chided.

***

THREE HOURS. I had three hours before I found out who wanted me so badly they would put out a bounty. This part was supposed to be easy: I sit nice and safe here at the warehouse and be Kitteren's puppet master.

I hated this plan.

I fully understood the slave trader crew had been replaced by TIO agents, but it still did not settle the unease I felt. I wanted nothing more than for this to be done and over with. I needed to deal with the lack of trust my family showed me.

I felt torn between wanting to feel betrayed and accepting they could not because of it being a Dark Ops mission. And also kicking myself for putting them in danger by staying silent, though I knew not what I could have told them to make a difference.

Sighing, I sat bored at a table in their small dining area, poking at the food on my plate. I should be starving, but I had no appetite.

"Hey, kid," Darius said and turned the chair across from me around to sit on it backwards. "If you don't eat, one of them will come in here and feed you."

"Just not hungry," I said quietly.

Darius started unwrapping his sandwich. "Yeah, I can guess why you wouldn't be. This whole thing is a disaster. Worse when it's family."

I pushed the vegetables around on my plate. "I just want to deal with one thing at a time."

"Makes sense. Maybe I can help with something?" He slid the extra bottle of juice he placed on the table over to me.

I stopped and looked at Darius. What was he up to? Seeing no loss in verbalizing it, I said, "Right now I just want to know who wants me - I'm not valuable." I returned to pushing the food around my plate.

Then the conversation between Kitteren and Lockonis I walked in on came to mind. What had Lockonis said? Something about a highly valuable asset. If not for the fact I should not have overheard the conversation I would ask for clarification.

Darius raised an eyebrow at me, his mouth full. Once he swallowed what he had eaten, he said, "Well, you would be wrong. At least to us as both an agent and a friend, you are extremely valuable. Hells, when we heard you were involved and how, the three of us fought for the assignment. Savanas managed to hold onto a couple of new agents and put in a request to the main office for support so we could all go. Said if she couldn't go, she'd make damn sure you'd be covered." He stopped and looked at me a moment before reaching over and cracking the cap on the bottle he had slid over. Not like I could have done it with one hand. "Any ideas on who else might want you this badly?"

I half-shrugged, my right arm being too immobilized to complete the gesture. Something at the back of my mind nagged at me enough to pay attention to it. "Previously the Arcane College has tried to recall me, but they wouldn't resort to this."

Darius started rhythmically tapping his fingers on the table. "You're right - this isn't their style, but they also acted weird when it came to Brown."

He had a point, but this seemed overly far-fetched even for them. "I should be there instead of Kitteren."

Darius paused in trying to inhale his food. "In your condition, you wouldn't last very long being tied up. She'll be able to break out easily, but your shoulder wouldn't be able take the strain. Besides, she needs to do this. Kitteren may not act like it, but she's taking what happened pretty hard. All of us are to tell you the truth." I could not recall ever having heard the sad tone in Darius' voice before. He always seemed cheerful. "The captain had some balls, I'll give him that. Had the three of you in his grasp and there was nothing we could do but sight in targets and wait for the order to continue."

I couldn't bring myself to look up at him. "What do you mean?"

"Ket, we all saw your fight somehow even if it was after the fact." I cringed hearing that. I forgot about the camera on the headset when I gave it to Kitteren. "You weren't supposed to be a part of this operation and there you were, fighting to protect those two hard-heads with everything you had."

"At least they stopped arguing with each other," Brad said as he came in. "Ket, you need to eat."

I did not feel like reiterating myself and continued to push my food around the plate.

"Anyone else you can think of?" Darius asked.

I half-shrugged again. "Everyone knows most of my secrets now." I think that truly bothered me. There was no more pretending to be normal, or at the very least not a monster.

"I wouldn't worry about it. Well, maybe," Darius started. "The Highlands guys have been talking about trying to get you onto their team."

I looked up at the men across from me, confused.

Brad took over, "Despite not being trained for something like this, your skill set impressed them, though I highly doubt the Director will break you and Silver apart."

I had not seen Silver since I woke. Given how angry he was the last time, I had a feeling this team Vince wanted to build would fall apart before it began. I returned to pushing the food around my plate. I could not seem to keep to dealing with only one thing at a time.

"Speaking of Silver, I didn't think he'd leave you alone," Darius commented. "Especially not with the injuries you sustained."

Brad shook his head. "Silver needs to clear his head. He's upset over the fact Ket managed to slip through his grasp and then..." He signaled at my current condition.

"A paladin and a tracker get taken hostage and are then rescued by a lab tech - sounds like a bad joke," Darius quipped and then laughed at his own remark.

Brad rolled his eyes. "Why don't you go talk to him, Ket? After you finish eating."

"Yeah, you don't want to have to eat the nasty blocks," Darius pointed out.

"Nutrition blocks," Brad corrected.

Darius shook his head and swallowed his food quickly to respond, "No, nasty blocks. Have you ever eaten one?"

I had not, but I figured I would not enjoy them. I forced myself to take another bite. They stayed with me, mostly carrying on their own conversation until I finished.

STILL HAVING a couple of hours until the buyer showed, I followed the directions Brad and Darius gave me to where they last saw Silver. Kitteren and the others taking the place of the slave traders had already left.

Silver had gone to check on the rescued children. I grew concerned they were still being held, but they needed to be hidden from the buyer just as I did.

It took me a while to get across the skywalk I had seen before to the other warehouse and then back down to the lower levels. Even with a little bit of magic to help speed things along, it was slow going with the crutch Fan ordered me to use. It hurt to put weight on my left leg.

Gently opening the door, I peeked in and saw the children looking in far better condition than when I last saw them - cleaned and fed with fresh clothes. They were laughing and playing. This room had been designed with children in mind - there were toys for various ages. A couple of adults I saw previously as part of the crew sat inside, watching and playing with the children, but no Silver from where I could see.

One of the two women looked over at me. "Ketayl! No need to hang by the door, come on in."

I felt bad I could not remember the Human woman's name. I quietly entered, not quite coordinated with the crutch under one arm. I stiffened up as I felt someone behind me. Looking up over my shoulder, Silver closed the door behind us. I could not read his face - he kept his head up so I mostly just saw the patch of silver hair under his chin.

He walked past me into the room. This had not been what I had in mind.

A few of the children came up and circled him, pulling on his hand toward whatever game they were playing. A familiar little girl looked up to see what the commotion was. "Fairie?" she asked and got up from where she had been coloring.

I stood still, not sure what to do as she came over to me. Everyone else in the room stopped and turned toward us.

The girl reached up and gently put a hand on the sling. "You got hurt because of us."

Silver turned his face away and it looked like something pained him. Perhaps he needed to tend to his own injuries.

I managed to shift away from the door and knelt on the floor.

"Are you still on that dumb story?" a boy next to Silver shot at her. "Give it up, it's not real."

Silver looked down at him and said, "It's as real as she is."

The little girl reached into her hair and pulled out the elastic I previously gave her as a promise. "Thank you for coming back. I'm sure you'll need to return it soon. I even washed it."

I nodded, my voice gone.

She latched herself around my neck and squeezed hard. "Thank you!"

Suddenly more children surrounded me and I found myself at a loss. I should not have come in here. She jarred my shoulder and I winced.

A Dwarven woman came over and gently pried her off. "Easy, honey. Just need to be gentle with her."

A flood of apologies poured forth from the girl's lips.

"It's okay," I tried to get in between her words. I became uneasy about the amount of children around me now. Had there really been this many in the hold? It seemed like there were more than what I teleported.

"Where are your wings?" another girl asked. "The statue has wings."

I looked up at the other women in the room and then over to Silver who made his way back over to me. He said, "I think some details might have been exaggerated in the story."

The children looked at me expectantly. The thought I had would likely be a bad idea, but I ran with it anyway. I put a finger to my lips, signaling to keep it a secret. I tucked my good hand inside the sling for a moment and started the simple illusion spell, trying to remember the details of the statue.

When I pulled my hand out, I cupped a handful of sparkling dust held together in a ball. Tossing it up, the little ball burst and showered myself and the children near me in the dust, outlining a pair of wings on my back. I fluttered them a little and then let the magic fade. It took more effort than I had been prepared for.

The room fell silent and little eyes were as wide as can be. I decided it had definitely been a bad idea as the moment ended and their voices got loud, all trying to shout different things at once.

The caretakers, Silver included, tried to calm the children down.

"See, we don't need to go to an orphanage," one of them said.

I held up my good hand and by some miracle, they all quieted. "How much do you know?" I don't think they had the truth.

"That you lived on the streets like us." I did not see who the voice belonged to.

"For a time, but eventually someone adopted my sister and I," I said. "Please don't think you should live like I did. I had a home and a family. I lost them and was forced to find my way. A new family found me."

"And now Ketayl is an agent with the TIO," the Human woman said.

"But what about the story? Those kids? Were they real?"

I nodded. "But I couldn't do it alone. Just like I didn't do it alone this time." I glanced over at Silver who sat next to me on the side of my injured shoulder. I held up the hair elastic to him.

The door opened again and I had not expected to see Joanna being escorted in by another agent. She looked around frantically until she spotted her son near me. "Matthew!" She immediately pulled him into a tight hug and began crying.

I felt a little guilty at having forgotten his name. At least she ignored me. I winced and started rubbing my hip. I needed to get up - sitting down on the floor like this had been a bad idea.

Silver picked me up easily and the Dwarven woman handed me my crutch. She said quietly, "We're slowly contacting the families we can. Making arrangements for the others. Just can't draw too much attention."

Joanna looked up and narrowed her eyes for a moment before covering her mouth. "What happened?" She stood up and reached out tentatively to brush her fingertips on the sling.

"Ketayl found us, mommy. They said she made sure that they'll never be able to do this again," Matthew chimed in proudly.

Then Joanna tilted my head to the side to look at the bruise on my jaw and then up. I could not move out of her light grip without falling backwards. Suddenly her eyes went wide and she backed off, "I'm so sorry. I'm a doctor in urgent care at the hospital - I'm afraid my manners are lacking after so many years there." She looked down at her son, placing her hand on his head. "I never did apologize for how I treated you before."

"It's fine."

I found myself in a tight hug and it sounded like Joanna started crying again. I stiffened up at the pain, but stayed still. My good hand gripped the crutch tightly and I hoped I could stay balanced.

Once she calmed enough, Joanna whispered, "Thank you. You brought him back to me." Then she let me go.

I began having a hard time managing the pain - I could feel the sweat beading on my forehead. I said, "I'm sorry, but I need to get going. Perhaps later?"

Joanna nodded and a chorus of disappointment rang through the children and many asked me to come back when I could. Silver escorted me out.

I managed to make it to the far end of the hall before having to stop. The pain got worse with each step and even with trying to stay off of the leg, my injured hip throbbed. I leaned back against the wall, clenching my teeth.

"I'm guessing you're off the pain killers," Silver said. "Where does it hurt?"

I shook my head.

"Dammit, Ketayl," Silver said sharply and his hand hit the wall next to my head. I looked up at him - he stood too close and I had nowhere to escape. "Knock off the tough act already - I know how much pain you're in. It's not a sign of weakness to let someone help. Let me do something. I've been on the sidelines watching you take on everything yourself."

"You fixed my shoulder," I pointed out.

Silver backed up a step. "I'm the one who should be taking the risks. I have a shield and armor, remember? I'm trained for a fight. And I never wanted to put you in so much pain, but none of us wanted you to lose the mobility in your shoulder either. You would have had to go through multiple surgeries and likely would still be in constant pain. You might have had to give up playing your violin. It is the only thing I have been able to do."

I had not known my shoulder had been in such bad shape. I sighed, the pain returning to a dull ache again and I started moving.

"No," Silver said and stopped me. He took the crutch away and leaned it against the wall before scooping me up. "I'll come back for it later."

"Put me down," I demanded.

Silver smirked and shook his head. "I like this. The last time when I carried you here, you kept curling up into me."

I felt the heat rise in my face. "Did not."

"How do you know? You were unconscious." Silver grinned mischievously.

I reminded him, "I don't like being touched." I tried again to be free of his hold.

It did not seem to take much effort for him to readjust me back to where I had been. "If you fight me, I'll tell everyone you're a snuggler."

"That's a lie," I shot back quickly.

"I have witnesses. Most of them in there." He gestured toward the room the children were in with his chin. "I suppose I can't count that then, huh? You were in risk of healing shock and probably just trying to stay warm. In the infirmary I guess wouldn't count either due to extenuating circumstances."

I glared straight ahead and stopped talking. At least he did not seem to be mad at me anymore.

As he walked, Silver asked, "Ketayl, why didn't you run when we told you to?"

"I couldn't," I said quickly and then stopped. More calmly, I continued, "I couldn't let them kill you. You were hurt and captured because of me."

Silver struggled to open the door while trying to carry me. As soon as he managed the latch, he said, "I guess we're going to have to spend some time training together to learn each other's skills. You didn't know I planned on putting a protective bubble around Kitteren and myself, but I was only going to be able to maintain it for short periods of time."

I stayed quiet. If I had listened, I might have heard him tell me.

"And I didn't know you knew how to disappear in a crowd. I figured with your hair color, it would have been easy to spot you," Silver continued his commentary.

I cringed. I learned that on the streets - not something to be praised.

Silver sighed, obviously frustrated with me. "Don't, Ketayl. The past is part of who we are. It may not be something to be proud of, but it happened for a reason and the best thing you can do is learn from it."

It did not make my past being put on display for everyone to see any better.

SILVER EVENTUALLY PUT me down in a chair by a console. As promised, he returned with the crutch. He also came back with my tablet and food.

At least it was only a bowl of fruit, but my appetite still had not returned. Reluctantly, I took a bite before Silver could give me a hard time about it. I paused at the first taste of the blueberries - these were fresh.

I still had plenty of time before the buyer showed. I managed to finish the bowl of fruit and had been left alone to read. Well, as alone as I could be in a room of working agents. The only interruption being Mother dropping off a pair of headphones so I could listen to music while I read. Silver sat beside me quietly. Perhaps not alone, but not being bothered at least.

Mother came over after a while and said, "Let's get you hooked up. Only Kitteren will be able to hear you." She held out a headset.

I moved to take it and stopped, unsure of how to fit it to my ear with only one hand. Mother quickly did it for me.

"I've already checked it, but I'm sure she would be happy to hear your voice. Just don't expect much in response from her once the transaction starts." Mother reached around and punched up a video feed on the screen in front of me and I looked away, though the image already seared in my memory.

Kitteren hung from one of the bars across the ceiling of the dining area. Her wrists bound and head hung.

Putting my tablet aside, I turned back to the screen, pushing the emotions back. "Kitteren, are you okay?"

"Yep, it's not as bad as it probably looks. Actually, it feels good to stretch out my back and shoulders," Kitteren said and I barely saw her lips move. "Glad you've got my back, sis. Especially since I haven't seemed to have yours lately."

"You shouldn't be doing this." My emotional control was strained. I could not stand seeing her like this.

"My choice." Right then I hated Kitteren's use of the phrase I used to explain my actions. *"You know, I only stole your hair pins and clothes since they have your arcane scent on them. Figured it would throw off anyone looking for you."*

"You could've just asked."

Kitteren sighed. *"I know. I screwed this up horribly. The fact you're still talking to me is a sheer miracle. When I ran into you outside the warehouse, I was certain what Vince, Lockonis, and Savanas all tried to warn me about what was going to happen. Then you came back even though you knew it was a trap."*

"The buyer is here," Mother said loudly. Her statement ended our conversation.

I leaned over to try and see her screen and froze. Darius and I dismissed the Arcane College, but there on the screen a female Arcane College mage walked up to where the boat moored. Two Human men in suits flanked her. There were a few more farther down the pier.

The audio from that location had not being fed to my headset. I could not hear what she discussed with the male Dwarf. Rathal and Darius flanked him, playing the two I previously fought.

Silver broke my line-of-sight. "What is it?"

I shifted to look around him and squinted, trying to better see her pin - she wore such decorative sleeves, or almost lack of sleeves, I did not want to base my analysis off of them. I could not make out the embroidery coloring on the screen. "I can't tell her rank from here."

Rathal coughed on the screen and then Mother said, "High Mage."

"You okay, Ketayl?" Silver asked.

I did not have time to be distracted, I needed to keep Kitteren safe somehow.

"Ket, talk to me," Kitteren whispered.

Taking a breath first, I returned my attention to her. *"There's an Arcane College High Mage and a couple of Human men in suits. They're on the dock talking right now."*

"Shit."

I agreed with her sentiment.

"They're headed to the dining deck," Mother called out.

"Kitayl, please don't do anything stupid. They're on their way to you." I did not care who heard me call her that. I needed her to know how serious I was.

I got silence as a response, but she could not speak now. Not with the High Mage so close. I needed to switch back to normal common to keep our communication clear.

"There's a lot of arcane usage in here," the High Mage commented as she entered the dining deck.

"Aye, like I said, your girl fought. Got a number of the crew good," the fake captain said. He looked far too much like the one they captured and I shifted uncomfortably.

"So the little fairy grew some claws. I'm going to enjoy removing them," she said. I had a feeling she used the derogatory term for Elves. Rathal clenched his fists when she said it.

I racked my brain for a name. I vaguely recognized the face, but there were too many mages to remember.

The High Mage walked up to Kitteren and tilted her face up so she could look at her. "Not much left to you now is there? You were quite expensive to capture, but at least you'll secure me a seat on the Circle of Magi."

The woman's statement confused me. Only Archmages could be selected to the Circle of Magi and only when a seat opened up.

Remembering I needed to talk Kitteren through it, I whispered, "Don't respond - she's looking for any reason to hurt you."

Kitteren jerked her face out of the High Mage's hand and glared at her.

"Don't. Don't set her off," I begged. I stood, leaning over the console toward the screen. I had no idea how fast she could cast. I knew I could beat Kitteren's reaction time.

Silver put a hand on my good shoulder and gently pulled me back.

"Your will is admirable," she said. "I shall deal with you momentarily. I believe we need to settle payment and collect the other merchandise."

"Aye, none of them leave this boat without it, High Mage Reinhart."

The name clicked with the face. I remembered her reputation at the Arcane College.

The High Mage signaled her men to present payment. "This will suffice I hope."

I did not take my eyes off of Kitteren. I dared not look away in fear I would fail my sister. Any information I had specifically about Reinhart would be useless here. Her desire for power had been matched by the low-cut front of her robes. It reminded me she would go to almost any length to get what she wanted. Though I vaguely remembered something about her rank and abilities did not match. She would use her body to gain favor with higher ranked mages. In this case, her actual ability to wield the arcane should be lower, but it did not mean she was any less dangerous.

Out of the corner of my eye on the screen I saw Reinhart signal the two men. "Go secure the rest of the merchandise, would you? When you're done, we'll take her."

The men left and I said nothing further. What could I say? The best thing right now would be for Kitteren to remain silent.

"This might take some time. I hear the person who wants the children asked for quite a few of them. So let us discuss you, shall we?" Reinhart smiled in a sickeningly sweet fashion. "Why would the Circle of Magi put a 'no touch' order on you? Hm?"

I cocked my head to the side, confused. Then I remembered I needed to feed information to Kitteren. "I don't know."

My sister repeated my words, her voice shaking. I did not know if she was scared or acting.

"All of the guards have been taken care of," someone called out in the warehouse.

"Rumor tells me it had something to do with an incident regarding High Mage Bettencourt."

As soon as the name left her lips, I felt the blood drain from my face. How did she find out about that? She was not old enough to have been in the Arcane College at the time. Likely not have been born would be more accurate.

"Ketayl?" Silver asked softly, his hand still on my shoulder.

Reinhart roughly grabbed Kitteren's chin and forced her to look up. "Tell me, did you kill him before or after he joined with you?"

I could feel everyone's eyes on me and I dropped my head, letting my curtain of hair shield me from their judgment. I gripped the console hard enough to turn my knuckles white. How dare she bring up something she knew nothing about. I felt my power start spinning wildly - the storm begging to be released.

Someone came over and took my headset from me. Mother said, "Kitteren, take her down."

I looked up at the screen in time to watch Kitteren grab hold of the rope above her for support and kick Reinhart in the chest with both feet which led to a flurry of movement. Silver pulled me back until I was sitting in the chair again. I refused to look at anyone. I needed to calm down first before someone got hurt.

I heard someone call out they had Reinhart in custody. Father appeared in front of me. "Ketayl, talk to me."

Closing my eyes, I shoved the emotions back, forcibly locking down everything in a manner I had not been able to before. I said flatly, "Contact the Arcane College and inform them of High Mage Reinhart's arrest. They will have a statement for you within a few hours. I would like time to prepare before speaking with her."

"No," both Father and Mother said at the same time. Father continued, "I will not put you in the same room as that monster."

Funny choice of term. Sitting up straighter, I said firmly, "I will speak with High Mage Reinhart once the Arcane College has issued their statement." I stood up and reached for my crutch. Then I tucked my tablet in my sling and made my way out of the room toward some place I could prepare quietly. Their questions would have to wait.

THE DOOR to the room slammed open. "Ketayl, what in the Hells happened?!" Kitteren yelled.

I did not look up from my tablet. "I'm sorry. I wasn't sure what to tell you."

Kitteren tore the tablet out of my hands and tossed it on the other end of the bed, out of my reach. I looked up at her. Rage filled her green eyes. "I don't care about that - I know how to cover my own ass. I want to know if what the bitch said is true."

I took a deep breath and recited the statement I came up with. "High Mage Reinhart was trying to get a reaction..."

Kitteren cut me off, "And she did! I wanted to drop her right then and there. And according to the others, you reacted pretty strongly too. So tell me she was lying."

I could not lie to my sister - not after everything she had been through, but I did not want her to know the truth. I worded my next statement carefully. "High Mage Reinhart was only trying to get a reaction and does not know what she spoke of."

"Damn your secrets, Ketayl," Kitteren growled and then stormed out.

I sighed and slowly shifted so I could get my tablet back. I hurt more than I wanted to admit, but I needed to wait until after I spoke with Reinhart before I could rest.

Silver walked in while I reached for my tablet. "Dayko wanted me to tell you they received a statement from the Arcane College."

I nodded and changed my direction to trying to get up. When I reached for the crutch, Silver moved it out of my reach. This had gotten old.

"Ketayl, what is going on? This isn't like you." Silver tucked my hair on one side behind my ear.

This Elven man barely knew me. I pushed back the anger wanting to rise and limped past him. I hated the damn crutch anyway.

It hurt far greater, but the pain helped me stay focused this time. Silver called for me, walked next to me, tried to give me the crutch back, but I kept going. I needed to read the statement.

I made my way through the door to the main area of the warehouse before Silver did anything more drastic. Father spoke with Rathal nearby and they ended their conversation abruptly.

"I'm sorry, sir, she wouldn't take the crutch," Silver said quickly.

Father looked down at me and I stood as tall as I could, trying not to show my pain. He said, "You'll do no one any good if you hurt yourself further. It'll still be a while before you can get the rest of your injuries fully healed and your shoulder is going to take longer."

"I came to read the statement from the Arcane College," I kept my voice even.

Rathal looked at Silver with a confused expression on his face.

Father sighed and went to get the sheet of paper. He handed it to me and said, "They didn't say much. Apparently she was acting of her own accord."

I read over the statement quickly. The Arcane College's reaction I expected. "This is common for them to send. I would like to speak with High Mage Reinhart at the earliest convenience. She will need to be informed."

"Someone else can do it," Father said.

I struggled to keep myself steady on my feet. "She also needs someone familiar with the Arcane College to act as an advocate."

"You can't be serious, Ket. And you can't be her advocate due to conflict of interest. You're not a liaison anymore," Kitteren looked down from the railing above. At least she seemed to have calmed down quickly. "What she needs is to be tied to an anchor and dropped into the harbor."

"Kitteren," Father warned. He shook his head and muttered, "These two..."

Rathal said, "Look, Reinhart is harmless. As much as I don't want to put her and Ket in the same room, she can't hurt her."

"Not physically, no," Mother said and I almost jumped at her sudden appearance. "I think there are answers we are all looking for at this point and standing around here is not going to achieve them. I'll allow Ketayl to go in on the condition she takes both Kitteren and Silver with her. I'll select more to observe from another room."

I wanted this to be private. I opened my mouth to tell them as such and then closed it when I saw the look on Mother's face. I had never seen so much barely contained anger in her eyes before.

"The condition is non-negotiable," Mother confirmed.

Clenching my jaw, I nodded. I had little left to hide at this point.

———

"Are you sure about this?" Silver asked as we approached the door to the rigged up interrogation room.

I stopped at the door and leaned the crutch on the side of it. I told the two following me, "Just don't react to her and if trouble arises, I will handle it."

Kitteren muttered something under her breath. I did not have time to play games with her. My attempts to lock everything down had been strained to its limit. I did not know how much longer I could maintain it.

I opened the door and strode in as steadily as possible. I did not want Reinhart to know how badly I had been hurt, but the sling and visible bruises were going to hamper the attempt.

The High Mage glared at me as I took my seat. She said, "Hmph, couldn't even take on a couple of miserable thugs. This is why you are still a Researcher. And what is this? Bodyguards? My, you don't think I'm dangerous now, do you?"

It did not take me long to see the spell used to bind her power. I vaguely wondered who crafted it for her. I guessed I got to be the only one lucky enough to try out the arcane restraint. The thought irritated me for a moment, but I let it pass for more immediate issues.

Kitteren and Silver took up spots in the corners of the room near the door. Silver stood out of my view, but Kitteren I could see easily.

"I don't," I said. "But I do wonder how you might fair in a fight with a Troll." I saw Kitteren smirk.

Reinhart's face paled immediately. "How dare you speak to a superior this way! I will not tolerate these insults!"

"Duly noted," I said flatly and pulled the folder out from under the sling. "I'm here to inform you about the statement we received from the Arcane College regarding your arrest." Putting the folder on the table, I opened it and turned the sheet of paper so Reinhart could read it.

She picked up the paper and I noticed they had not restrained her. A number of emotions flitted across her face faster than I could catch before she tossed the paper back down on the table and said, "This is fake."

"Your choice to believe what you will, but this is a common response from the Arcane College for anyone not an Archmage. There are many examples in the archives," I said, knowing the insult I made. I actually went through the archives instead of making someone else do it for me. "Now that you have read their statement, I am to inform you that due to a conflict of interest, I will be unable to act as your advocate. The Arcane College should be providing one for you shortly."

"You need to let me go back to the Arcane College. I order you to free me," Reinhart growled.

Busying myself with putting the paper back in the folder, I said calmly, "Given the severity of the charges against you, that won't be possible. And even if I acted solely on the will of the Arcane College, I would be in odds against their ruling."

Standing up, I tucked the folder under the sling. "If you require my presence during interrogation, please have someone notify me." I knew I went beyond what the others wanted me to, but she needed someone who understood both the TIO and the Arcane College and I was the only person who fit that.

"You never answered me from before," Reinhart said, her voice taking on an arrogant tone and she sat back in her chair, crossing her legs. She positioned her chest so the low cut would expose more of her cleavage. I did not think any of us in this room would be impressed.

I steadied myself before I said, "I'm afraid I don't know what you're talking about. I was not present at your arrest, she was." I nodded toward Kitteren. I began moving toward the door.

The look on her face told me she was not going to let this go. Reinhart leaned forward, "Did High Mage Bettencourt manage to derive his pleasure from you before you killed him? Oh, did you not want your friends to hear about that little incident?"

I started to walk away. "As this is not relevant to your case, our conversation is over."

Kitteren and Silver moved to the door and were most of the way out when Reinhart grabbed me from behind. Her hand squeezed the upper part of my right arm and I grunted at the pain through clenched teeth. "You weren't the only one to suffer through that kind of humiliation," Reinhart hissed.

The two accompanying me were back in the room in a second and I used my free hand to signal them to hold. I needed to take deep breaths to keep some kind of control. Panicking and accidentally killing her would only set this team back.

Reinhart's other arm wrapped around my left shoulder forcing me to be a shield for her. She continued, "I was just smart and decided to turn what I had to my advantage. I didn't need the Circle of Magi to put a 'no touch' order on me."

As calmly as I could, I said, "You have five seconds to let go before I remove you." I separated my fingers so Kitteren and Silver could see my countdown. And also so they could see the pure arcane energy I conjured in the palm of my hand.

"You can't do anything - you're just a Researcher. Now you will escort me out of here," Reinhart's voice told me she felt she had the advantage. She also used the same tone as when Brown had tried to command me six months ago, but with her power sealed she could not use it. If the pins were some kind of amplifier for the spell, mine sat in evidence thousands of miles away.

I ticked down three fingers while she spoke, forming a loose circle with my hand. Two. One. I changed the arcane energy to electricity and clenched my hand into a fist.

The bolts traveled up my left arm and headed directly toward where Reinhart held me. It had an instant effect. Turning, I held myself together as much as possible, watching her writhe on the floor for a few more seconds. Some part of me enjoyed it and took pleasure in being the one looking down.

"You dare to assault a superior?!" Reinhart moved to get herself back together to stand up.

Rathal and another agent made their way past Kitteren and Silver to hold her down.

"As a bit of advice, it is generally considered impolite to attack someone without provocation. Now if you'll excuse me," I kept my voice even and walked out of the room.

Kitteren and Silver followed me into the hall and away from where they were hauling the screaming High Mage back to wherever they held the prisoners. The serious expression on my sister's face broke and she started laughing. "Oh by the Gods, that was priceless."

Silver's expression had not changed. "I should look at your shoulder - make sure she didn't do any more damage."

I shook my head and handed him the folder. I needed to make it out of the hallway at least without losing my control. "Please excuse me. I would like to be alone." I needed to get away before I started showing outward signs.

As soon as he took the folder, I accepted the crutch and made my way down the hall toward the supply area. I remembered it being closer than the infirmary and about as private as I could get.

The pounding in my ears kept getting louder as I walked through the empty hallways and the pain worsened. I let the door to the supply room close behind me as I moved farther in. I only managed a few more feet before I started shaking too hard and dropped the crutch. I clutched at my injured arm and sank to my knees. I could not hold it in anymore.

I had enough control left to slam my hand on the floor and in doing so, put up a bubble to keep the sound contained before I left out the scream I held. My power stayed sated despite my emotional turmoil. I let myself cry. The years of holding it all in attacked me at once to add to the physical pain I felt.

I did not know how long I carried on before I realized two things: the pain started to fade and someone rubbed my back. I did not look up to see who when I told them, "You shouldn't be here." My voice shook as I spoke.

"Yeah, well, obviously neither of us is good at listening to you," Kitteren said. She paused for a moment before asking, "Silver, are you okay?"

"I'll be fine. The usual spell to try and dissipate the pain wasn't working - the only way to reduce it until she can take the medication is for me to share it," Silver said, his voice strained.

"Don't," I managed before my voice cracked.

I looked up to see Silver sweating and rubbing his shoulder. He said, "Too late now. It'll last for roughly an hour. Why didn't you tell us how badly you were hurting?"

"Ketayl has always been good at hiding these types of things," Mother's voice joined the conversation.

Between the shame from having been caught and the exhaustion of letting free my emotional turmoil, I kept my head down. My curtain of hair hid my face from the others and I curled closer to the floor.

Someone knelt down in front of me. "Ketayl, you can drop your soundproofing bubble," Mother said gently, trying to push this mass of hair behind my ear. "You don't have to hide."

Her voice soothed my frayed nerves and I strained to try and keep the bubble up in defiance, but it quickly flickered away. I curled down closer to the floor in shame. If only I could make myself smaller.

"That was an impressive bit of magic. I didn't know you knew that one," Mother said. "Also impressive how you handled Reinhart."

"That might be an understatement," Father said. How many more were in the room?

"Thank you," Mother said, and it did not fit the conversation above me. Feminine hands with calluses from so many years of playing music lifted my head up. Mother's eyes were soft and I wanted to move away to hide my face again. I could not look away despite the fact I knew I was a mess.

She shifted so my head rested against her shoulder and picked up something from her lap. Mother took the cool, damp cloth to my face. "Now, tell me if the incident with High Mage Bettencourt is real."

I nodded, shaking.

"Did he join with you?"

I shook my head.

"Did he try?"

I nodded again. My head felt heavy and I struggled to keep my eyes open. I just wanted to rest.

"When in the Hells did that happen?!" Kitteren's loud voice echoed in my ears and I winced at her volume.

"Kitteren," Mother warned. Her voice softened again, "I think it's time for you to rest. You should take the medication before Silver's spell wears off."

I nodded and accepted the pills and the bottle of water. I struggled to try to get up, but barely made it into a sitting position on my own.

"I've got her," Mother said. The thought of fighting her left as fast as it came. I could not concentrate anymore.

I managed to get out one more phrase before giving into exhaustion: "*I'm sorry.*"

2 0

"Come on, Ketayl, it's time to go," Mother's soft voice cut through the haze.

"We should leave her be and let her rest. They'll be fine until we get back," Father said.

Someone stroked my hair.

Mother replied, "We'll be gone quite a while with the prisoner transfer. She's rested enough to at least finish healing her hip and I'd rather she be able to wander around at Don's than be cooped up here. This place will not help her heal."

"I'm not going to argue with you there. The medication should be wearing off soon. I'll talk with Fan about what to send her with," Father said.

Then the door opened and closed with a couple of soft clicks. I still did not feel like moving. I enjoyed this nice in-between state.

Someone sat on the edge of the bed and continued to stroke my hair. "What other secrets are you hiding? What other weight are you bearing?" Mother asked softly. "I doubt you'll tell me any easier now - not with what we just put you through. Just don't be too hard on the others, okay?"

I did not care at this point. The world happened to be perfect right this moment and I refused to darken it prematurely. I did not hurt, my mind calm, and my power slumbered. These things Mother spoke of were out of my view at the moment and I enjoyed the bliss.

I breathed deep the ocean air and let myself continue to drift.

Eventually a dull ache started to anchor me back in reality. I tried to move my right arm to see if I could work it out only to be reminded it had been bound to me. Then other things came to the forefront, one after another in quick succession.

I sat up quickly and looked around - I needed to get out of here, embarrassed by what happened. How could I have not paid attention just a little longer to make sure no one followed me?

"Easy, lass, ye're back in the infirmary," Fan said. "Lindale and Dayko are makin' arrangements so you can go rest some place more comfortable."

She stood on the other side of the room. I could not seem to focus and cursed the pain medication again.

"How about we finish gettin' yer hip healed while you wait?" Fan smiled and walked over. "I'm sure you'll be glad to be rid of the crutch. Just lay back."

I did as she asked and stared at the ceiling only wanting to be free of this. I wish I could also get rid of this sling.

"You know, me an' the others been talkin'. Wanted to ask you to join our crew, but then we heard about the team ye're buildin'. Just know if you need any of us, we'll be more than happy to help out," Fan said as she wheeled a stool around to my left and sat down.

"Thanks," I said softly, hoping my voice did not sound too slurred.

Fan set the bed into a reclined position. "This will take a while an' then you might have to sit tight on yer shoulder. It'll heal fine on its own, but yer partner wants to try an' push it along as much as yer body can handle. Can't blame him - he should be able to cut your recovery time down to a couple of months or so."

Why would Silver care how fast I healed? Did he express this wish before or after the most recent events? I started to get hungry despite the worry. It was one more thing to deal with.

I heard the door open and I did not bother to turn to see who it was. Maybe if I ignored them, they would leave.

"Fan, I could have done that," Silver said.

The healing slowed while she waved him off with one hand. "Dependin' on how she feels, she might have enough for you to help her shoulder along. Her hip isn't as bad as I thought, but I'm glad I erred on the side of caution. Bet it hurt somethin' fierce to put yer weight on it."

She was not wrong, but I was not in the mood to be sociable. Silver came around to the other side from Fan and gave me a weird look.

"It's okay - she just woke up. I'd be pretty quiet too," Fan said as she continued her work. It started to get warm in here. Probably just my embarrassment.

Silver looked around for a moment before scooting another stool over. Once he sat down, he said, "We'll be headed out as soon as you two are done."

"Are you headed where Mackie was sayin'?" Fan asked.

I looked at her, curious as to what she was talking about.

Silver shook his head. "Lindale wants to try and narrow it down further first before dragging Ketayl from town to town up there."

I turned my attention to him and hoped I did not have to voice my question.

"Mackie apparently understood what you were saying to Kitteren," Silver explained. "She has a general area in the Highlands she says the two of you are from, but there are a number of communities in the region. It would be too much on your body right now."

I cared little for who might have understood me. I could not retrace my journey to find our village if I wanted to. I did not want to return. That being the last secret I held at this stage.

"I guess I'm going to have to learn your dialect of common, huh?" Silver asked.

"No," I whispered, unsure of my voice. I resisted the urge to fan myself as it quickly got warmer.

"Silver, can you help keep her cool?" Fan asked. "She's reactin' stronger than I expected with the medication still in effect. She's gonna to end up with a high fever at this rate."

He left my side, and I wanted to breathe a sigh of relief. "I'm fine," I said as Silver searched through the cabinets.

"I think not," Fan chided. "Ye're gonna to be drenched in sweat here soon. I'm sorry, Ketayl."

It meant I would need to clean up again. I only hoped I would have enough concentration left to do it magically once Fan finished. I closed my eyes and thought through everything that occurred recently. If those two men had not abducted the girl in front of me, I would not be here. Or if I had not cared. I would likely only be aggravated over my family acting weird.

Because I could not let go of the past, I now stood here with it all on display for everyone to see. I only had myself to blame.

Something cool and wet touched my forehead and I looked up at Silver. I thought he looked concerned, but even with the cool cloth, the heat was starting to get to me and I did not know if I imagined it.

"Sorry I dragged you into my mess," I said.

"I followed willingly. Just rest," Silver said, wiping my face. I wanted to pull away, but I felt too drawn to the coolness of the cloth. He looked at Fan. "I've never seen this kind of reaction before."

I tried to ignore them and think about other things. I needed to help get Sparky settled in the lab when I got back. Would my shoulder be healed enough by then so I would be able to use my arm? How long did Fan estimate again?

"Aye, it's uncommon, but the medication is what is causin' it. With forcin' her body to heal faster, it's also attackin' what's left of it in her system at the same time as if it was an illness an' is causin' the spike in temperature. Anythin' she listed not havin' a reaction with wasn't gonna to cut it with pain management. I had to take a chance when I chose what she's on."

"She didn't react like this when I was healing her shoulder before the numbing agent wore off completely."

What day was it? The Summer Solstice took place on the 20th this year. I wondered what else might be going on in town for the festivities.

"Vastly different things, lad."

Maybe I would just stay at the hotel. I had been really tired lately.

"I'm going to hold off healing her shoulder more - I don't like this," Silver said.

I wished they would stop treating me like glass.

Fan's voice strained as she said, "Yer gonna to like it less when I send her with more of the medication. I want her to take a dose before she leaves an' to get rest when you get there. It'll last about four hours. Give yerself a window between doses to get her shoulder healed."

"It's still going to take weeks to fully repair between everything else. I already risked her life restoring it - I won't do it again." Why did Silver sound worried? Was there something going on?

Fan pointed out, "Sometimes lettin' it heal naturally is best. I'll leave it at yer discretion."

"Do you really want to put up with her being a stubborn pain-in-the-ass for even longer if you let it heal that way?" Kitteren's voice joined the conversation.

I cracked my eyes open to look over at her.

"Oh, you're awake. We brought you a change of clothes," Kitteren smiled. Mother stood next to her with a bag which looked like it came from a store.

"Clean these," I managed to get out.

"What's going on?" Mother asked, coming over to touch my sweat-dampened hair.

Fan explained her theory to them.

Mother nodded and opened her hand to Silver. "Give me that for a moment please."

Silver handed her the cloth he just soaked in the bowl of water next to him. "I'm sorry, ma'am. I didn't want to chance my spell interfering with Fan's healing."

She looked at him for a moment. "You're doing more than enough. I should be the one apologizing to you."

I closed my eyes again thinking of cooler things like snow or at least a chilled lavender tea. I had no warning before the cold cloth slipped under the collar of my shirt and I squirmed - it felt like ice.

"Easy, Ketayl," Mother soothed. "I don't think you're going to be in any shape to clean your clothes. And once Fan is done, it'll be easier to cool you off in the shower."

"Just a few more minutes, lass," I heard Fan assure.

It was so hot. I could not hold onto a single thought for any length of time. I vaguely understood what Fan said.

Those few minutes felt like days.

As SOON AS the cold water hit me, the world came back into focus. I shivered - it felt like ice against my overheated skin. I tried to move away.

"No way, I got soaked with you - you're staying," Kitteren said. Then I realized she held me up under my good shoulder and had undressed to her undergarments. I took a moment to take stock of the situation. No sling, but I was still fully clothed. And now soaked and freezing.

"Why?" I asked through chattering teeth.

Mother came into view and said, "You were incoherent. We needed to get your body temperature down quickly once Fan finished. How do you feel?"

"Cold," I managed. This vacation had to be near the top of worst vacations ever taken. It was definitely on my list. Granted, I had no others to measure against.

The water turned off. Mother came further into the small space. "Let's get you out of those wet clothes and cleaned up. Kitteren, go dry off and check on the final preparations - I'll help your sister."

Kitteren guided me to a small bench nearby and patted me on the head. "You be good."

I glared at her, still shivering, wrapping my arms around myself. I found my right arm sluggish to respond and started to ache.

A hand stopped the movement before I could complete it. "You shouldn't move your arm yet. Let me help you out of those wet clothes."

Reluctantly, I let Mother help me since I shivered too hard to do it on my own. She wrapped me in a large, fluffy towel I suspected might have been pilfered from the hotel and then sat still in the main area of the small locker room while Mother brushed and dried my hair. I stared at my reflection in the mirror and the massive bruise covering my right shoulder. The rest of me looked fairly beaten as well.

Kitteren came back in while I sat on the bench, letting Mother fuss with my hair. She winced when she looked at me. "That looks painful."

I did not much care anymore and just stared at the floor. I just wanted this to be over.

"Hey, Ket," Kitteren said softly - she knelt down to get in my line of sight. "Dad, Brad, and I will be taking you and Silver to Papa's house, okay? We'll all be back in time for your birthday, I promise."

I stayed silent. What did it matter?

"Come on, Ket. I'd rather have you angry at me than this. What is going on?" Kitteren put her hand on mine.

"I think that is a question for another time, little one," Mother said gently. "Ketayl needs time to heal, both physically and mentally."

"No," I said before I could stop myself. My voice low I said, "I'm not glass." A phrase I had been using fairly frequently lately and I meant it every time, but I started to think I spoke an alien language. My anger rose again - Kitteren might just get her wish. "I need everyone to stop digging into the past. I kept it hidden for a reason and now..." I choked on the rest of what I wanted to say.

"Ah," Mother said, "That's what I was missing." She continued to brush my hair gently. It turned my anger into sadness and I did not want a repeat of earlier.

"Dammit, Ket, stop thinking you're shielding us from something bad or evil. You went through the Hells and back for me and all of us," Kitteren said angrily. Her face then softened. "Stop taking this on yourself. I'm not glass either."

"You're going to need to learn to share with having a partner now. Especially one who cares so much about you," Mother added. "You're going to learn how to share also, Kitteren. Ketayl is your sister, but she's still her own person."

Kitteren sat back on her heels and smirked at me. "Yeah, I guess I can live with him being your partner. Just don't expect me not to give him a hard time whenever I can."

"Kitteren," Mother warned.

My sister shrugged and I smiled at her antics - I never could stay mad at her for long. "There you are!" I winced at the volume of her voice. "Now let's get you dressed and ready to go. You'll be staying with Papa for the day. Just try not to give Silver a hard time, okay? I can't believe I just said that."

"He might think you like him if you keep this up," I said.

Kitteren made a face of disgust. "Ew, no. You keep the paladin. Not my type."

Mother dug through the bags. "I think you'll want to wait until the bruising on your shoulder disappears for some of this." She pulled out an airy looking black short-sleeve shirt and a pair of shorts I would not have chosen for myself - they were not long enough for my tastes.

I sighed and let them fuss. Just as I would return to my normal wardrobe, life would return to normal as well. I hoped.

21

FAN MADE me take more of the pain medication before I left despite my request to wait until I got to my destination. My belongings at the warehouse were packed up and loaded into the car for me. And now I sat in the middle of the backseat between my sister and Brad.

I leaned my head against Kitteren's shoulder. The medication kicked in again almost immediately and we were maybe halfway to Don's house. Father glanced at me in the rear-view mirror, but said nothing. Silver sat next to him and turned to see what caught his attention. Brad held an ice pack to my shoulder.

The silence was deafening. The least they could do was talk about me like I was not here.

"Are you okay?" Brad asked as he readjusted his hold on the ice pack.

"Yeah," I muttered, making myself comfortable. It had been a long time since I let my guard down this much around Kitteren. I found I missed the closeness we used to share. I thought it only born out of necessity.

Kitteren wrapped her arm around my waist and pulled me as tight as our seatbelts would allow. So long ago we would huddle together for warmth - I had not seen it as more than that because of my sense of duty to try and keep her alive.

Father glanced at us in the mirror again and I saw a soft smile on his face.

I closed my eyes - the medication already started to make focusing difficult. I would rather have waited to get to Don's house before taking it so I could sleep off the effects. Kitteren rested her head on mine.

After a few moments the sound of a shutter made me look up again and I saw Silver handing a phone back to Father. "Hey," I said, my word sounding off.

"Did you expect me not to want a picture of that?" Father smirked as he glanced back at me in the mirror.

I grumbled and closed my eyes again. He could have at least waited until I did not look quite so beaten. Maybe by resting I could slow down the effects of the medication. Not likely, but it gave me a reason to remain still.

Time passed and eventually I felt the road turn from pavement to dirt under the car's tires. It meant we were close, but I had no desire to move. I knew I would have to because Kitteren probably grew tired of me leaning on her.

I leaned on Kitteren, right?

As I opened my eyes, the car slowed and pulled into a driveway. Don stood out on the front porch as if he waited for us. But he also enjoyed just sitting on the front porch. I could not make up my mind on which version would be true.

Kitteren helped me sit up and unbuckled my seatbelt. I needed to go inside, right?

My body sluggishly responded and I slid across the seat with help from my sister. The others were already out and going about their business, though Silver stood outside the door waiting.

Standing up, I noticed Don with a sad expression on his face, but I could not understand why. Father and Brad spoke quietly with him.

I managed a couple of steps before my legs gave out and I got caught on something on the way down. A silvery weave hung in my vision. My voice was slurred when I said, "*It's pretty and shiny.*" I wanted to touch it, but could not figure out how to move my arms.

Kitteren snorted and then started laughing hard enough it almost sounded like she started crying.

"What did she say?" Silver asked.

Kitteren calmed enough to answer him, "Don't worry about it.

She's basically drunk. Probably why she didn't want to take the medication again."

"I'm not drunk," I tried to argue, but it came out weird. *"I don't drink, but I'm thirsty."* Maybe it would fix how I sounded.

Kitteren continued to snicker. "Let's get her settled and probably some water."

I finally managed to grab the silvery thing and held onto it as I was picked up. I flicked the end around, amused by the feathery tail.

"What did you give her?" Don asked.

Brad said something and I stopped paying attention. The words were too difficult to follow. They started talking back and forth. Alice came out to see what the commotion was.

Kitteren led the way inside and I tried to get down, but I could not figure out how to get down so I went back to playing with Silver's braid.

Once we got upstairs to one of the guest bedrooms, Silver put me down on one of the beds. He nearly fell back on top of me because I still held his braid. I giggled at his stumble.

"I take it this is why she doesn't drink," Silver said and looked to Kitteren as he pried my prize out of my hand.

"Probably." Kitteren wiped her eyes. "I've honestly never seen her like this before."

"Then don't look." It made sense, right? I yawned. Sleep sounded good.

It sent my sister into another round of laughter. Silver muttered something about needing to learn a new dialect.

"If you want to get her settled, I'll get a glass of water for her," Kitteren told him. "Ket, can you at least switch to something Silver can understand? Like common or Elven?" She looked at him on that last one. He nodded.

"I'm speaking common."

Kitteren left laughing and shaking her head. Silver at least smirked at whatever was funny.

I curled up on my left side and promptly fell asleep.

A GENTLE BREEZE greeted me as I woke. Distant voices carried up the stairs, too low to be understood. I sat up and looked around to get my bearings, still feeling groggy from the medication. I swore never to take it again if I could help it.

Scooting to the edge of the bed, I put my feet on the floor, testing how solid I felt to stand. I decided to take it easy and managed to get up and looked out the window - it looked to be about midday, maybe early afternoon. Clouds covered most of the sky.

The last time I slept in this room and this bed was after I got hurt taking on the slave traders 50 years ago. Mother decided to take myself and Kitteren in then. I still did not understand her motivation for doing so to this day.

Shifting from one foot to another, I was restless, but I did not want to disturb anyone. I looked around for my shoes and had no idea where my belongings were. I supposed it did not matter - I ran around for so long as a child without shoes.

I opened the door quietly and looked around the small hallway. The doors to the other bedrooms were closed and the distant voices became more distinct, but they were not near the stairs.

Taking a chance, I stepped out and closed the door quietly. While I peeked down the stairs a stray thought caught my attention: I should go for a walk in the forest.

The voices started to get louder and I backed up, the invisibility spell falling into place almost instinctively. Don and Silver walked by the bottom of the stairs.

Silver stopped and looked in my direction. "I should go check on her," he said and started making his way up. I plastered myself to the wall opposite the door to the bedroom I had been in.

"Leave my brownie be. The medication she's on is too strong for her to handle properly - she needs to be able to sleep it off," Don chided.

They continued past the stairs. I took it as my signal to move, though I left my spell in place. I could feel the broad grin on my face. This was fun - sneaking about with nothing truly on the line other than getting caught and sent back to bed.

Alice worked in the kitchen, humming while she cut up something. The once normal door on the back had been replaced by a sliding glass door, which had been left open. This was almost too easy.

She turned and looked in my general direction. "Donald, I said... Odd, I thought I heard someone." Then she returned to her cutting.

I held my breath and stayed completely still. I quickly padded my way out to the backyard once she returned to her task. I sprinted as much as I could on the balls of my feet through the grass, hoping no one noticed the temporary indentations of where I stepped.

Joanna headed back inside with Steph and Elizabeth just after I left and I caught sight of Jon and Alex under the pavilion as I ran, but did not stop to satisfy my curiosity. The children played with a ball on the other side of the yard.

Once I reached the backside of the shed, I stopped and leaned my back against it, grinning madly and a little breathless. It had nothing to do with being out of shape.

I also dropped my spell. Here the path into the woods began. I would not be seen by anyone at the house from here and walked more sedately into my former domain.

This time I could enjoy the cool earth beneath my feet. Take in the sound of the breeze as it rustled the leaves above my head. The life around me. No concerns about keeping my sister alive and where our next meal would come from.

As I walked, the breeze picked up and I stretched out my unbound arm and lifted my face, letting it play with my hair. Eventually I came to a familiar stream. Someone took the time to build a small bridge. I hopped its width easily when I was far smaller, but I stopped to admire the craftsmanship of the little bridge.

It looked like perhaps bicycles had ridden over it. I could not be sure, but I decided I should cross it also. Reaching the other side, I jumped off and misjudged my balance, wobbling on the balls of my feet until I steadied. I giggled.

Then I shook my head - I really hated this medication.

I walked further through the familiar territory. Even 50 years later, little seemed to have changed. Sure there were new trees and other plants - others gone, but the feel of this forest remained the same. I just had not the peace of mind to truly see the world around me then.

Soon enough a small shack emerged from the forest. The little wooden structure had been fixed up - the holes were gone, windows looked to be relatively new, and the roof maintained all of its shingles. I walked up to it slowly, worried I might start seeing the past and it would ruin my current mood.

I looked in the window and saw an all too familiar set up. Blankets laid out over a small cot. I blinked and now the cot had become a small bed. A little table sat next to the bed which had not previously been there. The fireplace remained cold, but not uninviting.

I went to the door and tried the knob, finding it locked. I looked around, debating if Don might hide a key out here. I reached above the door frame, remembering how I managed to find the key to get into his house when I was little. Though often enough he forgot to lock his doors. Cleaning had been the only way I could repay him for the use of the shack and everything else that followed.

My fingers found the small object and I fumbled to open the door with my non-dominant hand. I placed the key back where I found it before going in. I huffed against the musty smell in the little shack and left the door open to air it out. Standing in the center, I slowly looked around. My height made it look so different and yet I still found it familiar. My fingers reached out and touched the blankets on the bed.

It seemed like for so long Kitteren had been trapped here. Shaking my head, I grabbed the top blanket and made my way to the corner of the shack - as far from the door as I could. I tossed the blanket around my shoulders and sat down with my back to the wall - injured shoulder toward the corner and pulled my knees up under the wrap.

This had not been so bad. It was just how things had to be when we were little. It kept us alive to be where we were today.

I yawned and dozed back off.

I TRIED to curl tighter into the blanket, but my bound arm making it difficult woke me. I rested a lot lately. I briefly entertained the idea I would be able to work a week straight without a problem when I got back.

I cracked open my eyes and saw the sun had not moved much, if at all. I should not have been missed.

"You pick the oddest places to rest," Silver said.

The sound of his voice made me jump. How did he find me out here? Did Don tell him? How long had I been resting? He sat on the small bed, his phone cradled in his hands.

I lowered my head back into the blanket and closed my eyes again. Maybe he'd be gone and this had been the dream.

I sensed movement and the blanket slowly pulled away. "I think we need to talk, Ketayl."

"Everyone wants to talk," I muttered.

"I don't doubt it, but I want to know why you slipped out of the house and came all the way out here." I opened my eyes when Silver brushed my hair out of my face.

I backed away from him as much as I could.

Silver held up his phone in front of me, anger flashing across his face. "If it wasn't for the fact I was able to track you, I would have no idea where you went. Hells, I still wouldn't know you left if it hadn't alerted me to you getting out of the range they set." His phone displayed a map of the area with a blinking blue dot in the center.

"I came here to be alone," I shot back. "I feel like I can't think lately without someone being over my shoulder. And now I'm being tracked?!"

"You've been trying to run away from your past and yet here you are in what I would think would be the last place you would come to," Silver snapped and waved at the shack around us.

"*What does it matter where I go?!*" I shouted and then sank back. I took a deep breath, returning the conversation to normal common, "I'm tired of running and it only chasing me. I never wanted..." I trailed off.

"Ketayl, I don't think any of us wanted this." Silver sat down next to me and fiddled with his phone. "Until you disappeared on me in the market, I didn't know the real reason I had been asked to help keep an eye on you, though I did question if there was more going on." He showed me the message again from Lockonis. "This was all I received. Dayko gave me something of a clue when he told me to stay close and report on any problems. Lindale warned me to try and keep you away from the warehouses on the waterfront if possible. They had me continue to search with the others en route to meeting them at their base of operations. Only then did I find out about this mission."

I sighed and asked, "Would it have changed anything?"

"Yes, it would have," Silver said quickly. "I wouldn't have kept from you that you were being used as bait or information or whatever it was they wanted of you. I would never have let you out of my sight for even a second, though I'm thinking it wouldn't have stopped you."

"Probably not." I rested my chin on the arm I put across my knees. Not the most comfortable position, but it did not matter.

"At least we're both being honest here," Silver commented offhandedly.

I rolled my eyes. "Even if I had known, I would have let myself be bait," I said before I really thought it through, but I found it to be true. "I just don't think I have any information that would have been of use to them."

Silver raised an eyebrow at me and noted, "I doubt you would have been content to remain as just bait. Not with what I've seen."

"No, I wouldn't have."

Silence fell between us for a few minutes. It gave me time to think about the conversation thus far. Even if I knew, I would have done the exact same thing even knowing the high probability of exposing my past. Somehow, the realization helped put everything into perspective.

"Thinking about it, all of this took place in the span of only a few years, right?" Silver asked.

I had not been expecting the question. "About a year and a half if you're just talking specific events. Maybe closer to two years." My memory on the actual time frame had become fuzzy.

"That's a lot of years left for other events in your life," Silver pointed out.

I rested my head back against the wall and breathed deep the scent of the forest. "I'm afraid I have little else of interest. Being a Researcher for the Arcane College wasn't eventful. What about you? It seems only fair."

Silver remained quiet for a moment. "I'm afraid prior to six months ago, my life has been fairly straight forward. No adventures taking down slave traders at a young age." He paused and smirked at me. "Though I may have some tips for the next time you want to face down a Troll."

I rolled my eyes at him. Learning to deal with Silver on a regular basis would be an adventure in and of itself. Though his comment about fighting a Troll had my interest. There had to be more to it. I filed it away to ask on later - I was tired.

Silver's face turned solemn. "Blaise Sutton took me as his

charge when I was a baby - I only ever knew life within the church. I didn't think I was missing anything until I started working with you."

I could not decide if it was a compliment or not. Even though I did not raise the blade, in meeting me his life had been torn apart. To this day I still did not fully understand why he chose to leave the church and join the TIO. My change of occupation came from an unexpected transfer, though I had still yet to get the rest of the story from Lockonis. It just seemed unimportant by that point given everything else. Then work picked up.

"I heard you teleported all of the children off before coming back for us," Silver commented. "I wasn't sure you could do that. I sort of assumed for some reason, but I didn't know."

I half-shrugged. "It was my first attempt. I didn't have enough arcane energy left to take you and Kitteren. And I would never have been able to safely target one of the boats." Somehow I still felt like I failed.

Silver leaned forward to try and look at my face. "Your first attempt?"

I tried not to look at the wide blue eyes staring at me. "I knew how it worked, I had just never tried it before. I didn't expect how intense it was to pull so many with me even with only teleporting a short distance."

"You mean to tell me you teleported on board, cloaked, teleported yourself and roughly 20 children off, teleported back with enough energy to cloak yourself again, and then picked a fight with slave traders?" Silver seemed surprised or impressed. Either way he gave me far too much credit.

I shook my head. "Not without Rathal transferring his arcane energy to me before I went back."

"Odd he hadn't mentioned it when he told me about you teleporting the children," Silver said and leaned back.

Obviously things worked out between him and Rathal. I sat back and simply listened to the wind rustle the leaves.

After a while, about the time I started to doze back off, Silver said, "I never did thank you for helping me through training."

I did my half-shrug again. I did not want to admit I needed to learn the information also. And to also admit I had not received the same training.

I had not even told Silver I did not receive a badge of my own until Savanas gave it to me the morning before I handed him his.

"I was about to ask you a personal question, but I have a feeling you're not in the mood after this mess," Silver said.

That would be an understatement.

"I mean," Silver started and then paused. "All those calls over the past six months and we never really discussed anything outside of work. Everything else was fairly trivial."

"I'm not exactly good at conversation," I explained. We talked about inane things from time to time, but never anything of significance.

Silver grunted. "I guess most of this will have to wait. You'll probably need some actual time-off after this. You should probably spend it with your family to sort everything out."

It was not something I wanted to think about right now. "What about you? Do you have anyone in Ocean's Edge?" I knew he left the church, but there had to be someone else in the city he wanted to reconnect with.

"Hm? No." Silver's short answer surprised me. Often I thought he liked to hear himself talk.

"No love interest?" I asked, closing my eyes again, not sure why I went to something so inane. I also didn't want to specify gender of a potential mate as I had not bothered to inquire previously.

Silver snorted and then started laughing. "For some reason, I didn't think you would bring that up. No, I don't have a girlfriend. My few attempts at a romantic relationship failed rather spectacularly."

I cracked open an eye to look at him. I could not read his face and he kept his attention straight ahead. "For some reason I find it hard to believe."

Silver looked at me, surprise on his face. He stopped and looked to be giving it actual thought. "I seemed to attract the ones who only wanted to be able to claim they were seeing a paladin. I am far more interesting than my title." His voice changed to that cocky, self-important tone he sometimes used on his last sentence as he touched the tips of his fingers to his puffed up chest.

I covered my mouth to hide the smirk. I did not know why I found it funny whenever he did that.

"Now I know that wasn't the medication," Silver grinned broadly and rocked to bump my good shoulder gently.

My mood soured quickly. "I'm never taking it again."

Silver sighed and suggested, "How about only before you rest for the evening? Don said he was going to make a few phone calls to find you a solution for during the day."

I made a non-committal noise. I did not want to, but it would be a reasonable compromise. We fell silent again.

After a minute or so, I found a different question to ask, "If you were notified when I got out of range, why didn't you stop me before I got out here?" I had not moved quickly, even with my hip healed. Granted, I also did not know what the range was.

Silver brought one knee up and propped his elbow on it. He admitted, "If Don hadn't come with me, I might have, but then I would have missed seeing you relax finally. You seemed so content on your walk. He told me a little about this place after you fell asleep, but not why you chose the corner instead of the bed."

Stretching my legs, not as used to the position anymore, I admitted, "This was my usual spot. Occasionally I'd share with Kitteren, but it was easier to let her get rest without having to deal with me."

Silver said nothing and I debated simply leaving. I just wanted to be left alone and to keep all of this private, and here I was talking again. It made no sense.

"We should go find something for lunch. Maybe head into town later and check out the Summer Solstice festivities if you're feeling up to it," Silver said softly as he got up. "Besides, I just found out your birthday is in a couple of days." His eyes spoke of mischief.

I felt my face turn red in embarrassment. "It's just a random day that was chosen - I don't celebrate it."

"No, it's only fair. You sent me something for mine." Silver helped me up even though I had no plans of moving.

I argued with him on the way back to Don's house. I could get used to things being this way. I still needed to figure out how to deal with my power now, but for some reason, for the moment, it seemed content.

EPILOGUE

I LEANED my head against the window of the car, taking in the lush green of Ocean's Edge. I knew Brad, Darius, and Rathal were stopping here, but why did the rest of us need to as well? I only wanted to get back to the main office, find my bed, and pretend this had all been a bad dream.

Savanas and Melody picked us up at the airport. Currently I rode with Savanas and her team.

Melody drove for the others. She said something about getting them settled in at the hotel.

Savanas insisted I go with her so Doc could take a look at me after the long flight. Her voice had been clipped the little she spoke.

The three men in the car with me fought for who would get the front seat. It had been mildly entertaining at the time, watching them argue like children. Savanas' patience seemed to be limited because she told me to take the front. I went to say I was fine in back, but something in her face held my tongue. The hard set in her jaw and narrowed eyes in the direction of my family members concerned me.

I simply wanted time to myself to sort things out. It felt like even after all was said and done with the mission in Mystic Port, I could not be left alone. Someone always kept showing up when I finally found a moment. This included Don and his family. They were nice people, but I just wanted peace.

Too soon we pulled into the underground parking garage for the Ocean's Edge branch. I took a deep breath before starting the slow process of getting myself out. The door opened before I finished getting the seatbelt off. Brad stood there with his hand out.

"You three head to my office for debriefing," Savanas said, her words clipped. She still sat next to me in the driver's seat.

Brad looked through my door at her. "Do you want me to escort Ket to Doc? I can give him…"

Savanas cut him off. "No, he's read the files. All three of you upstairs now. I'll get her to where she needs to be." It sounded as if she growled at him. Her hands gripped the steering wheel tightly.

"Oh shit…" I heard Darius mutter. "Better move."

The men quickly obeyed her orders, gathering their gear out of the back of the truck before leaving.

I sat still, the waves of anger emanating off of Savanas were tangible. I did not want to remain in her presence at the moment. "Let's go," she said.

Swinging my legs out, I tried to put forth as much speed as I could manage. I did not want to be the one to unleash her barely contained anger. I cringed when I bumped my injured shoulder.

"Ket, take it easy," Savanas said gently. I had not even heard her get out and come around to my door. I looked up, not expecting the tone, still concerned about what I would encounter. "You're not the one who needs to be worried."

I directed my gaze downward.

"The others aren't in trouble, at least not yet - they did what they were ordered to do. Come on, Doc is expecting you." Savanas paused a moment to help me out of the truck before continuing. "We need to focus on you for a while - get you back to normal."

"I'm not sure what that is anymore," I whispered and adjusted the loose black tank top. At least the bruising did not look as bad, but it had begun to turn a sickly yellow color as did the other bruises. My clean clothes were few and I ended up stuck with a pair of khaki shorts I wished were longer. When I got to the hotel later I could deal with the problem. Perhaps after a short nap if I could be left alone.

Savanas closed the door and started prodding me toward the elevator to head upstairs. "Well, seeing how soon we can get your arm out of that sling will be a step in the right direction. The rest will simply take time and unfortunately a lot of soul searching."

I opened my mouth to say something, but the thought left me before I could get it out. We were on our way upstairs when I asked, "You tried to warn me about what was going on, didn't you?"

Savanas folded her arms. "I should have just told you outright and damned the red tape."

Mother said the same thing. I shook my head. Dark Ops were that for a reason - they operated outside of the normal protocols because of the sensitive nature of the mission. "I understand - I didn't have clearance."

The sound of Savanas punching the stop button on the elevator made me jump. "Dammit, Ket! I've gone over the case files - watched the videos, listened to the audio, read through the reports. I don't know how you can 'understand' what was just done to you. My own guys are on record asking permission to get you on board and end the charade. They watched you jumping at shadows because you could sense the people following you. People who were supposed to be there for your protection. It's no wonder you broke away from the entire security detail - I wouldn't have been able to tell friend from foe."

I lowered my head to let my hair hide the fact I shook in an effort to control both my emotional state and my power. Yes, I was upset about how things happened, but it was done and over with and I needed to hold onto the logical explanations to keep it together. "We shouldn't keep Doc waiting," my voice wavered and broke as I spoke, betraying what I tried to hide.

"Alright," Savanas said softly and pushed the button to let the elevator resume.

Silence hung between us and I tried to use the time to pull myself back into some semblance of order.

The elevator deposited us onto the first floor and I followed Savanas down the hall. She spoke once we turned the first corner, "After you're finished, we'll go get something to eat. It'll be my treat." She smiled at me over her shoulder, but her smile did not reach her eyes.

"I'm okay."

"No getting out of this one I'm afraid," Savanas said and smirked. "I know you're going to be in town for a couple of days at least. And listen, if you want to get away from people, you're welcome to crash at my place. Just don't mind the fur - I'm still trying to get Roh to stay off of the furniture. He'll be about the only one to bother you."

I nodded. I might seriously consider taking her up on the offer. It would depend on how things went. And Roh seemed like a sweet puppy.

Savanas knocked on the door to Doc's office before letting herself in. "Brought you someone," she said cheerfully.

Doc quickly put down the file he had been reading. "I take it vacation didn't agree with you," he quipped, but his voice sounded strained. "I hope you don't mind if I perform a full exam - I'm having a hard time believing what I've read so far."

I sighed, resigned to my fate for the time being. He signaled for me to follow him. Savanas trailed behind us into one of the exam rooms.

"I'm just here as an extra pair of hands. Besides, you don't want me upstairs when the others arrive," Savanas said flatly.

Doc shook his head. "And you complain about Rathal's temper."

Savanas shrugged. "He's mellowed out since we started letting him and Silver spar with weapons. Not sure what will happen once Silver heads for the main office."

Doc placed the examination clothing on the table. "I'm sure he'll figure something out. Just be gentle with Ketayl's shoulder. Don't try to move it too much." He directed the last part at me before leaving.

Hopefully this would not be too long or painful.

ONCE I FINISHED with all the tests Doc wanted to run and dressed again, he returned with something black wrapped in plastic. "Looking at how your shoulder has been healing, I don't see why we can't put you into a lighter-weight sling. I'll send my reports along to the main office and contact Mogan about starting to work with you in a couple of weeks. She's been excellent with rehabilitating injuries. You'll still want the old sling for when you rest."

I tried to put a face to the name, but found I could not.

"I'm also recommending medical leave."

I looked down at my hands on my lap. Not exactly what I wanted to hear. I needed to do something to keep myself busy.

"Do you honestly think she'll listen for very long again?" Savanas asked. She picked up the old sling and searched it for something. As soon as she found what she was looking for, she pulled a knife out of her pocket to work at it.

"No," Doc admitted after he paused to look at me for a few moments, "But I'm still going to recommend it. Ultimately it will be up to Ketayl's superior."

Which meant Lockonis. She might be easier to persuade.

It did not take Savanas long to remove the small fabric pouch. She made a face of disgust at it before tossing it in the trash. It made a loud thud against the metal wall.

"And I would like Silver to continue to progress the healing on your shoulder and other injuries as he sees fit."

He was insufferable enough - barely leaving me alone since we had our discussion in the shack. At least he seemed content to just follow me around instead of dragging me along.

Savanas' phone dinged with a message. She had been getting a few during the time we were down here, but said nothing. She glanced at the message and rolled her eyes. "Are you done with her? I have some people upstairs impatiently waiting."

Doc nodded and helped me get down from the table before helping me put on and adjust the new sling. "I'll keep in contact with you. Give me a call anytime if you need anything."

I nodded and bowed. Savanas quickly ushered me upstairs. I readjusted the badge clipped to my waistband while we were in the elevator.

Savanas noticed the gesture. "And here I told you there was nothing hiding in it. I should have warned you about what was hiding behind it."

"I didn't trust Kitteren wouldn't think worse of me to tell her what she wanted to know either," I said, keeping my eyes straight ahead. The new sling certainly breathed better and I suppressed a shudder at the coolness of the elevator. "I'm as much at fault."

"Still, she could have explained she needed to know for an assignment even if she didn't give specifics," Savanas said, her tone conversational.

I shrugged and winced - I would need to remember to not do that with my right shoulder still for a while. "Hindsight."

Out of the corner of my eye, I caught the surprised look Savanas gave me. "I suppose you're right."

I looked curiously around the empty floor while silently following Savanas upstairs to the next level and into her office - the silver nameplate next to the door being the only thing to tell me. Once Savanas opened the door, I saw the others - not only Savanas' team, but also my family and Silver. All eyes turned in my direction and I had a feeling the silence had been going on for a while. Stepping in, Vince sat behind the desk in the room with Lockonis next to him - both of their faces grim.

Those two I had not been expecting to deal with until I returned to the main office.

The silence continued and I shifted uncomfortably. I kept my focus on Vince - the head of the TIO being the most powerful in the room.

Finally Vince broke the silence, "So you're teleporting groups now?" He seemed curious, not angry. "And a few other surprises I would certainly like to discuss at a later time."

I did not know what he referred to, but I answered him regarding the teleport, "It was my first attempt, sir."

"Are you serious?!" Kitteren voiced loudly. Apparently Silver had not shared that information. She straightened up when both Vince and Lockonis leveled glares at her and she said, "Excuse my outburst."

As their attention returned to me I tried to stand taller.

Vince continued, "I'll be traveling to speak with the rest of the team after this, but right now, Ketayl, I want to know if you wish to file grievances against any of the agents involved."

I blinked. File grievance? The thought had not even crossed my mind. I looked over at Kitteren who turned her face away from me, but I caught her wiping a tear. My attention then went to our adopted parents who both stood stoically to my left. The Ocean's Edge crew were behind me and I did not feel the need to continue this evaluation to them. Silver stood to my right and I looked at him for a moment hoping for an answer.

Finding none, I turned back to Vince and firmly said, "No."

"No?" Vince asked. "You are well within your right." He gestured at me and I presumed the injuries sustained.

I raised my chin and I could see Kitteren looking at me out of my peripheral vision confused. "No. This was my choice and I will deal with any other issues personally."

"Hm, you certainly are a curious one," Vince mused, leaning forward to flip through a file before him. "We might be in trouble with an agent as stubborn as you going into the field regularly." He still sounded like the events unfolding amused him.

I closed my eyes for a moment, thinking through my next action. My power pushed at me as I tried to reign in the conflicting emotions. The badge on my waistband felt heavy. They put too much faith in me.

I glanced sideways at Silver before I strode forward and pulled the badge off of my waistband and placed it on the desk. "Thank you for the consideration, but I haven't earned this."

Turning on my heel, I walked quickly toward the door to leave before something broke through my control.

"You're resigning?" Silver sounded hurt.

I stopped with my hand on the doorknob. "I'll continue my work, but I don't deserve that badge."

"The rest of you are dismissed for now. I need a conversation with Ketayl. Savanas, if you and Silver would also stay," Vince ordered.

I stepped back to allow the others to leave, never lifting my head to look at them.

The door closed behind the last person and I refused to turn around. "Why?" Lockonis asked. Apparently she stayed also.

I took a shuddering breath before speaking, "I never completed any formal training which was obvious during this assignment."

"Is she serious?" Lockonis asked someone. "Ket, first of all, you shouldn't have been on this assignment - Dark Ops or not you were supposed to be off-duty. Second, I never did any training either. Same for the big guy and Savanas received vastly different training. Sure, we've developed the system we use now, but you've learned way more than you would have through the training course. Hells, we were talking about setting up an advanced tracking seminar on the flight here just to see who could keep up with you."

I turned back around to see if Lockonis' comment had been in jest.

She continued, "Look, I know this is hard to accept, but honestly, if you wanted to take the tests for the training, I'd let you except in your helping your partner study, you've proven you know the material. Probably better than he does as I know you weren't reading from the books most of the time."

Vince stepped in. "We should probably also talk about the latest Terran Council ruling regarding you."

I never viewed the videos of the last one Lockonis spoke of. I did not think myself ready to hear this.

"Archmage Donovan dragged us down there again a few months ago," Lockonis sighed. "He seemed very adamant about getting you recalled."

I cocked my head to the side. No one mentioned anything about recalls after I last talked to Lockonis about it six months ago.

"The short answer is you are no longer a part of the Arcane College," Vince said, his voice even. "I'm fairly certain most of it was due to the Archmage pissing off the Council, but the official ruling came down due to the complete lack of support from the Arcane College since you came to us as well as their lack of ability to care for you. This gave us the freedom to move you from liaison to agent."

"The change happened immediately in the system, but Savanas followed the proceedings and begged us to let her give you your badge," Lockonis teased her former partner.

Savanas shook her head. "I asked. Nicely I might add."

Silver walked over to the desk and asked, "May I?" His hand hovered over my badge. Vince nodded and my partner picked it up, looking at it carefully before walking over to me. Grinning broadly, he clipped it to the sling. "It seems only fair."

I rolled my eyes at Silver and gave him my best look of annoyance as I took the badge off the sling and put it back on my waistband. I guess I was stuck with the thing. Though it started to feel more like it belonged now that the weight of the Arcane College left. I did not expect to feel freedom at the announcement. At least not so quickly.

"Ooh, I didn't know Ket could get sassy," Lockonis said, sounding far too entertained.

"Ketayl," Vince said, getting my attention. "When you return, check in with your assistant and then I want you to take some time-off. Dayko has requested for you to spend time with your family. Get what you need to in order. We're setting up a new space for you and Silver to work in and you'll have your hands full sifting through what the cyber team has found so far."

"We'll keep feeding you what we think might be relevant information as we find something," Lockonis chimed in. "Right now it's all rumors and isolated incidents - nothing I can piece together as a lead."

I nodded. It seemed reasonable enough. Though I wondered why Father was requesting the time-off. There was no point in arguing - I was not going to win about not taking leave.

"Are we good?" Savanas asked.

The question surprised me. I did not know if I needed to answer or not.

Vince signaled for us to leave. "I want to speak with Silver anyway and I'll call the others back in here at some point."

I silently followed Savanas out and back downstairs. As we got closer to the loose group formed, Kitteren pushed herself off the wall to speak to us. Savanas rushed her and shoved her back against the wall, pinning my sister across the shoulders with her forearm. "I don't want to hear anything out of you," the head of the Ocean's Edge branch growled. Then she let go and continued toward the elevator.

"Why are you so angry?" Kitteren called after her. "I brought your team back in one piece."

Savanas stopped and stood still for a moment before returning and swinging hard, connecting her fist with Kitteren's face. My sister fell back and onto the floor. "You've got a lot to learn," she ground out. "When we warned you about how you could lose a lot more than you gained, you weren't going to be the only one to lose. She's your sister for the Gods' sakes! Act like it!"

I stared at the two, unsure of what just happened. Everyone else around me seemed to be in the same stupor.

Kitteren got back on her feet and started toward Savanas, her hands already balled into fists. As she wound back to take her own swing, I reacted, opening my left hand toward the two to cast my shield spell around each of them.

"Enough!" Almost everyone looked up at the same time to see Lockonis at the railing of the upper level. Vince and Silver were to the side observing. I shook my head and returned to concentrating on holding the two women.

Savanas touched the shield with her fingers - her face curious as the hexagonal pattern of the shield lit up where she touched. Kitteren swung at hers, making it harder for me to maintain the spell. It required more energy the harder and faster she hit.

I knew it was only a matter of time before I would not be able to hold it.

"Dammit, Lockonis let me go!" Kitteren shouted. "If Savanas wants to have it out right here and now, I'm game."

"I'm not the one casting it," Lockonis said calmly. "Though it was impressive timing."

Kitteren stopped and turned in my direction. I had my hand out and knew I started to sweat from the strain. I should have more in me than this to keep it going. "Ket..." she breathed.

Father put his hand on my arm. He pushed gently, but did not force me to stop. I gave up a moment later, figuring both women had calmed down enough to let out.

"Dayko, if you would escort Ketayl and Savanas," Vince ordered. "The rest of you I want reviewing the case files."

A hand touched my back, gently pushing me toward the elevator while I tried to watch the others. Savanas' team made their way to their desks - Rathal jumping his to get to his chair faster. The rest found somewhere to be. Except Kitteren who simply watched us leave. She rubbed her face where Savanas struck. It looked like we might have matching bruises at this rate.

I stood awkwardly between my adopted father and the head of the Ocean's Edge branch during the silent ride down.

Savanas led us to her car this time instead of the fleet vehicle she used to pick us up in. Father opened the door for me and I sighed, wishing people would let me do things for myself.

He smiled gently. "You can put up with some coddling." He patted my head.

"Given what just happened upstairs, I think she's proven she can handle herself," Savanas said flatly.

Father leaned down so he could see Savanas. "I know, too many of us keep underestimating her. But given the circumstances..."

Silence hung like a crooked picture.

"Sorry about hitting Kitteren in front of everyone," Savanas said.

Father shook his head. "Don't tell her, but she needed it. You just did what many of us were thinking, though we were mostly waiting to see what Ketayl here would do. Take care of my girl." He patted the top of the car and shut the door, quickly walking back toward the elevator.

As soon as she started the car and pulled out, Savanas said, "Ket, I really am sorry about what you witnessed back there. Though I'm not sorry I hit her."

I shook my head. "I kind of wanted to myself for a while." Kitteren had been obnoxious most of the trip and part of me decided she deserved what she got. The other part cringed at seeing her in pain.

Savanas laughed. "Okay, let's go find a late lunch."

———

"Hope you haven't been waiting long," Savanas said cheerfully. "I'm afraid we got caught up in some drama at the office."

I walked behind Savanas, taking in the outside patio of the Waking Dawn which faced out over the water. Green canvas triangles shaded the tables and the one we were being directed toward was out of view of the main dining area. Roh came up and bounced around our feet before going back the way he came.

"Is that why you warned me to stay away from the office today?" I had not expected to hear Retanei's voice. I nervously remained behind Savanas, not wanting my friend to see me like this. I ducked my head, letting my hair try to hide as much as possible.

"Something like that."

The hostess bowed and told us our server would be with us shortly. She gave me a sad look as she took in my injuries again. I wanted to say I had grown used to it after being dragged around everywhere in Mystic Port, but it still bothered me.

Savanas sat down and I moved slowly to take a seat.

"Gods, what happened?" Retanei asked. "Savanas, why didn't you tell me?"

"Dark Ops gone wrong," Savanas said flatly.

Retanei made a face of annoyance and moved my hair to get a better look. She cringed when she saw my shoulder and then gently push my head so she could look at the bruising on my neck. "You look like you got into a fight with a Troll. At least it looks like a Troll hand print around your neck."

"She did. And slave traders," Savanas' voice sounded tired.

Retanei sat back down. "Geez, Ket. You're tougher than you look if you're still standing. I probably would have seen the thing and ran. If I end up dealing with another out-of-control werewolf pack, I'm taking you along."

"I thought the Alpha Prime dealt with them," Savanas inquired.

"First indication of a problem ended up under our jurisdiction," Retanei answered. She turned back to me, frowning. "What on Terra happened, Ket?"

How much was I allowed to talk about? I stared at the table and the closed menu in front of me. Out of the corner of my eye, I saw Artemis curled up in the corner, chewing on a bone. Roh had one as well though he rolled around while he chewed, being far more lively with it.

"What happened is a little more complicated than we have time for, but shall we move onto figuring out food? I'm starving," Savanas said.

"Sorry," Retanei said and looked at me again. "Just... damn."

I flipped through the menu, not really hungry. Glasses of water began appearing on the table. I looked up to see Trevyn setting them down. "Lass, you look like you could use somethin stronger than water this time." He smirked at me.

I managed a small smile at his joke.

Savanas jumped in, "I certainly could. Got a good summer special?"

Trevyn winked at her. "I know just the thing."

Retanei ordered a sweet tea and I copied her. She asked, "Are you sure, Ket? Usually you avoid stuff like that."

She knew of my sensitivity to things like caffeine and sugar. I did not even try to hide the tiredness in my voice when I answered, "I think I need something to get through the rest of the day. I didn't get much rest on the flight here."

It had been a private flight and a smooth ride, but with the agents around me and someone always close to my side, I could not relax.

Savanas raised an eyebrow but said nothing. She turned to Trevyn and asked, "So when did you start waiting tables?"

He laughed. "I let one of my waiters have a couple of weeks off - his mate just gave birth to their first child. Plan on givin' the lad as much as he needs really. I also have a few takin' days off here an' there for appointments an' the like. It's easier for me to fill a spot than possibly overwork an' anger my employees. I've got a good crew - I want to keep them." He patted me on the shoulder. "Let me get those drinks an' I'll get an appetizer tray for you lovely ladies on the house."

With that he left.

Savanas shook her head. "Good ol' Trevyn," she mused.

I felt lost as to what was going on.

"Should you be drinking on-duty?" Retanei asked.

"Pretty sure I went off-duty the moment I dropped Kitteren," Savanas said flatly.

Retanei shook her head and then something made her look at me. "Wait, she said you two were going on vacation..."

I looked down at the menu, not really seeing it. I thought quickly, trying to figure out how to avoid talking about what happened. "I guess you were helping out here." I cringed at my horrible attempt to change the topic.

Silence hung awkwardly for a few moments.

"Yeah, there was a volunteer request at the main office," Retanei said idly. "Figured I'd come give Savanas a hand while the Orc tribes get themselves reorganized."

Savanas mused, "Who knew Ted could be a diplomat."

Retanei started laughing. "Only among Orc tribes does brute strength and a very large axe constitute diplomacy."

I settled back while I half-listened to them talk. Flipping through the menu, I felt I could breathe with the attention off of me.

My mind drifted to what I needed to do when I got back. I knew what my orders were. I knew where I had to be. I did not know how to deal with rebuilding my relationships. So far I mostly acted like nothing changed and I knew it was a temporary solution, but I did not know what else to do.

Things would not be the same between my family and I, but I could not fathom just walking away. I had been so torn about what I had done to cause the rifts that I ignored what they had done. Savanas pointed out in a way that if mine and Kitteren's positions had been reversed, I would not have taken the same path.

At this point, I think I just needed to listen to all sides of the story before acting. I just knew I needed to stop letting Kitteren get away with so much.

Though I would be happier to sit and sift through whatever the cyber team managed to pull together for me. Spend hours in the lab. Anything but face what happened in Mystic Port.

But then I would never move on. Taking a deep breath, I knew what few secrets I still kept needed to remain that way as long as I could manage. At least what my biological mother made me promise.

As our meal wrapped up and Trevyn collected the plates, something else appeared in front of me. I looked at the small individual-sized cake with a candle on top flickering in the light ocean breeze.

Lou hovered behind me, a satisfied smirk on his face. "Savvy asked if I wouldn't mind since it was your birthday recently and you've had a rough patch. By the looks of it, quite a bit rougher than I got the gist of."

"Thanks, Da," Savanas said.

"You didn't have to." My attention was torn between Lou and Savanas.

Trevyn still stood nearby. "It's not like he had to go far, lass. The bakery is right next door."

"Speaking of, I have your order ready to come over." Lou turned when he spoke to Trevyn.

The Dwarf's eyes lit up. "Perfect. I'll bring a couple of people over within the hour."

While the two men talked and walked away, Retanei pointed at the cake.

I stared at the flame, trying to make sense of the cake before me. This was odd.

"It's a Human tradition - you're supposed to make a wish and blow it out," Savanas said gently. "You don't have to say the wish out loud."

"I'm not sure if I have any room left for this," I admitted, delaying what I was supposed to do. The little round cake sat before me with its white frosting and purple flower along the edge. The thin white candle getting noticeably lower.

Both women waited patiently. I did not know what to wish for. This was as bad as trying to think of something to write for the burning of the scrolls during the Winter Solstice.

Something struck me. While Retanei may not be aware of what happened, Savanas knew and she remained. So did the others. Vince nor Lockonis said anything about my part, though certainly would be an ongoing conversation for a while, but more on my capabilities rather than on the monster I believed myself to be. Even with the illusion gone, people were still here.

Taking a deep breath, I blew out the candle.

ACKNOWLEDGMENTS

Joshua Jackson for encouraging me along and indulging me in this crazy adventure.

My local critique groups: Brandi Burns, Kenneth Jorgenson, Patrik Martinet, Skip Knox, Loni Townsend, and many others. A number of them also were subjected to being beta readers as well.

And all of my friends and family who have been cheering me along.

ABOUT THE AUTHOR

J.C. Jackson is originally from New England and currently lives in southwestern Idaho with her husband and daughter.

On top of writing, she enjoys gaming whether that is picking up a controller or throwing down some dice in a tabletop RPG (as well as other board games). She has also been a fan of science fiction and fantasy since she was little.

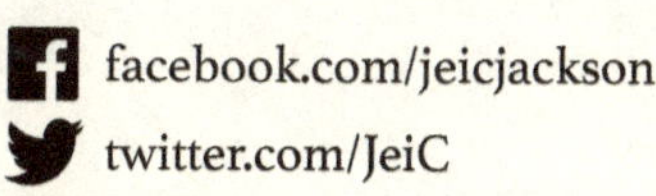

facebook.com/jeicjackson

twitter.com/JeiC

instagram.com/jeicjackson

ALSO BY J. C. JACKSON

Terra Chronicles

Twisted Magics

Shattered Illusions

Twice Cursed

Conjured Defense

Mortgaged Mortality